when love comes to town

For my friends.
—Tom Lennon

First published 1993 by The O'Brien Press Ltd., Ireland.
Foreword copyright © 2013 by James Klise.
Text copyright © 1993 by Tom Lennon.

Library of Congress Cataloging-in-Publication Data

Lennon, Tom.
When love comes to town / Tom Lennon.
p. cm.
Summary: Neil Byrne, a teenager in Dublin, Ireland,
in the 1990s, comes to terms with the fact that he is
gay and seeks acceptance from his friends and family.
ISBN 978-0-8075-8916-8 (hardcover)
[1. Gays—Fiction. 2. Coming out (Sexual orientation)—Fiction.
3. Ireland—Fiction.] I. Title.
PZ7.L5394Wh 2013
[Fic]—dc23
2012020160

Published in 2013 by Albert Whitman & Company.
ISBN 978-0-8075-8916-8

All rights reserved. No part of this book may be reproduced or
transmitted in any form or by any means, electronic or mechanical,
including photocopying, recording, or by any information storage and
retrieval system, without permission in writing from the publisher.
Printed in the United States of America.

10 9 8 7 6 5 4 3 2 1 LB 17 16 15 14 13 12

For more information about Albert Whitman & Company,
visit our web site at www.albertwhitman.com.

when
love
comes
to town

tom lennon

albert whitman & company
chicago, illinois

FOREWORD
by James Klise

Meet Neil Byrne—Dubliner, rugby star, soon-to-be graduate.

He's weeks away from his eighteenth birthday. Many of his friends have joined up in romantic pairs (the "rhyming couplets" he regards with jealous cynicism), but Neil remains single. He's got, in his own words, "a problem that won't go away." He's gay. And for Neil, being gay is both a secret and a burden.

After all, consider the year: 1992. Neil connects with friends using a telephone booth instead of a cell phone. He listens to music recorded on cassettes and played on a Sony Walkman. Neil and his peers may legally (if not always responsibly) drink beer in pubs, where the music of U2 and Sinead O'Connor play over stereo speakers.

Much has changed in the two decades since an Irish educator calling himself "Tom Lennon" published this groundbreaking book. (To protect his Catholic school teaching career, the author never revealed his identity.)

The novel reminds us how isolated many gay people felt in the pre-Internet age, before connecting with others was as easy as a click. That isolation was only increased by the near-invisibility of role models: no out actors or musicians, no out politicians or sports heroes—in fact, not many out and proud ordinary people either. In the novel's first chapter, the only visible gay person Neil sees is a shadowy stranger who propositions him in a public bathroom. Not a super inspiring vision of a young person's future, is it?

We may be tempted to judge Neil for his at-times-bleak outlook, but think of his situation: no gay-straight alliances in schools, no Ellen Degeneres on TV, no uplifting talk in the media about how "it gets better." And imagine the risk of telling his parents, when "always in the family, nothing was ever said when it should have been." Neil's parents have no more resources than he does, because they're stuck living in the pre-Internet, pre-PFLAG world too.

For most young people now, it's not that way anymore, but it sure felt that way then. When I was a closeted gay teen in the late 80s, I felt the same intense isolation that Neil feels, along with the same ugly, internalized homophobia. My fear controlled my life. I remember this endless, confusing flirtation with a cute guy I'd see in my college library. Sitting at separate tables, we'd steal glances across the room. He'd catch me looking at him, I'd catch him looking at me, back and forth, on and on…for two years! We never spoke. I never even knew his name. The behavior seems crazy to me now. (By the end of the 90s, the first time I laid eyes on Mike, my partner, I walked straight up to him, introduced myself, and said, "Let's get coffee sometime.")

I don't mean that it's easy for young people to come out now; it may never be easy. But with the Internet, more role models, more resources in schools, more protection under the law, and a greater ability to simply talk about sexual identity and diversity, the process has improved for many people.

This funny, suspenseful, and heartbreaking book is a welcome reminder of how far we've come since 1992. We read it now to be entertained by the story, to feel moved by Neil's difficult circumstances, and to be grateful that things have gotten so much better for all of us.

Plus, when you're young, it's always fun to ask that timeless question: When will love come to my town?

chapter one

Neil rested his elbows on the window ledge, sank his chin into his hands, and stared out across the neighborhood gardens. Clothes flapped on clotheslines, birds squawked, small kids played soccer in the garden that backed onto theirs, and a couple of semi-naked diehards lay sprawled on deck chairs soaking up the watery rays of early May sunshine. At the end of his own garden, a rope with a car tire attached to the end of it dangled from the tree house that his father had built years before. Everything in the garden was in bloom. But even the fresh flowery scents couldn't change Neil's mood; Sunday afternoons were always a low point in his week.

Certain that no one was looking, he leaned out the open window and tossed the soggy, sperm-filled tissue into the next-door neighbor's bushes. Third of the afternoon. *God knows what sort of flowers will sprout from that bush*, he thought, lighting up a cigarette and slipping on the headphones of his Walkman. Sinead O'Connor's haunting vocals brought tears to his eyes.

Nothing can stop these lonely tears from falling

Neil made sure to blow the smoke out the window; he didn't fancy facing another of his mum's investigations. He looked at the books spread out across his desk and closed his eyes in a grimace. There was so much he had to review before the exams, but he just couldn't concentrate today. Then he glanced in the mirror, pouted, and made a face at his reflection.

Nothing compares
Nothing compares to you

Narrowing his moist eyes into slits, he focused on a flock of gulls gliding past distant telephone lines. *Lucky things*, he reflected. What he wouldn't give to be able to just fly away with them. Flecks of dandruff cloud speckled the horizon sky. It was definitely a day for the beach. But the thought of being the spare prick yet again had made him use the study excuse when Gary and Trish had called.

"Jesus, you can't study all day," Gary insisted.

"The break'll do you good, Neil," Trish added, touching his arm gently.

"Plenty of time for catching rays over the summer," Neil replied with a grin. Neil always grinned, that was what they liked about him. All the fun of the fair when Neil was around. Gary and Trish, Tom and Andrea, Joe and Mary, Paddy and Niamh ... Tweedledum, Tweedledee, all the rhyming couplets were off to the beach—with Neil. "We'll have to find you a girlfriend, Neil," one of the girls would say, and Neil would lie back on the sand, cup his hands under his head, and make some smart-aleck comment like, "Only one?" And, of course, everyone would laugh. And Neil would laugh with them. But inside he felt the clawing emptiness. Sometimes he felt like he wanted to break down and tell them all about the real Neil. End all the pretense. Scream it out at the top of his voice for all the world to hear.

The bedroom door burst open and his young niece stood in the doorway, her bottle in her hand. Neil removed his headphones, switched off the Walkman, and stubbed out his cigarette quickly.

"How're you, Anniepoo?" he said, holding his arms out.

3

"No, Anniepoo. Nee's shoe, Nee's shoe." The sturdy two-year-old was pointing at his runners.

"Neil's cool Reeboks," Neil said, lifting his beaming niece up onto his knee. He could hear the commotion downstairs. His oldest sister Kate and her husband, Dan, along with their two kids, had arrived for their Sunday afternoon visit. His mum was showing Kate the new curtains in the dining room, his dad was chatting with Dan in the living room, while Danny, his three-year-old nephew, was running from room to room, shooting bad guys with his noisy machine gun.

"You crying?" Annie was pointing at his eyes.

Neil nodded. "I crying."

This was a signal for his niece to lean forward and place a sloppy kiss on his nose.

"I better now," Neil assured the little girl.

"Teddy, teddy," Annie said, pointing to the small teddy bear sitting on top of the chest of drawers. Neil had been given Ted by Santa Claus when he was a baby, and at his mum's insistence, it had remained in his bedroom ever since. He knew it was because he was the youngest in the family; it was her way of clinging on to the memory of happier times.

"Ted is watching you," he said, gently pressing his finger into the child's button nose.

"Nee's books, Nee's books," she said, now pointing at the desk.

"Neil's books," Neil nodded, as he stood up and hoisted the delighted child onto his shoulders.

"My bot-bot, my bot-bot," Annie squealed. Neil picked her bottle off the table and went downstairs with Annie bouncing up and down on his shoulders.

He stood outside the living room door and listened. His dad was holding court.

"You've met Chris, haven't you, Catherine?" his dad asked.

"I think so," his mum replied absently. "Doesn't he work in the advertising department?"

"The very one," his dad agreed.

"You always find them in advertising," Dan, Neil's brother-in-law, said with a guffaw.

"I mean, he doesn't hide the fact that he's one of them," his dad added, and again Dan guffawed.

Outside the door, Neil was struggling to fight back a blush.

"But, you know, a better listener you'll never find," his dad continued.

"Is that right?" Dan said in his kiss-arse voice.

"People queue up outside his office for advice on their marital problems."

"Don't exaggerate, Dad," Kate said.

"I'm telling you, they do," his dad insisted. "The man's a born therapist."

"So long as he sticks to therapy," Dan quipped, and he and Neil's dad laughed.

Neil took a deep breath and walked into the living room. Dan immediately came over to Neil and slapped his back in his rugby-club manner. "Couple of weeks now and we'll be able to go for a pint together," he said, winking to the others.

Neil grinned, trying to conceal his horror at the thought of being stuck in a pub alone with his brother-in-law.

"Our little Neiley Nook's going to be eighteen!" Kate exclaimed histrionically, clapping her hands to her face. "Oh my God, I feel ancient!"

"I must say, I'm looking forward to discovering what pubs look like from the inside," Neil said in a deadpan voice, bringing a burst of laughter from the others, especially Brendan, his dad.

"Don't mind that white lie," said Catherine, his mum, smiling uncertainly.

"The most worrying thing is that this fellow and all his pals are going to be able to vote," his dad said, and another friendly peal of laughter circled the room.

Then Neil's little nephew charged into the living room, spraying the place with imaginary bullets from his clacking machine gun.

"You're dead! You're dead!" Danny shouted.

Everyone had to moan and pretend that they were hit before the noisy gun fell silent. Then the little fellow's eyes lit up. He had spotted Neil. He dropped his gun, hurtled straight for his uncle, and wrapped his arms around his legs.

"Hulk Hogan!" Danny roared, attempting to lift Neil up off the ground.

"And the Warriors of Doom," Neil said, keeping his head bowed, afraid that his dilated pupils would betray his squalid bedroom activities.

"They love their Uncle Neil," Kate said.

"Mind the baby, Neil!" his mum warned, watching anxiously as Annie jigged up and down on his shoulders.

"So, how's the studying going?" Dan asked.

"Fine," Neil replied, adopting his best fake smile. Since Christmas, his brother-in-law had asked him the same question every time they met. He usually singled Neil out for a friendly chat, but Neil always felt awkward. Except for rugby, they had absolutely nothing in common.

"Danny, stop that!" Dan caught hold of his son who had begun to grab figurines off the mantelpiece and toss them across the room as imaginary grenades.

"Danny!" Kate shrieked.

"You're a bold boy!" Dan said to his brazen-faced son.

"It's all right," Catherine said, stooping down to pick up her precious figurines

Brendan chuckled heartily as he rubbed his grandson's hair. "No damage done."

"Don't encourage him, Dad," said Kate.

"You'd need eyes in the back of your head," Dan said.

"Did he break them?" Kate asked.

"No, no, they're fine," Catherine said. Neil saw his mum slip a broken china elephant into her pocket. Her brother, Frank, the missionary priest in Africa, had given it to her. Neil knew that he'd hear the complaints about Kate's children later. But as always in the family, nothing was ever said when it should have been.

"I've got a bit of news." Kate held her hands up theatrically, "Dan's getting a new company car next week."

"Really?" Neil's mum pretended to sound delighted.

"What type?" his dad asked, his eyes lighting up.

Kate turned to Dan. "What type was it again, pet?"

"Well, it was a choice between a Volvo and a BMW," Dan said. Neil could see that Dan was bursting with pride, though doing his utmost to appear modest.

"We're taking the Volvo because we think it'll be safer for the children," Kate told them.

Brendan nudged Dan. "You let her choose, did you?"

"You know yourself, Bren," Dan laughed.

"Don't mind him," said Kate.

"Well, I think this calls for a celebratory drink," Brendan announced, taking a bottle of his homemade wine from the liquor cabinet. "And we'll even allow the young fellow a taste of things to come," he added, nodding toward Neil.

But Neil shook his head. "No, Dad, I won't, I'm just going out." Escape was imperative. There was only so much happy family chat he could endure. It was as if the same record were replayed every time they met.

"Where're you going, love?" his mum asked.

"Just out on the bike for a bit of air."

"Oh, some young one, I'll bet," his dad teased.

"Is there something we should know?" Kate looked to Catherine inquiringly.

His mum shrugged. "Sure, he tells us nothing."

"A break from my studying, Kate." Neil blushed as he lifted Annie down from his shoulders and purposely avoided his mum's searching look.

"A good-looking fellow like you should have a girl-friend," Kate said, prodding him gently.

"Only one?" Neil felt suddenly nauseous as he muttered the well-worn reply and brought the predictable macho laughter from his dad and his brother-in-law. But he was still conscious of his mum's stare.

"Whatever happened to Becky what's-her-name that you brought to your debs?" asked Kate, tweaking Neil's nose.

"That'd be tellin'," Neil said, ducking out the door. He

couldn't get away fast enough now. He glanced back quickly and saw them all watching him leave.

While Neil was wheeling his bicycle out of the garden shed, he could hear his mum's voice drifting out through the open window. "He likes to go out for rides on his own," she said, but Neil could sense the pain in her voice. She knew that there was something troubling her youngest. Neil had once overheard his dad blaming his exams, but he knew that his mum wasn't convinced. Her motherly intuition told her that it was something a lot deeper than that. But her watchfulness drove Neil even further away from her. The boy who had told her everything during his younger, more carefree days was like a stranger to her now.

Neil forgot his troubles as soon as he felt the summer breeze on his face, blowing away all the bedroom cobwebs. He took a shortcut through the deserted suburban oasis of Blackrock College, past all the rugby fields that held so many vivid memories of past glories for him. He smiled as he recalled his brother-in-law Dan charging onto the Lansdowne Road field in front of twenty thousand spectators and embracing Neil after he had scored a goal in the Schools' Cup final. Neil had teased him about the lengths people go to to get their mug on television. But Dan was so taken with the achievement that he actually brought Neil's medal into his office and down to his rugby club to show it off. *Look what the missus's kid brother won! Passport to any job in the country, this medal is.* Neil imagined the reactions behind Dan's back. *Swear he had won it himself. Idolizing a kid, what a dork.*

Neil's thoughts were interrupted when Father Donnelly stepped out into his path and flagged him to stop. His brakes screeched as he skidded his bike to a halt.

"Trying to run me down?" Father Donnelly joked.

Neil grinned. "Sorry, Father, didn't see you there."

"You look like a man who's very worried about his graduation."

"Short break from the studying."

Father Donnelly rested his hand on Neil's shoulder. "I want an A on that English paper from you," he said.

"At least," Neil smiled. Father Donnelly had taught him since First Year and Neil had always been one of his favorite students.

The priest's face became serious. "Have you decided on your major?"

Neil nodded. "Liberal Arts."

"And have you told your mother and father?"

Neil shook his head. Father Donnelly squeezed his shoulder gently. "I think you should, you know."

Neil blushed. "I will after the exams are over."

The priest relinquished his grip on Neil's shoulder. "You should tell your parents these things, Neil, they'll understand. They know you a lot better than you think they do," he added absently before he bade farewell and continued on his stroll.

What was Donno getting at? Neil wondered. Had he been talking to his mum? Neil knew the priest well enough to realize that what he had just said was laden with undercurrents. Surely the old codger couldn't have guessed. No way. He was just worried that he would be seen as the one responsible for Neil's decision not to do engineering. That was it, he decided as he pressed down on his pedals and set off again through the empty school grounds.

A man with a bushy mustache was standing by the urinals, supposedly pissing, when Neil stepped cautiously into the gents' toilets on Blackrock seafront. Keeping his head down, Neil ducked into a stall and locked the door.

Water was hissing through the overhead pipes, and the faint sounds of people on the beach drifted through the vent in the concrete wall. Ignoring the pungent odors, Neil started to read the graffiti. It struck him how sad most of the comments were. Notes of desperation. Presumably sane people organizing dates on the back of a toilet door. After he had read the complete toilet-door works, he flushed the toilet and opened the stall door. His heart jumped when he saw that Bushy Mustache was still in the rest room, now pretending to wash his hands in a dingy handbasin that looked older than himself.

"You wouldn't have the time, would you?" Bushy Mustache asked in his suave voice.

"Eh, it's just past three o'clock," Neil replied, avoiding the man's lingering look. His face felt like it was on fire as he walked out of the rest room. He stayed out of view while a DART train, packed with happy day-trippers, shuttled past. Then, as he was unlocking his bicycle, Bushy Mustache appeared at the doorway of the rest room.

"Lovely day, isn't it?" he said.

"Yeah." Neil's hands were trembling as he fiddled with his combination lock. He felt the man's eyes burning right through him. He kept his head bowed, certain that with his luck, someone he knew was bound to be passing at this embarrassing moment. "Hey, Neil, saw you chatting to this bloke outside the bog in the park. You'd want to watch it, you'll get a bit of a name for yourself." *Don't worry*, Neil reassured himself, *you'd fob them off with a grin and a joke.* "Oh, he was some goer," you'd say with a mock sigh, "me arse was sore for a week after." They'd laugh, and all suspicion would be dispelled immediately.

"You don't have a light by any chance, do you?"

Oh shit, he's not giving up easily. Maybe you're giving out signals without even knowing it.

"Sorry, don't smoke."

That's it, up on your bike now and cycle away back into your safe little world, Neil thought. *Leave the toilet fiend to*

13

his own devices. God, what a life, spending your Sunday after-noons in a stinking toilet. Imagine if his mother knew. Imagine if the doctor delivering the screaming baby said, "Oh missus, this boy of yours is going to spend every Sunday afternoon in a dingy toilet, attempting to lure younger men into the cubicle with him." Aaaah, she'd scream, "Murder him! Drown him like a kitten. Slit his throat from ear to ear. Gag him till he suffocates. Just get rid of him."

Quickly Neil squashed any thoughts of what his own mum would say if she could see her little fellow now.

Later that evening, Neil crossed the road as he cycled past Hollywood Nights. He didn't want to be spotted by any of the rhyming couplets who went there most weekend nights. Anytime he did go there, Neil ended up standing at the edge of the dance floor with Mal and Tony, two cynical guys from his class who spent their nights commenting on the ugliness—and the sexual availa-bility—of the female talent. Two cynical guys with whom no self-respecting girl would dance even if they did have the nerve to ask. It was Mal who, during one of his more inventive moments, had coined the phrase "rhyming couplets." Neil hated himself for fraternizing with them, but it was better than feeling completely left out.

After locking his bike to a railing in the carpark of the Stillorgan Orchard, Neil skipped up the steps that led to the cinema. Quarter to nine. Good, he thought, he wouldn't have to stand in line and pretend he was waiting for someone.

"Neil!"

Neil's heart sank. All the people in the line turned to look at him.

"Hey, Neil!" It was the unmistakeable voice of his sister Jackie. Neil turned around and saw her and her boyfriend, Liam. There was no escape.

Neil grinned as he joined them. "How's it going?"

"How're you, Neil?" Liam beamed his friendly smile. Both Liam and Jackie were wearing odd shoes again. It was their latest craze. They had started off wearing odd socks, before graduating to odd shoes. One day Neil had bumped into the pair of them on Grafton Street, when they were wearing one running shoe and one Doc Marten each.

"Who're you here with?" Jackie asked, searching around for her younger brother's friends.

"I'm supposed to meet Gary and Tom," Neil lied, "but I'm a bit late. You haven't seen them, have you?"

Jackie and Liam shook their heads vaguely. Then Jackie's eyes lit up as she grabbed Neil's sleeve. "Did the old pair say anything about me not coming home last night?" Both Jackie and Liam were second year science students at UCD. Liam had a flat in Rathmines and Jackie often stayed the night there. She would phone home after the pubs closed and tell her parents she had missed the last bus and was going to stay with her friend Michelle.

Neil shrugged. "Nah, just the usual martyr act from the old dear."

"Oh, what have we reared?" Jackie was doing an exaggerated mimicry of their mother.

Liam smiled. "Which film are you going to?" he asked, flicking his long hair back from his face and jangling the huge collection of love bangles on his wrist. Both he and Jackie gave each other a bangle to mark each new week of their relationship.

"*The Crying Game*," Neil told him, wishing he had someone to wear bangles for.

"That's what we're going to," Jackie said. "You might as well sit with us, looks like the lads have gone in already."

The line had started to move. Neil sensed that Jackie knew that he had come alone. She was probably wondering what was wrong with her little brother. Why didn't he hang around with the crowd? Neil saw a flicker of the same look of pity that he'd seen on his mum's face earlier. He wished he had hidden away with his books as usual, invisible to the world.

chapter two

A carnival atmosphere swept through the Sixth Year classrooms as the end of term drew closer. Everyone knew that it was the end of an era, a benchmark in their lives, and a strange aura of camaraderie and goodwill pervaded. Fellows who had hated one another's guts for the past six years exchanged pleasantries. The coolest bloke in the class, Mick Toner, who had behaved like a rock star for the past few years and made a particular point of not speaking to anyone who played rugby, now dropped his guard and babbled away like an excited kid on Christmas morning. The two cynics of the class, Mal and Tony, were barely recognizable without their sneers. Even despised teachers were treated as friends.

But a great cloud of nervous anxiety hung over everything. Neil smiled to himself; he and his classmates were like unborn infants reluctant to leave the womb, afraid of the great unknown that was beckoning and that they had all been looking forward to escaping into for so long. Now, even the classrooms that had always been seen as torture chambers suddenly became appealing. They personified safety and certainty. All decisions were made there for you. Maybe it wasn't such a bad place after all, he thought, but it was like something he had read somewhere once, that most people only realize how good times were when they are over.

"I don't like saying good-bye," Father Donnelly, flanked by all the other teachers, was addressing the Sixth Years, all of whom had assembled in the hall, "so I'm not going to say good-bye."

"Say au revoir." The voice from the back of the hall was clearly audible, and a ripple of amused laughter filled the hall.

Up on the stage, Father Donnelly smiled benevolently, biding his time, waiting for the noise to subside. Then he pointed down at the grinning culprit. "Keep that sense of humor, Mr. Toner, God knows you'll need it." This was greeted by a burst of laughter, as every head turned to look at the now-red-faced Mick Toner.

Father Donnelly rambled into his end-of-term speech.

He reminded them how fortunate they were to have been educated at Blackrock Academy. This was met by low mumblings of protest from the back of the hall. He told them that they must show compassion to those less fortunate than them, that they must take Christ's message out into the world with them.

"His rule is simple…" Father Donnelly paused.

"No baseball hats in the classroom," a deep voice at the back of the hall interrupted, and this was greeted by another burst of laughter.

Father Donnelly chose to ignore the comment, "…Love God and love thy neighbor."

"Even Mal and Tony?" The deep voice was again followed by sniggers, quickly silenced by Father Donnelly's icy glare. Neil felt sorry for Donno; it was obvious that the ceremony meant more to him than it did to his students. He had admitted as much to Neil and a couple of others on the Co-Operation North weekend. He had told them that summer was the saddest time of the year for him. The graduating class, which he had known since they were twelve-year-olds, would walk out the school gates, and very few of them ever came back to see him again. Neil decided that he was definitely going to drop in and visit Donno regularly.

Father Donnelly signaled for attention. "Now, all that's left for me to do is to open these envelopes here in front of me and announce the winners of this year's prizes."

The tension in the hall mounted. Father Donnelly didn't lift his eyes from the gathered assembly as he tore the envelopes open. He seemed to enjoy watching them squirm. There was a prize to be awarded for each subject and each recipient had to suffer the long walk up to the stage to collect his prize. Drops of perspiration trickled down Neil's rib cage, his heart pounded. The prize for English was about to be announced and he was one of the hot favorites.

Big deal, he thought, *who gives a shit if I win or not. It'll all be forgotten about by tomorrow anyway.*

But try as he might, he still couldn't ease his anxiety. No point in fooling yourself, Neiley Nook, you're a competitive fucker and you want that prize.

Father Donnelly held the piece of paper up in front of him. Half an hour seemed to pass before he revealed the winner's name.

"Neil Byrne."

Neil froze. Everything went hazy.

"Yo, Byrner!" someone shouted.

Gary hugged him in congratulation. All around him his classmates turned their heads to look at him. He was a popular winner. Thunderous applause, piercing whistles, and the din of stamping feet rang in Neil's ears as he walked the seemingly endless distance to the stage. Arms reached out to slap him on the back and punch him as he passed. Even ice-cool Mick Toner was applauding wildly, and the sneers were strangely absent from Mal's and Tony's faces. Neil struggled to fight back the tears of pride. But he felt uneasy as he turned to show the crystal bowl to his admirers. Would their adulation be so enthusiastic if they knew the truth about him? What would they be shouting at him then?

His parents' delight turned to silence when Neil broke the news to them. He picked at the little specks of dirt lodged beneath his fingernails while he waited for their response. He realized that it would come as a shock.

"Liberal Arts?" His dad almost spat the words out in disgust.

"Well, English and history…"

Another long silence followed. The martyred look creased his mum's pinched face. His dad's face was red with anger.

"I mean, that's what I'm interested in," Neil pleaded. "I won the prize for English, didn't I?" he added.

His dad stood up, rested his backside against the draining board, and stared intently at his son. Through the kitchen window behind his dad, Neil counted seven magpies perched on the thick branch supporting the tree house. "I'm interested in classical music, Neil, but I'd never be able to make a living out of it," his dad replied calmly.

Neil bowed his head and stared at his feet. He knew the line his father's argument was going to follow. You'll get a job anywhere in the world with an engineering degree. Liberal Arts is for rich kids who can step into Daddy's company when their fooling-around days are over.

One for sorrow, two for joy, three for a girl, four for a boy, five for...Neil's mind went blank, he couldn't get past four in the rhyme his mum had taught him as a child.

"English and history books should be read as a hobby, in your spare time...An arts degree isn't worth tuppence when it comes to the jobs market."

"You need one if you want to become a teacher."

"A teacher?" His dad's voice was laced with incredulity.

"You want to become a teacher?" his mum asked in surprise.

"Well, I wouldn't mind it," Neil lied. He had no idea what he wanted to do after college; he never looked that far into the future.

"In case you haven't noticed, there're more teachers in the unemployment line this country than there are working," his dad snorted derisively. And once again, Neil felt like breaking down and telling them all about the monsters that stalked him. About the sadness, the despair, the hopelessness, but worst of all, the horrible loneliness that he kept hidden deep in his heart. *Try to understand*, his eyes pleaded. *Hug me and tell me that you'll love me no matter what.*

His dad prodded his shoulder. "Are you listening to us at all?"

"Yeah." Neil swallowed to clear the lump in his throat.

"Look, just do your bloody exams first. We'll discuss this again some other time," his dad said, and left the room. The front door slammed shut behind him.

Neil remained seated as his mum started to clear the dishes off the table. Eventually, she broke the awkward silence. "Your father isn't too pleased with your sudden change of heart."

"It's not sudden." Neil's reply was sullen.

"Well, it's very sudden to us, Neil…I don't know, but d'you have any idea how much it costs to go to college these days?"

Neil said nothing.

"I mean, we're not made of money, your father only has a limited salary," she sighed. "With both you and Jackie at college, things are going to be very tight…"

Neil dug a teaspoon into the sugar bowl and stirred the white granules around slowly. How could she worry about such stupid things at a time like this? Why didn't she understand?

"But we don't mind making sacrifices if we know that you're going to have a chance of getting a decent job at the end of it."

"Well, if I get a Morrison Visa, I won't need to go to college at all, and you won't need to spend a penny on me," Neil countered cruelly. This sparked a brisk upsurge in his mum's work rate. She got down on her hands and knees, shook some Vim onto a scouring pad, and began her assault on the greasy interior of the oven. "Martyr overload" was what Jackie called their mum's habit of diving into her least favorite chores when she was upset. But America was a particularly sore point. Both of Neil's older brothers, Paul and Joe, had got visas a couple of years before, and the pair of them now lived in New York. She never admitted it, but Neil knew that their leaving broke his mum's heart, and the last thing she wanted was for her youngest boy to emigrate.

But this silent suffering angered Neil. Why didn't everyone just say what they felt? Instead of listing off a million-and-one reasons, why didn't his mum just admit that she didn't want him to leave because she loved him? How could she expect him to be less secretive with her if she wasn't prepared to be open with him?

"I better do some studying," Neil muttered, standing up. He needed to have a smoke and listen to some music. His mum kept scrubbing, ignoring him as he crossed the kitchen. Neil lingered at the door a moment, smiling inwardly as he watched his mum's furious scraping.

But then the unexpected happened. His mum spoke.

"Your friend Becky phoned for you earlier."

"Oh really, what time?" Neil asked calmly.

"Earlier, I don't know what time," his mum said, resuming her scrubbing at a slower pace.

Neil left the room. As he dialed Becky's number, he grimaced. He had finally recalled the last lines of the magpie rhyme: Five for silver, six for gold, seven for secrets never to be told.

———————

Neil and Becky went on a spree using Neil's English prize as their excuse. Neil couldn't stop talking once he went over two pints. The words tumbled out so fast that he sometimes had trouble understanding what he was saying himself. But Becky was obviously enjoying his company. She kept rolling back on her seat in laughter. Neil always felt relaxed when he was with Becky; she was different to all the other girls. To her, he was simply her friend Neil and not the Blackrock winger who scored a goal in the Schools' Cup final. He could be himself with her; there was no need for his usual game-playing.

After their fourth pint he made the most difficult

decision of his life. The secret never to be told. The time had come, he decided; someone had to be told before he went mad.

He held Becky's hand and beckoned her closer. "Becky," he slurred, "if I tell you something, will you swear you'll never tell a soul as long as you live?"

"Of course."

"No, you've got to swear."

"Neil, you can trust me." There was a hint of indignation in her reply.

Neil held his head in his hands. "Oh God, I don't know how to say this."

Becky eyed him patiently. Neil put his lips up to her ear and purposely made his whisper incomprehensible.

"What?" she muttered.

"Got a problem that won't go away," he said, and an anxious look crossed Becky's face—the type of look that people give when they're told that someone is terminally ill.

"No, it's nothing like you think. Like, I'm not sick or anything," he added quickly. Then he took a blurred look around the half-empty pub to ensure for the hundredth time that no one was within earshot. He had to go through with it; he couldn't live with this secrecy any longer. He had rehearsed this moment countless times in the privacy of his bedroom. Again he put his lips up to

Becky's ear and whispered, "I think that…I'm gay."

As soon as the admission had passed his lips, he wanted to retract it. He watched Becky's face closely. Tears welled up in his eyes. He wanted the ground to open up and swallow him. He was crazy. She was going to shriek and run out of the pub and tell everyone. His life was over. He'd definitely have to go to America now.

Pretend it was a joke, he thought. *Becky, I was only messing. Had you going, though, didn't I?* But he needn't have worried. She shook her head and smiled warmly.

"I thought as much," she said calmly, almost giving Neil heart failure. Who else knew? Was it common knowledge? That's why all his friends were so friendly; they felt sorry for him. Maybe he walked in a way that gave it away, or maybe it was the way he held his cigarette, or even the way he spoke…That was it, it was his voice—it was too soft. Gary's mum had commented on it once. What was it she said? "Neil, you've got a lovely voice." Hah, what the old lady meant was, "Neil, you've got a gay voice."

"Don't worry, no one else suspects." Becky smiled as though she had read his thoughts.

"But . . . How did you know?"

"Feminine intuition. And I am a friend of yours, Neil." She smiled, patting his knee.

"But why didn't you say anything?"

Becky shrugged. "I hoped you'd tell me in your own time," she said, stroking his cheek gently.

"Would you have guessed at all if, say, you didn't know me?" Neil asked, relieved now that his panic attack was unfounded.

Becky looked puzzled. "What d'you mean?"

"Say if you met me as a stranger." Yet again Neil checked that no one was eavesdropping. "Could you tell that I was gay?"

Becky laughed. "Why, what does a gay person look like?"

"Ah, you know what I mean."

"Well, you don't look effeminate, if that's what you're worried about." Becky smiled. "Quite the opposite, in fact."

Neil sat back and sighed. Then Becky leaned over, wrapped her arms tightly around his neck, and kissed him. All the years of pain and frustration seemed to drain from inside him as though a ten-ton weight had been lifted from his shoulders.

"I love you just the way you are," Becky whispered into his ear.

"You should write songs," Neil replied with a grin, earning himself a gentle blow on the shoulder.

A lounge boy gave them a quick glance as he passed. Neil leaned over and whispered into Becky's ear. "Lovely bum, hasn't he?"

Becky's face went into contortions. Neil dug a tissue out of his pocket and blew his nose. The couple at the next table were giving them strange looks, but he didn't care now. He felt like standing up, punching the air, and shouting in jubilation. Instead he took a long gulp of his pint.

"I'm glad you told me," Becky said, pressing his hand.

"So am I," Neil grinned.

"I mean, it's great; now we can go out eyeing up the prospects together." She added with a smile, "D'you know something, Neil? You've got the sexiest eyes."

Neil's face went crimson. "Stoppit, yer makin' me go all scarlet," he joked in a strong Dublin accent, trying to conceal his embarrassment.

"Don't worry, you're not my type, but it's great that I can say these things to you now without you getting the wrong idea."

"Don't be so sure, babe," Neil purred.

"You're going to drive all the old queens wild," she said, and Neil's laugh was a mixture of nervousness and excitement, "And the young queens."

Neil looked at her uncertainly. Surely she didn't mean what he thought she meant. But she did.

"So when are you going to go into town?"

"Huh?"

"Into a gay bar," she whispered.

Neil laughed incredulously. "Are you kidding?"

"You're the one who said you wanted to be in love."

"Jesus, but a…"—Neil checked that no one was listening before he mouthed the words that sent a tingle of excitement down his backbone—"…a gay bar?"

"Well, everyone will have three heads with horns growing out of their foreheads, but apart from that I'm sure they'll all look pretty normal."

Neil shook his head. "I couldn't, Becky, no way."

Becky shrugged her shoulders. "You've only got one life. If you want to die wondering, that's your business."

"I'd be sure to be spotted. Can you just imagine if my parents found out?" Neil gave a long sigh.

"Never know, you might meet your dad in there," Becky replied in a deadpan voice, causing Neil to double up with laughter. He pictured his dad with a bushy mustache and his hair cropped, sporting a lumberjack shirt, leaning against a bar. The thought repulsed him. But at the same time Becky's apparent familiarity with the gay scene was beginning to puzzle him.

"You sound like you know the place," he said with a laugh.

"I do," came Becky's reply.

"What?" Neil's eyes opened wide in amazement.

"I've been in there," Becky added calmly.

"Go 'way." Neil's mind was working overtime. Surely Becky wasn't going to tell him that she was gay!

"With Jimmy."

A pause followed as Neil caught his breath.

"Your brother, Jimmy?" he whispered.

"Hmm," Becky nodded.

"Is he…?" Neil asked incredulously.

Becky smiled as she nodded. Neil leaned back in the seat and sighed.

"And you thought you were the only one." Becky poked his ribs playfully.

Neil grinned, he couldn't hide his delight. At last he knew of someone else who was definitely gay. He tried to form a picture of Becky's brother. He had been in Sixth Year at Blackrock when Neil was First Year, in the same class as Neil's older brother, Paul. He was the school's main cheerleader for the rugby matches, and he used to dive into the packed crowd of squealing Rock supporters and belt anyone who wasn't cheering loud enough. After he left school, he set up a rock band, Neil remembered them opening for the Hothouse Flowers in Blackrock Park one hot summer's afternoon. The band moved to London soon after, following a vague promise of a recording contract that never materialized. But now Neil understood why Becky's brother had settled in London. Away from all the neighborhood tongues. That's what he'd do himself, he decided. As soon as he could afford it, he'd go abroad. Live his life the way he wanted to live it without all the hassle and pretense he'd have to put up with at home.

"But listen, keep that to yourself," Becky spoke in a low voice.

"Of course." Neil was still reeling from the news. But the thought of escaping from the country made him feel good. It was the obvious thing to do.

"So, if you want me to come into town with you," she continued, "just ask; I know the ropes."

"Ah, I don't know," Neil said vaguely, but the thought of having Becky with him was appealing. "Tell me, does your whole family know about Jimmy being gay?"

"Nah, he just told me when he was home last Christmas."

"And, does he, eh . . . have a boyfriend in London?"

"Yeah, Jamie. He's been living with him for five years now."

"God!" Neil couldn't prevent his display of surprise.

"Practically married," Becky said.

Neil grinned. He loved when Becky behaved so matter-of-factly on subjects that most people would've had kittens over. Suddenly emigration had lost all its sad connotations.

Then, a blond-haired lounge boy smiled and nodded shyly at Neil as he rushed past their table with a trayful of drinks. Becky pressed her leg against Neil's and muttered her approval.

"Oh my God!" Neil gasped, nodding after the lounge

boy. "I never realized he worked here."

"You know him?" Becky licked her lips.

"Know him? I've been crazy about him for years," Neil whispered, all thoughts of emigration deserting him. Becky raised her eyebrows.

"His name's Ian. He's a class below me at school," Neil explained.

Becky smiled. "Well, one thing I'll say for you, there's nothing wrong with your taste."

"Cute, isn't he?"

"A little dreamboat," Becky said.

"I was only fourteen or fifteen at the time. . .and I remember, 'Nothing Compares 2 U' was being played on every radio station."

"So that was your song?"

Neil nodded. "Yeah, well, more like my song. But I felt so happy, I wanted to rush home and tell my mother all about this gorgeous bloke I had seen at school." Neil laughed wryly and Becky squeezed his hand. "I was afraid to speak to him in case people accused me of trying to chat him up.

"But then, a couple of months ago, after one of the cup matches, he came up and spoke to me."

"The little slut." Becky nudged him teasingly.

"Just to congratulate me."

"Oh yeah, that's what they all say."

Neil laughed. "Anyway, he looked even better close-up."

"I hope you gave him your phone number," Becky teased.

"Someone in my position has to be responsible," Neil said.

"Of course." Becky was smiling.

"Anyway, there I was, the supposed rugby hero, practically melting with passion, wobbly legged, butterflies in my stomach as I spoke to this vision. Nearly wetting myself. I mean, I never felt as nervous before any rugby match. But as usual, Gary and the rest of the lads were waiting for me, and instead of staying with the angel, I had to make some joke for the lads about the hassle of autograph hunters, and go off to the pub and listen to them go on and on about their girlfriends."

"They were probably just jealous because Ian was chatting you up."

"Definitely." Neil smiled inwardly as he remembered how he used to wish that he had blond hair and how he pretended that he was left-handed after he discovered that Ian was left-handed. In some strange way it made him feel like him. But he knew that there were certain things that were too silly to tell even Becky.

"Anyway, what did your admirer say to you?"

Neil sat up, shaking himself from his pleasant memory.

"I haven't a clue; I just stood there staring." Neil stopped and grinned when he noticed that Becky was pretending to play a violin.

"Never seen eyes so blue…But d'you know, the funny thing is, I'd say if I had the nerve to suggest a little hanky-panky, I don't think he would've objected," Neil said.

"Really?" Becky's eyes widened.

"But of course you've ruined my chances now."

"Me?"

"Yeah, he's seen you. He'll assume you're my girlfriend."

"I'll tell him the truth."

"Yeah, I can just imagine. 'Here, young fella, yer man over there fancies you.'"

"Give me a break, I'm a little more subtle than that."

Neil smiled wanly. "It's a crazy situation. Sometimes I wish I'd never set eyes on him."

Becky laughed, but then she looked away as she said in a solemn voice, "I know exactly what it feels like, Neil."

Neil winced; maybe she was going to tell him she was gay.

"It's the night for baring our souls," she said, turning to face him, and holding both his hands gently. "D'you swear you won't tell anyone?" she added in a slightly mocking tone, and Neil smiled to acknowledge the silliness of his earlier insistence.

"D'you remember that bloke I was going out with the

time I went to your debs with you?"

"Yeah," Neil nodded. He remembered all right, the fact that Becky was going out with someone was one of the reasons he had felt safe in asking her.

"Well, he's married."

"Really?" Neil gasped, doing his best to contain his surprise.

"Hmm," Becky muttered, her head bowed now, her face clouded with anguish.

The events of the past few months all fell into place for Neil. Now he realized why he had never met the famous Brian. And why he saw so much of Becky even while she was going out with Brian. The one time he had broached the subject, Becky had been vague, telling him that Brian worked odd hours or something.

"Oh, he promised me the usual," Becky rolled her eyes, "the earth, moon, and stars...And like an idiot, of course, I believed him."

Neil said nothing; it was his turn to listen with compassion.

"But when it came to the crunch, he said he couldn't leave his kids."

"I'm sorry." Neil knew it was a stupid thing to say, but he could think of nothing else.

"One thing I'll warn you about, Neil," Becky turned to look at him. "Most men are fickle."

Neil nodded, not really understanding what Becky meant.

"But the worst part is that I'll never feel like that about anyone again."

Neil patted Becky's arm gently.

"That's why I have to get away for the summer." Becky was going to France as an au pair.

"I'm going to miss you," Neil said, and he meant it now more than he ever did before.

"I'll miss you too," she murmured, squeezing his hand tightly.

"You better write every day," Neil smiled.

"And you better write and tell me all about your adventures in gaytown," Becky said, wagging her finger at him playfully.

"Uh-oh, we have company," Neil whispered, nodding toward Gary and Trish, who were making their way over to their table.

"Let's get some tongues wagging," Becky whispered, grabbing hold of Neil's hand and resting her head against his shoulder.

"How's it going?" Neil beamed, watching the surprised expressions of the two new arrivals.

"Who's for a drink?" Gary asked. Neil shook his head, pointing at their full glasses. He smiled inwardly as Trish sat down opposite them and did her best to pretend that nothing was amiss. But he could sense her delight; at last Neil had joined the rhyming couplets.

"You remember Becky, don't you?" Neil said to Trish, doing his best not to slur.

"Yes, we met at the debs," Trish said, formally extending her hand for Becky to shake. Becky nearly overturned the table when she stretched for Trish's hand. Neil and Becky burst out laughing and Trish forced a faint smile onto her face.

"I believe congratulations are in order," she said to Neil.

Neil blinked in surprise. Surely she wasn't referring to his apparent new romance.

"The prize for English," Trish added quickly, as though she had read his mind.

"Ah yeah, thanks, Trish." Neil grinned drunkenly.

"My little genius," Becky said, leaning over to plant a slobbery kiss on Neil's cheek, but still Trish didn't bat an eyelid.

Neil noticed Gary giving him the thumbs-up from the bar. Neil winked at him conspiratorially. The ridiculousness of the situation amused him. Here was the guy he had lived next door to since the day he was born, his closest friend over the years, an inseparable pal with whom he had gone everywhere and done everything, and even he didn't have a clue. Neil recalled the

loneliness he felt after Trish had arrived on the scene a
year before. His pal was rarely seen after that. If he wanted
to see Gary, he had to see Trish as well. And he soon got
tired of being the fifth wheel.

"Gary should've ordered the drinks off one of the
lounge boys," Becky said, squeezing Neil's hand tightly.

"Yeah, the lounge staff here is pretty good," Neil said,
and both he and Becky giggled.

"How long have you two been here?" Trish asked,
with the short uncomfortable laugh of someone feeling
left out.

"That long." Neil held his hands miles apart.

"Stop boasting, Byrner," Gary said, rejoining them.

Neil knew it was stupid, but his apparent romance
made him feel good. Accepted. Normal. He assumed his
friends had discussed the lack of romance in his life. They
discussed everyone else so there was no reason to think
that he should be excused. *He gets too nervous when he's
alone with a girl, he's too shy, he lacks confidence, he wants to
study all the time, maybe he can't get it up.* He could imagine
their conclusions. But the real reason probably never
occurred to them. They knew he wasn't that type. A
rugby player! For God's sake, he won a Senior Cup medal
with Blackrock! No way. And, he had slept with Yvonne
Lawlor, hadn't he? Anyway, there isn't the slightest hint of
effeminacy about him. They could point the finger of

doubt at a number of other blokes in his class all right, but not Neil Byrne. No, no, certainly not Neil.

Becky stood up and stumbled across the lounge to the toilets. She had lapsed into a state of boredom since Gary and Trish's arrival. The conversation was much too superficial for her. The moment she disappeared into the ladies' room, Gary grabbed Neil's leg.

"You're a dark horse!" he exclaimed. "How long's this been going on?"

"Oh, now." Neil grinned evasively, conscious of his reddening face. Gary licked his finger, touched it against Neil's cheek, and made a hissing sound.

"You make a good couple," Trish said approvingly. Neil looked at her to see if she was being sarcastic. No, he didn't think so. Trish didn't have a sarcastic bone in her body.

"Here's to a long and happy relationship." Gary held his pint glass aloft.

"And a spring wedding," Neil said, clinking glasses, bringing the expected polite laughter from Trish.

But Neil couldn't believe that he was actually clinking glasses, joining in one of the sickliest of couple routines, a routine that always reminded him that he was alone. After his admission to Becky, he knew his days of hanging around with the couples were numbered. He sighed with relief when he saw Becky reemerge from the ladies' room.

Then, just as she sat down, the blond lounge boy came over to their table. Neil winced when he felt Becky's foot press down heavily on top of his.

"How's it going, Ian?" Gary said.

"Hiya." But the blushing lounge boy was looking at Neil, returning his friendly smile. Under the table, Becky was rubbing her foot slowly up and down the inside of Neil's calf.

"Forty pints of Guinness, please," Neil said, bringing a delightful grin from the lounge boy, who had now begun to wipe down their table. As he stretched to reach the dirty ashtray, Neil had to struggle to prevent himself from touching his hairless arms. Just a friendly little stroke, he thought. No one would notice. And even if they did, he could blame the drink. But he was beaten to it. Gary reached over and patted the perfectly shaped bottom.

"You've got a lovely bum," Gary said with a laugh. "D'you know that?"

Poor Ian's face went crimson as he grinned and pushed Gary away playfully. Neil felt like screaming.

"God, he's beautiful looking," Trish said to Becky, after Ian had gone.

"Hmm, he is," Becky nodded.

Neil bit his tongue so hard he was sure he drew blood.

"And d'you see how blue his eyes were?" Trish added.

"Wouldn't you die for them?" Becky sighed, again

nudging Neil's foot under the table.

"I'd say he's a bit…" Gary said, swiveling his hand in a semicircular motion.

"What?" There was a hint of disgust in Becky's tone.

"You know, a fag," Gary added in an effeminate voice, letting his wrist hang limply.

"Why?" Becky asked like a shot. Her fiery stare was making Gary feel uncomfortable.

"Because he's so gentle," Gary laughed, trying his best to conceal his embarrassment. "I mean, did you see the way he picked the empty glasses up?"

"So that makes him gay?" Becky wasn't letting him away that easily. Neil sipped his pint anxiously; he knew Becky could get very headstrong when she had been drinking. But it was fun watching Gary squirm.

"Now, don't get me wrong, I've got nothing against gays," Gary added with another laugh, quickly deciding that the liberal stance was the one to take with Becky.

"That's big of you," Becky muttered.

"So long as they keep well away from me." Gary guffawed.

"Don't flatter yourself." Becky almost snarled.

Gary glanced at Trish and Neil in bewilderment during the awkward silence that followed. Neil knew he'd have to crack some stupid joke to dispel the potentially nasty situation.

"I hope he's not gay, 'cause I slept with him last week," Neil said, bringing the expected laughs of relief from Gary and Trish. Becky sat back and took no further part in the conversation.

Neil made sure that they passed Ian on their way out of the pub. Even though Becky was humming "Nothing Compares to You," Neil felt his heart flutter when he and Ian exchanged parting nods. They made their farewells outside under the clear sky, and as Gary and Trish promised to meet them again soon, Neil heard Becky muttering something derogatory under her breath.

Neil reflected on the evening as he strolled home alone from Becky's house through the ghostly, silver moonlight. Maybe his timing was wrong, a week before his graduation was hardly the time to be laying his soul bare. But what the hell, he was glad he had done it. Maybe things weren't as bad as he thought. Jimmy McGann was gay and he seemed to be enjoying himself. Neil's step slowed. His house had come into view. It looked like something out of a postcard with the moonlight shrouding the rooftop. But underneath that roof, the secrets would linger. He knew he'd never say it. Nothing would ever change. Seven for secrets never to be told.

chapter three

The following week was a blur of studying, eating, and sleeping. Time passed in a dreamlike fashion. But the dreaded day drew closer. Neil couldn't get to sleep the night before his first exam, English. The more he tried to sleep, the more awake he felt. His head was running riot with a jumble of poems, characters, metaphors, similes, symbolism, imagery. Imagery? What does it mean? He realized that he didn't really know the meaning of the word. How was he supposed to answer a question if he didn't even know what the bloody question meant?

Neil sat up in his bed. Maybe he was going mad. It was four o'clock in the morning, a couple of hours to the start of the most important exam of his life, and crazy, jumbled conversations were going on inside his head. He shook his head and slapped his face sharply. One thing was sure: No one else doing the exams was still awake.

A prayer, he decided; it was time for a prayer. The last resort. He wiped his damp forehead and sighed. It was best to do a deal with Jesus or whoever.

Right, here's the deal, Jesus, he bargained. *You let me get to sleep and I promise that I won't wank for a week. Okay? That's fair enough, isn't it? You know that'll be a struggle for me, so come on, be fair.* Neil laid his head back down on his pillow and closed his eyes. No sound. Just the faint ticking of his clock and the rhythmic drone of his dad's snores in the next room…

He was definitely feeling sleepy now, he would curl up fetal-style, pretend that he was a little kid again, and everything would be all right. In the morning his mum would make him a special breakfast, and she would probably kiss him before he left the house, and yes, he would kiss her back, and no, he wouldn't be embarrassed, and yes, he would even tell her that he loved her. And she would smile and ruffle his hair like she used to do, and tell him that he was her special little boy, that there was no need for him to feel unhappy. And she would say that no matter what, she still loved him. And maybe he would go caddying for his dad like he used to do. Yes, and his dad

45

would smile, drape his arm around his shoulder, and call him his little chatterbox. "Mister Happy, d'you know what you are? You're my little chatterbox." And of course he'd say it in such a way that he'd want Neil to continue chattering...Mister Happy. He'd forgotten that name. Mister Happy with the perpetual grin on his face.

Neil tensed. No, surely he hadn't heard what he thought he had heard. He held his breath and listened. A few seconds passed. Then he heard it again, clear and distinct. Birdsong. *Tweet-tweet, chirp-chirp.* A lone voice, slightly husky, but it would rise to a crescendo in no time. Then he heard a dog bark. This was followed by the sound of a foghorn way out at sea, and the distant rumble of early morning traffic. He looked out the window and saw the row of singing birds perched on top of the tree house. Forget about getting any sleep now. He had to talk to someone.

He crept into Jackie's bedroom. She was fast asleep, curled up on her side, with one hand hanging limply out over the edge of the bed and the other hidden somewhere beneath her duvet. Neil looked out her bedroom window. The first gray streaks of dawn light were falling upon the road outside. The sky was beginning to brighten out over the sea. He crossed the room and shook his sister gently.

"What time is it?" Jackie awoke with a start. When she lifted her head, her long strands of silky hair seemed almost reluctant to leave the pillow. She propped herself up on her elbow and rubbed her sleepy eyes with her knuckles. The multicolored collection of love bangles slipped down her arm, making a jangling sound.

"I can't get to sleep," Neil whispered, and the annoyance drained from her face when she remembered what day it was and how upset her younger brother was.

"I'm going to be too tired to do the exams." Neil was close to tears.

Jackie sat up and calmly motioned him to sit down on the edge of her bed. She reached out, held both his shoulders, and stared into his eyes. "You'll be fine, Neil," she said quietly. "Loads of people stay up studying all night before exams and they get top marks."

Neil forced a thin smile onto his face. He knew she was just trying to humor him.

"I'm telling you, Liam does it all the time. You see, it doesn't matter how tired you think you are; the moment you step inside that exam hall your adrenaline will start pumping and you'll feel as fresh as a daisy. Anyway, you'll have no problem, you've got brains to burn."

Neil looked away and blinked back his mounting tears. He felt so disoriented now, he was tempted to tell Jackie what he supposed she already suspected. But she could never suspect how lost and lonely he sometimes felt. Tonight, however, was hardly the time for major revelations. Instead he muttered good night, went back to his own bedroom and finally fell asleep.

———————

Neil's heart missed a beat the following morning when he walked down the corridor to the exam hall. Ian, the lounge boy, sporting a red baseball cap, faded blue jeans, and an extra-long checked shirt, was sitting outside the door along with a couple of other Fifth Years who were there as assistants to the exam proctor. Neil smiled to himself; he knew that their main duty was to accompany examinees to the toilets.

"How many jobs have you got?" Neil joked when Ian flashed him one of his boyish grins.

"Someone has to stop you all from cogging," Ian replied, and Neil gave him a friendly punch on the shoulder.

Jackie was right, once he was handed the exam paper, any trace of tiredness disappeared instantly. The sight of Ian was guaranteed to awaken him from the deepest slumbers anyway. A quick perusal of the questions, and it became obvious that Father Donno's predictions were uncannily accurate. Neil smiled to himself when he saw the question on the use of imagery and symbolism in *Wuthering Heights*. He realized that he knew the meaning of the word, all right; the problems would arise only if he had to explain it to somebody else. So much for wanting to be a teacher. But the essay question was where Neil excelled; the title he chose leaped off the page at him. Loneliness. Donno had warned them to be specific if they did this sort of essay and to try and write from their own experience. Neil grinned; whoever had set the paper must have being thinking of him. His pen couldn't move fast enough as he scribbled down all his experiences over the past year. It was like therapy, and the presence of Ian outside the door certainly helped to focus his thoughts. He couldn't wait to tell Becky. But then he realized that she was more than likely doing the same essay herself about her adventures with Brian, the married man. The correctors were going to have some fun reading their scripts. But halfway through, Neil got a panic attack. What if the exam corrector was a bigot? What if they decided to trace it back to the school and then to the student and told Donno that he had a queer in his midst? Donno would probably try and hop him if he knew. Neil sniggered aloud at the thought, bringing a puzzled look from Mick Toner, who was chewing his pen and staring into space at the desk alongside his.

Neil put his hand up and attracted the proctor's attention. It was bathroom time. His own reward for doing what he considered a decent essay. Much to Neil's relief,

Ian was up out of his seat in a flash once he saw who it was who was leaving the hall.

"How's the exam going?" Ian asked shyly while they strolled down the wooden corridor together.

"Ah, not too bad." Neil tried to sound casual.

"I heard the choice of essays is pretty crap."

"Bet you've been talking to Mick Toner," Neil said, laughing as he sneaked a look at the sky-blue eyes.

"Yeah," Ian smiled, "he was really pissed off."

Neil wondered what Ian's reaction would be if he told him that he had been the inspiration behind his essay. *Hey gorgeous, I'm dedicating my work of art to you, what d'you think of that? And another thing, I've written poems about you, what d'you think of that?* But Ian wasn't thinking of anything, he was holding the bathroom door open for Neil with his left hand.

"See you," Neil said, heading straight for one of the stalls, deciding that he couldn't really go to the urinals when he didn't even want to go to the toilet. He stood inside the dark, pungent-smelling cubicle, thinking of the expression that would have formed on Ian's face if he had asked him in for a quickie. *He seems so innocent,* Neil thought, *he probably wouldn't even know what a quickie was.* After about thirty seconds, Neil flushed the toilet and left the stall.

"Ah, nothing like a quickie," he quipped, washing his hands. Ian smiled. And Neil wanted to whisper *I love you* like Yvonne Lawlor had whispered into his ear a couple of weeks before at Hollywood Nights. It had been an awkward moment, which, true to form, Neil had gotten out of by making a joke. "Love is subjective," he had said with a laugh. It was cruel, he knew, but Yvonne would recover, and anyway, people like her had it easy; she could go around declaring her love openly without having to move to another country. After that incident he made himself scarce at Hollies, insisting that the place was only for kids, that Yvonne Lawlor was a bitch, that he was sick of meeting the likes of Mal and Tony, and that the music they played there was woeful. Then Neil had what he considered to be a flash of inspiration.

"D'you ever go to Hollies?"

Ian looked puzzled. Of course he was puzzled, Neil thought, what was this Sixth Year bloke doing asking him a question like that? In the middle of his final exams, for God's sake!

"Sometimes," Ian said with a shrug of his slender shoulders.

"Great place, isn't it?" Neil added, drying his hands.

Ian nodded nonchalantly, and Neil felt his heart surge. It was obvious that Ian hated Hollies, more than likely because there were women there. He was definitely gay.

Then Neil sighed inwardly. How pathetic could you get? Just leave the poor kid be. How would you like it if he was your little brother, and someone was chasing him like this?

But he knew it didn't matter how pathetic he was being; he wanted to know everything about Ian.

"I better get back and finish my masterpiece," Neil said, leaving the bathroom with Ian tagging along behind him, and he smiled as they parted company.

———————

At lunchtime, Neil opened the front door and heard the blazing argument between his mum and Jackie in the kitchen. His mum had discovered that Jackie was going to Amsterdam to work in the Heineken factory for the summer with Liam and not with her pal Michelle as she had said. He stood in the hallway listening.

"I'm just getting sick and tired of all your lies," his mum said in a weary voice.

"It wasn't a lie. Michelle was going to come with me," Jackie insisted.

"Lookit, Michelle's mother told me that Michelle never had any intentions of ever going to Amsterdam. She wouldn't allow her." His mum sighed. "It's just getting to the stage now, Jackie, where I'm not able to believe a word you say."

"Yeah, well, maybe there's a reason for that." Jackie

sounded sulky, and Neil knew what was coming next.

"I beg your pardon?"

"I'm twenty years old. It's time you and Dad stopped treating me like a kid."

"We'll treat you like an adult when you start behaving like an adult."

Neil heard Jackie clicking her tongue and sighing noisily, and he knew that she was rolling her eyes upward, a gesture guaranteed to anger his mum.

"I wish you'd have a little manners when you're speaking to your mother."

"What?" came Jackie's reply of feigned indignation, her bangles rattling as she pushed her hair back from her face, a sure sign that she knew she was in the wrong.

"You know full well what I'm talking about," his mum replied angrily, but this was only a signal for her daughter to go on the offensive.

"Why aren't you honest? Just admit that you don't like Liam."

"This has nothing to do with Liam."

"Oh yes it has."

"It's your own problem if you decide to hang around with someone who smokes drugs," his mum replied. She still hadn't gotten over the shock of Jackie using the fact that Liam smoked pot as a clinching argument during heated dinner-table discussions. Liam always got first class honors in his exams, and this was Jackie's conclusive proof that her parents were wrong again; smoking pot didn't have an adverse effect on the brain.

"Jesus!" Jackie muttered, laughing scornfully.

"Don't be taking the holy name in vain please," his mum snapped. "Not while you're living in this house."

"Everyone in college smokes pot." As usual, Jackie was resorting to her calculated hyperbole.

"You'd be far better off going into a church and saying a few prayers, missy."

Neil heard the clanking sounds of pots being dumped into the sink. Martyr overload time. Jackie had launched into her reasons for not going to Mass. Patriarchy, power-broking bishops having flings, brainwashing, women being churched after childbirth because they were considered dirty, the sudden convenient disappearance of Limbo, the celibacy lark, the Billings method…She recited her well-worn list.

Neil smiled and shook his head. He could never understand why Jackie made such a fuss about religion. He had given up going to Mass himself a couple of months before when the pope encouraged active job discrimination against gay people in certain situations. It was the only way he could protest against the insensitive statement. But he didn't see the sense in making a big scene about it at home; it was his decision, not his parents'. At the time, he had been one of the few blokes left in his class who still went to Mass. But then, he had his reasons for being a holy Joe. He remembered the priest telling the congregation that Christ died to restore life, while he was praying that people would move ever so slightly so that he could get a better view of Ian. And when the choir sang, their celestial voices were rejoicing his beauty. That heavenly hair, that sweet neck, that angelic dreamy stance. Beauty that poetry was invented for.

Of course, Jackie had raised the topic of the pope's statement every day at dinner for weeks, using it as yet another stick to beat their parents'—particularly their mother's—staunch beliefs. Neil wished he had the nerve to contribute to the discussion, but he was too embarrassed, too self-conscious, and imagined that his parents would start suspecting he was gay if he did. It was ridiculous, he knew, but at the back of his mind there was another fear—the fear that if he started to speak on the subject, the floodgates might burst open, causing the volcano inside him to explode, ripping the cozy little family apart at the seams.

Neil tiptoed upstairs to his bedroom. Jackie's imminent departure depressed him; he didn't relish the thought of being the focus of his parents' attention for the entire summer. And to add to his woes, Becky wasn't going to be around either. He put his headphones on and lit up a cigarette. The dj on the local pirate station was reading out good-luck requests for students doing their final exams. Every request was from a male to a female or vice versa. The rhyming couplets had even hijacked the airwaves. Some day he'd have the courage to phone in a request to break these conventions. "For Ian from his ever-doting boyfriend," he muttered, slipping his hand into his school trousers and circling it around his mounting erection.

The swagger in the faded jeans, the checked shirt with the white T-shirt underneath, the cute little nose that he'd never noticed before. Then the old, faithful image entered his thoughts—the time he had glimpsed Ian standing in a dressing room after rugby training, naked except for a pair of white cotton briefs. A momentary vision of heaven. The fleeting image evaporated, and a new one took its place. They were marooned on a desert island together. Their world was a haze of languid sunshine and open love. Now naked, moving those pale, bloodless lips closer, he glides his hand down along that hairless chest, across that dreamy stomach; panting, he caresses the firm, milky-white bottom, and . . .

Oh fuck, not now, Neil, he told himself, whipping his hand abruptly from his trousers and standing up. *For God's sake, not in the middle of your fucking exams. You'll fall asleep during the afternoon paper, or worse still you'll keel over with a collapsed lung*. And the family doctor would give his hushed diagnosis: too much sex. Family life would never be the same again.

Downstairs, the kitchen door slammed. Footsteps stomped up the stairs. Neil sighed with relief. He recognized Jackie's distinctive step. Her face was ablaze when he slid his bedroom door open. He saw that she wanted to fill him in on her litany of woes, but she bit her tongue. It was his day.

"How'd it go?" she asked, forcing a smile onto her face.

"Cinch," he grinned.

"And you didn't feel tired?"

Neil shook his head.

"See, told you."

Neil was pointing downstairs. "And you told me that you were going to Amsterdam with Michelle," he said, imitating his mum.

"Jesus, that woman!" Jackie sighed, "I'm definitely moving into a flat with Liam next year, and then she'll just have to face up to the fact that we're bonking the brains out of each other."

Jackie opened her eyes wide and gritted her teeth, pretending she was crazy. Neil laughed, more in embarrassment than anything else. Then a concerned look furrowed his sister's face. "Oh, I meant to tell you," she said in an urgent tone, jingling her bangles as she held her hands to her face. "Did you hear about Becky McGann?"

Neil raised his eyebrows quizzically.

"She's having an affair with a married man," Jackie whispered.

"What?" Neil blustered.

"He's in his forties, so I heard anyway."

"Who told you?" Neil was angry at his sister's casual attitude to the gossip she was spreading.

"Yvonne Lawlor told Mary." Jackie was slightly taken aback by Neil's abruptness. She began to assure Neil that she didn't see anything wrong with Becky having an affair, that it was the man's fault. But her voice sounded faint and faraway. Neil felt dizzy. He knew it was all his fault. Yvonne Lawlor was using Becky to get her revenge on him. It was a major mistake spending the night with Yvonne last March. But he was drunk, she had a free house, and it just happened. Took a little while to get started, but then they did it six times in the one night. Crazy passion. Bonking the brains out of each other, as Jackie would say. And he had enjoyed it. But it was the weeks following that were the problem. Doing the rat on her, as Donno used to say at school. He was woken from his trance by the sound of jangling bangles. Jackie was waving her hands in front of his face to attract his attention.

"You better go down and get your lunch, Neil. Her Highness has it prepared for hours," she said before going into her bedroom.

Neil felt strange as he went downstairs. He didn't know how he was going to break this news to Becky. She'd definitely think it was he who'd leaked the news. That night on the phone to Becky, Neil's conversation was full of awkward pauses.

chapter four

Move your body
Move your body to the rhythm of love

The smooth, rhythmic, tinny piano beat of K–Klass pounded from the speakers, and the colorful, hi-tech lights flickered and swirled in synchronicity, sending the gyrating mass of dancers into overdrive. The exams were finished and every graduating student south of the Liffey, except Becky, seemed to be packed onto the dance floor of Hollywood Nights.

It was crazy. "A heaving mass of drunken sex maniacs," Neil muttered to himself, taking a long gulp of beer as he watched from the bar. He felt good now—a bit drunk, but good. The exams had gone well.

"Would you look at your one?" Mal slurred beside him.

"Not bad-looking, is she?" Neil said, following Mal's pointing finger.

"She's a fuckin' dog!" Tony shouted from the other side of Neil.

"Woof, woof!" Mal barked.

"Jesus, Byrner, your taste is up your hole!"

As usual, the three desperadoes were eyeing up the talent from a safe distance. All the typical horseshit chatter went on around them. Whose daddy was rich. Whose daddy drove the most expensive car. Whose daddy owned the biggest house. Whose daddy knew the most important people. Who was going where for the summer. Who was bonking whom.

Then Neil's heart sank. Yvonne Lawlor and her friend Carmel were making their way toward him. It was too late to run to the sanctuary of the gents' toilets; they knew he had spotted them. As they drew closer, he noticed that their heavily caked-on makeup was glistening under the dance lights.

"How's it going?" Neil moved away from Mal and Tony and draped his arms around both girls' shoulders, hoping that by being extra-friendly he would disarm their bitchy intentions. They were both in Becky's class at school, and Becky had warned him that Yvonne was out for blood. But when the girls flinched and slipped out of his grip, he knew he was in for trouble.

"How's Becky?" Carmel asked pointedly, bringing a smile to Yvonne's face. Mal and Tony strained their necks to hear.

Neil feigned puzzlement. "Becky who?"

Yvonne and Carmel exchanged glances, then both of them clasped their hands to their mouths and laughed falsely. Neil felt uncomfortable as he watched them closely for clues. Without warning, Carmel grabbed hold of his left hand and held it out for close examination.

"Ah, it can't be him," she announced loudly, causing Yvonne to double over in hysterics. Neil smiled grimly, trying to figure out where their well-rehearsed charade was leading.

"D'you have any children?" Carmel asked drunkenly, again bringing the predictable burst of laughter from her pal.

"That's for me to know and you to find out," Neil replied coldly, realizing now what they were playing at.

"Ah, we're only messing." Yvonne guided her pal away. "See you later."

Like fuck you will.

"Bye, Neil," Carmel smiled falsely, holding her hand up and wriggling her fingers at him.

Neil didn't reply; instead he gave a nonchalant nod, but he was very tempted to comment on their enormous, waddling backsides. *You left all your problems behind you, girls, or was that your jeans I heard screaming with pain?* Something like that would wipe those supercilious smirks off their faces.

"You're playing the game there, Byrner." Mal pushed Neil's shoulder drunkenly.

"Has she got the hots for you or what!" Tony sighed before taking another long gulp from his bottle of Corona.

"Been there, done that," Neil muttered, faking a grin as Mal slapped him on the back.

"Does she bark in bed?" Tony asked, bringing the usual guffaw of laughter from Mal. Outwardly Neil was smiling, but inside he was disgusted with himself. What was he doing here? Hoping to see Ian walk in that door? Yeah, that was it.

"Jesus, would you look at Gary and Trish!" Mal sneered as he pointed at the couple kissing in the middle of the dance floor with a large clapping group gathered in a circle around them.

"Fuckin' exhibitionists!" Tony muttered.

"I'd say he's porkin' her," Mal said.

"That's if he knows what to fucking do with it." Tony laughed, steadying himself as he swayed drunkenly.

"She's a dog, isn't she?" Mal said.

"Great Dane," Tony added.

"Woof, woof," Mal barked.

It was pathetic, Neil thought. Here he was, hanging around with two guys that no one else would be seen dead with. None of his real friends could understand why he did it. Trish and Andrea refused to even speak to Mal and Tony. But they didn't realize that the two cynics had their uses, serving as a buffer against female company.

But try as he might, Neil couldn't ignore Yvonne and Carmel. They were watching him from their high stools at the bar to the back of the dance hall. Every time he as much as glanced in their direction, they had their wriggling fingers up in the air, waving at him. And on one occasion, he was certain that he saw Yvonne direct a limp-wristed gesture toward him.

At nine o'clock, Neil left Hollywood Nights, unable to take any more of Mal and Tony. Near the exit he bumped into Tom and Andrea and told them he was just leaving his denim jacket in the cloakroom. Ducking his head, he rushed past the long line outside, praying no one would spot him. He jumped into the back of a taxi, and kept his head down while it did a U-turn on the main road. Hoards of revelers were messing around on the grassy embankment in the middle of the road. He recognized a few of the faces. It looked like better fun than inside the dance hall, but Neil knew he had to escape.

The more he had to drink, the more adrift he felt from the crowd.

"Where in town, boss?" the taxi driver asked, turning his head to look at Neil.

"Dame Street," Neil answered in a deliberately gruff tone designed to discourage any further conversation. Normally, he would have discussed anything from the weather to Ireland's World Cup prospects with any friendly stranger, but tonight he had other things to think about.

The car sped along the six-laned motorway, beneath the Belfield overpass, past the television station, through Donnybrook, past all the places Neil was so familiar with, but which now looked so different. He felt like a stranger passing through his own city. When they got to Stephen's Green, he almost told the driver to stop and let him out. His stomach was in a knot, his palms were sweaty, and his head was in a tizzy.

Oh Jesus, what am I doing? he asked himself over and over again. A million images flashed through his head. His mum and dad sitting at home watching the television, Kate and Dan's wedding, the madness in the airport last Christmas Eve when he went with his dad to collect his two older brothers, the party in school the night they won the Senior Cup, sitting between Jackie and Liam at the cinema, and, of course, Ian in his faded blue jeans…

"That's six-fifty, boss," the taxi driver said, fixing his mirror to get a look at Neil.

He's afraid I'll do a runner, Neil thought, digging his last tenner from his pocket and realizing that he didn't want to leave the taxi at all. Maybe he could sit there for the rest of the night. Tell the taxi driver that he'd keep him company. Go all around the city with him, meet all the late-night weirdos. Why was he so different?

He stood on the pavement, watching the taillights of the taxi cruise up toward the lofty spire of Christ Church. Overhead, the darkening twilight sky was streaked with spectacular glows of pink and orange. Colors caused by the city smog, his dad once told him. *Beep, beep, beep, beep*, the little green man was telling him it was safe to cross. Hesitant, he watched the carefree, smiling swarms of passersby. Couples, mainly, walking hand in hand.

They'll think you're going to the Olympia, he reassured himself. *Yeah, just keep walking.*

Up ahead, he spotted a lumberjack shirt approaching. Skipping out to the edge of the pavement, he stared at the bald head and the mustache. *Hah, say no more, is the pope a catholic?* Their eyes met as they passed. *Hey, you're going in the wrong direction*, the voice in Neil's head felt like saying.

Skip down the cobblestone road as planned, Neil thought, eyes peeled for gangs. *Oh shit, you're going to bump into someone you know. Hey Neil, how's the form? What're you doing around here? Same as you, Sunshine. That's your answer.*

Around the corner and there it is. Faster, faster. Oh fuck, it looks like a kip. Thump-thump, thump-thump. Shut up, heart. People are staring. Too late to turn back now. Full moon over-head. Wish it was winter. Dark and wet. Put on your baseball cap. Tip the visor down over your face. No traffic. Run across. Quick now, head down and in the door.

Conversation stops as every head turns to look. Cropped heads, gray heads, bald heads, all ancient, sitting on stools at the bar, staring at the fresh new face as he strolls casually through the old timers' bar.

Oh God, what the fuck did I come here for? Just stare at the floor and keep walking. Through that door and up those stairs there. Quick, for God's sake. Probably an orgy going on up here. Can't be worse than downstairs. Legs feel wobbly. Should've gotten Becky to come with me. Should've gone out with Becky to meet her married man. Oh Jesus, help me. Open the door. Dim lights, loud music, younger crowd, girls as well, looks just like an ordinary pub, except for the blackened windows. People aren't staring; well, not obviously anyway, but they all seem to know one another. The barman's giving you a friendly smile. Relax and order a drink.

"Pint of Budweiser, please."

There's a bloke drinking Guinness. *Tell him Gary's joke, about the doctor telling the queer to drink fifteen pints of*

Guinness and to eat five loaves of brown bread, and then the punchline that you laughed at. That'll show you what your arse is for. Ha, ha, ha, that'd go down well here. In the corner a video jukebox. *Sip your pint and watch the video. Pretend you're a regular. Jesus, that guy just pinched the other guy's bum. For God's sake, don't stare. Those three blokes over there, dancing to the video, they can't be more than sixteen. Too camp looking though. Keep your eyes peeled for Ian. Can you just imagine? Heaven has sent me an angel. Dream on, I doubt that anyone else from Blackrock has ever set foot inside this joint. Except for Becky's older brother, of course. Down the back, look, two girls kissing. Well, who did you expect to see snogging? The rhyming couplets on tour? Move over toward that door, the bloke with the tartan stripes on his jeans, laced up red Docs, spiky hair, and earrings. What a getup. Nice face though, and he's around your age, and it looks like he's on his own.*

"How's it going?"

"Hi."

God, what a fairy voice. Go on, say something else, you started the conversation.

"Good crowd here, isn't there?"

"Wait'll you see it at ten o'clock."

"Get packed, does it?"

"Yeah."

Smile and walk on. He's not interested in you. Anyway,

imagine walking down the street with him. Spare me. Where to now? Around the corner. Stop smiling, you don't want to attract undue attention. There's a ledge. Put the pint down and light up. Dying for a smoke. What now? Oh fuck, why didn't you just stay in Hollies? This is awful. Can't even smoke, hands shaking so much. Armpits are a mess as well. River of sweat. Oh no, need to take a leak. No way, not here. Oh Jesus, make a deal. Promise you'll start going to Mass again if you can just disappear. You'll even help with the collections.

"Haven't seen you here before."

Fuck, he's talking to you.

"Jack's the name."

Just smile and shake his hand.

"So, don't you have a name?"

"What? Oh yeah, I do, it's…eh, Gary."

Nice one, Neil, nice one.

"It's all right, Gary, relax. I'm not going to bite your head off."

Return his friendly smile. This is a laugh, he's the same age as the old fellow and he's chatting you up. Now you know how Jackie felt that night in Leeson Street.

"First night here, is it?"

"Yeah."

Shit, what d'you admit that for? Dickhead.

"I could tell…Suppose you have to start sometime."

"Suppose."

"You can blame it on the full moon."

Just smile at him. Always humor a weirdo, that's what they told you at school.

"What's that?"

What the fuck's he pointing at?

"Your drink?"

"Oh, eh, a Budweiser."

"Smithwicks and a Bud when you're ready there, Gary."

Hope he doesn't expect one in return. What's he doing now, tapping my shoulder?

"Forgot to ask you, will you have a pint?"

Just grin and let him think he's hilarious.

"So what part of Dublin d'you come from?"

"Eh...out toward Bray."

"Thought so, you can tell by your accent."

Oh, can you now, Mister Accent Expert? Suppose you're waiting for me to ask you where you come from? Well, you can wait, pal.

"I'm from Clontarf myself."

Oh, are you now? How interesting. Jesus, what am I doing here? Mum, I want you now. I want to be ten years old again, sitting at home watching television with you and Dad.

"Relax, Gary, it's not as bad as it seems."

Easy for you to say, you probably live in the fucking place. Oh Jesus, I've never felt so weird. Let me die now, it'll be better for all concerned. Think of the coroner's report. He died in a gay bar. Can you just imagine them all whispering at your funeral. Gary's mum, Mrs. Meehan, Mrs. Burke, every tongue in the neighborhood, waiting outside the church. "Did you hear where it happened?" "Oooh, I did, isn't it awful." "Desperate." Heads wagging in feigned concern. "His poor mother, she'll never recover." "He was always a bit strange though. Hmm, there was something peculiar about him, you know, you could tell…" Another flurry of concerned nods. "I always had my doubts…And he was with an older man, I believe. Old as his poor father, I heard. Terrible, isn't it? Desperate. What's the world coming to!" Sighs all around. "Ssssh, here's the family. Adjust the faces. Forlorn looks now. Sorry for your trouble, Catherine. He was a lovely fellow, your Neil, one of the best. An absolute credit to you. It's God's way, Catherine."

"It's not God's way," you'd shout from the coffin, and all the neighborhood tongues would stiffen with fright. "It's not God's way that anyone should feel the way I do!"

"I never told my parents myself, but you youngsters these days are a different lot."

What's he talking about now? Just smile and pretend you're listening to him.

"Things were different then, but attitudes have changed since, thank God."

"Yeah, they have." Neil nodded vacantly.

71

A new video came on and Neil smiled when he saw Bono and B.B. King appear on the numerous screens. If only they knew the type of pubs they were frequenting.

The gutsy vocals, ripping guitars, and pounding drums filled the pub, much to the delight of the three young dancers. It was obviously a pub favorite.

When love comes to town, I'm gonna jump that train
When love comes to town, I'm gonna catch that flame

The barman gave Neil a friendly wink as he left the two pints down on the counter. Sugar Daddy took his bulging wallet from his tweed jacket, peeled a tenner from a bundle of notes, and paid the barman.

Pathetic attempt to impress, Neil thought as he thanked him. The guy in the tartan jeans was right, the pub was beginning to fill up. All arriving under cover of darkness. Neil told his elderly suitor that he was twenty and had just finished his second year of science at Trinity. Another two pints followed, and when Neil made a feeble attempt to pay, good old Sugar Daddy wouldn't hear of it.

"I was a student myself once upon a time," he said, patting Neil's arm, signaling to him to put his money back in his pocket.

Just as well, Neil thought, he didn't have enough to buy a round.

He was more relaxed now, he knew that Sugar Daddy was trying to get him drunk, and he was succeeding, but he didn't feel threatened. The drink had lessened Sugar's inhibitions, and every so often he would drape his arm around Neil's shoulder, or touch his bare arm, and once when Neil said something witty, he leaned over, kissed his cheek, and told him he was great company.

The bristle of stubble reminded Neil of the bedtime kisses his dad used to give him as a kid. "Night now, Neiley Nook," he would say, leaning across his bed and tucking him in. But what would his dad say if he saw him now? What would Gary and the others say? What would Mal and Tony say? Or Father Donno and the other priests in Rock? And Gary's mum and the rest of the tongues on the road? There was such a thin line between respectability and disgrace, he reflected. But what the hell, he didn't care now, he was enjoying himself, and Sugar Daddy wasn't such a bad type.

The pub was definitely one of the most exciting and different places he had ever been in. It gave him a sense of freedom, a feeling that he could behave as he wanted to at last. Still, a part of him didn't want to be there. What was he doing with this crowd of strangers? he asked himself. Bad and all as the rhyming couplets were, at least they were his friends. They were the people he had grown up with. Like it or not, they were his life. Maybe he should just get off with Yvonne Lawlor and forget about being gay. They could go to the movies together, he could bring her around to the house on Sunday afternoons, and then they could go to the beach with all the others. But not for the first time, his gaze was caught by one of the numerous photographs of scantily clad guys hanging on the pub walls, and he knew that Yvonne Lawlor would have to take a backseat for the time being.

When he looked around, Sugar Daddy was chatting to one of the many friends he had in the bar, all of whom had lingered in conversation long enough to get a good look at Neil. *This is how girls feel when guys ogle them*, Neil thought, meeting all the lecherous looks with his best glare of disdain. But his thoughts were interrupted when Sinead O'Connor came on the video screens, singing "Nothing Compares 2 U."

"You obviously like this song, Gary," Sugar Daddy said, smiling as Neil sang along quietly with the words.

Neil started to sing louder, much to Sugar Daddy's amusement. When the song finished, he wished he had the nerve to put the video on again. But there was a crowd around the jukebox, and drunk as he was, he still felt shy in these new surroundings.

"Will you have one for the road?" Sugar Daddy asked, and Neil swayed, steadied himself, then shook his head, aware that his indifference was upsetting his admirer. It was stupid, he knew, but he felt guilty chatting to Sugar Daddy, as though he was being unfaithful to Ian. To lessen his guilt, he switched his glass into his left hand. He would be left-handed for the rest of the night, he decided and, like Jackie and Liam's bangles, this would be the symbol of his unspoken love. If people knew, they would more than likely consider him a sad case, but they didn't know the warmth he felt inside from this simple little gesture. He wondered what Ian would say if he knew.

The spell was broken at precisely half past eleven when glaring bright lights were switched on to clear the pub. The anonymity of the dim lights was shattered and people shielded their eyes as they fled for the door.

"D'you want to go clubbing?" Sugar Daddy asked.

Neil hesitated, then he shook his head, deciding that he had taken enough chances for one night. "Nah, I better head home…Listen, thanks a lot for the drinks and all that," he said, slightly taken aback by the plethora of wrinkles that lined the older man's face. The harsh light did him no favors.

Sugar Daddy waved his thanks away. "I'll run you home, my wheels are just outside," he said, jangling his car keys on his index finger.

"Ah no, you're going to Clontarf. I'll get a taxi," Neil lied, conscious of the slight slur in his speech.

"It's no problem."

Neil thought quickly. "I'll tell you what, could you drop me to my cousin's house in Blackrock?"

"I'll drop you home, Gary. It'll be my pleasure, believe me."

"No, I'm a bit too buzzed to go home, I better stay with my cousin."

Sugar Daddy laughed. "Whatever you like."

True to form, Sugar Daddy drove a brand new BMW, and his tape rack was full of classical tapes, just like Neil's dad's collection. Despite strong temptation, Neil turned down the offer of a cup of coffee in Clontarf. But all the way home he kept thinking of the lure of that comfy little bachelor pad. Sugar obviously wasn't a psycho, and he certainly wasn't going to make unwanted demands. As the powerful car purred its way through the city, Neil had to struggle on several occasions to restrain himself from grabbing Sugar Daddy's arm and telling him to go to Clontarf. Repulsive, maybe, but sex was sex. What harm was there in lying back on the bed, closing his eyes, and enjoying a slow, sensuous massage, all the time imagining that it was Ian's fingers touching him. Sugar was silent, pretending to concentrate on the road in front of him, but Neil knew that he was just waiting for the horny command to do a U-turn.

However, Becky's words of warning were still ringing in his ears. "Whatever you do, Neil, for God's sake be careful. Promise me that," she had pleaded, looking deep into his eyes. And nice and all as Uncle Sugar was, he was certainly no novice. Twice around the block at least, Neil guessed, sneaking a quick look at the aging profile. Sparse graying hair, sagging chin and jowls, leathery complexion, shiny black hairs sprouting from the bulbous nostrils, a little tuft of chest hair peeping out over the collar of his casual shirt, thin spindly legs lost inside his trendy, baggy trousers. Neil couldn't help smiling to himself; for all the talks about AIDS at school, situations like this were never mentioned. After all what would a nice little Rock boy be doing with a man as old as his dad?

It dawned on him how much power he had over this middle-aged man; the poor fellow would have done anything for him. Ever willing to please, he wore his heart on his sleeve, awaiting the slightest whim from his new obsession. And Neil knew that he, of all people, should have been more sympathetic, but he also knew that any displays of sympathy were bound to be misconstrued by his lovelorn suitor. Instead he played the role he was well used to. The innocent that he had played so often with so many would-be girlfriends over the years. The trick was never to let the conversation stray from the banal, keep cracking silly jokes, and never ever show even the slightest flicker of understanding as to what was really going on. It was flirtatious and cruel, he knew, but what else could he do?

"Here's my number anyway." Sugar did his best to sound casual as he handed Neil his business card. "If you ever feel like having a chat or anything." They were parked on the quietest part of Cross Avenue, half a mile from Neil's house.

Neil noticed that the poor fellow's hands were trembling. "Yeah, definitely, I'll give you a shout," he tried to sound enthusiastic as he slipped the card into the pocket of his jacket.

"Which house is your cousin's?"

"Ehh, it's just over there." Neil pointed vaguely toward a cluster of new houses.

"Lovely place to live."

"Yeah…" Neil clicked the doorlock open. "I suppose I better go in before they all go to bed."

"D'you want me to wait till you check?" Sugar's eyes flickered with faint hope.

"No, no, it's all right. They're still up, the light's on." Neil hoped that his voice didn't sound too panicky. "Thanks again for—" Neil flinched when he saw the older man leaning across to kiss his cheek. "Jesus, not here," he said in an urgent whisper. Alarm bells clanged in Neil's head. Sugar was looking deep into his eyes.

"You're beautiful, Gary, d'you know that?" he whispered, his voice tinged with desperation.

Neil grimaced. He had seen this coming.

"I mean that...and I really enjoyed meeting you," Sugar added, his voice now pained with the hopelessness of the heartbroken.

Neil met his stare and thought that he could be honest with this guy. This wasn't Yvonne or one of the girls in Hollies; this was a guy who knew about him. But what could he say? Sorry, I like you and all that, but unfortunately you remind me of my old man. There was no easy way, he decided; he had to keep up the innocent act.

"I enjoyed meeting you too."

"Do call me."

"I will," Neil promised, climbing out of the car.

"I've got some good videos you might be interested in seeing."

Neil grinned and gave one last Yvonne-style, wriggly finger wave before he closed the door. He stood on the pavement and waited for Sugar to drive off before he crossed the road and started his trek home.

What a sad case, he thought. What would he do if he ended up like that himself? Not a chance; he had his family, and anyway he'd probably end up marrying Becky. And they'd have two kids just like Danny and Annie. His step lightened. A thick carpet of pink and white cherry blossom petals lay on the pavement, cushioning his footsteps, giving the impression that he was walking on snow.

He smiled to himself as he remembered how he had inadvertently discovered where the gay bar was. It was after a rugby match in Castleknock and Dan, his brother-in-law, was driving him and two of his teammates home.

"Don't ever go into that place there by mistake, lads," Dan had said, laughing as he pointed at the drab-looking pub.

"Why not?" one of the lads in the backseat inquired innocently.

"It's one of them funny pubs," Dan had said in an effeminate voice, flapping his wrist limply. Neil had felt his face burning as he joined the others in forced laughter. Neil "Judas" Byrne.

The full moon peeped out from behind a cloud, pouring its eerie, silver light down upon the leafy neighborhood. So many times, he had taken this roundabout route home in the hope of a chance meeting, but so far, one fleeting glimpse through the frosted-glass front door was his only reward.

A dim light glowed upstairs. Maybe it was his beloved's bedroom, Neil thought, stopping at the gate and concentrating. He would communicate by telepathy. *Thump-thump, thump-thump. Shut up, heart, you'll waken the entire neighborhood. Right, if you're there, Ian, give me a sign. Climb out of your bed, walk over to the window, open those curtains, and give us one of your angelic smiles. I wrote two poems for you last week. They're tucked away in the bottom of my sock drawer.*

Car headlights suddenly swept around the corner, causing Neil's heart to flutter. The return of Sugar Daddy. Back for one last desperate attempt to win his heart. Neil quickly donned his baseball cap, dug his hands into his pockets, lowered his head, and strolled on. As the big car roared past him, the man and woman in it turned their heads to inspect him. *Aging rhyming couplets on Neighborhood Watch*, Neil thought, watching the car round the corner and speed off into the night. *Hah.* He laughed inwardly. *That's what lay ahead for Gary and Trish and all the other couples.* Beady eyes glued to the blinds of their semi-D, on constant lookout for strangers stalking their neighborhood. He sneaked a parting glance at Ian's house and clenched his fist in silent jubilation. The bedroom light had been switched off. At last, a sign. The telepathy had worked. They were definitely destined for each other.

His own house was in darkness when he eventually got home after one o'clock. Neil tucked into a couple of toasted cheese sandwiches, laced with mayonnaise. Then he gulped down the remainder of the milk and left the empty bottle back in the fridge, even though he had given his mum his solemn promise never to do this again. On his way to the TV room, he could already feel the first niggling traces of a hangover. Or maybe, he thought, it was the early signs of a brain hemorrhage.

Plonking himself down into an armchair, he flicked through all the late night channels. "Damn all on," he muttered, letting his eyes drift to the rugby team photos hanging on the wall. Junior and Senior Cup winning teams with Neil standing at the back, on the extreme left, in both photos. Away from the glare of the limelight. They took pride of place over all the other family photos, including his parents' wedding photo and the photos of his nephew and niece. Then he glanced at the video collection and Sugar's deliberate little hook started to play on his mind. "I've some good videos you might be interested in seeing," that was what he had said. Neil had pretended not to hear, considering it a bit pathetic. But Sugar knew what he was doing; he had more than likely planted this same seed with thousands of other young fellows, Neil reflected, knowing that few could resist the lure of that visual excitement.

Neil stood up and slipped one of the many family holiday videos into the video player. It was taken on a sun-soaked Donegal beach, where they used to rent a holiday home for three weeks every summer. Neil smiled as he recalled his dad's futile attempts to get his offspring to perform for the camera. Holding on to his director's cap (it always seemed to be windy), his face ruddy as he roared his instructions. "Where is Kate?

Stop messing! I said walk, not run! Don't look at the camera!"

The picture came on the screen. "Neil Byrne at five years of age, struggling against the Atlantic Ocean," his dad's wry commentary announced. Neil grinned when he saw himself as a five-year-old, squatting at the water's edge in his swimming togs, happily building a sand castle. All of a sudden a freak wave broke over him and drenched him. Little Neil stood up, dripping wet, and started to bawl with shock. Then the picture jumped as his dad retreated from his youngest son, who had automatically run toward him for comfort. Paul and Joe were in the background, bony-ribbed nine- and eleven-year-olds dancing hysterical jigs of joy, cheering as their little brother decided to change direction, and his fast little legs ran toward their mum instead. She wrapped a big towel around him, snuggling him close to her while she shouted to her husband to turn the video off. Jackie, sitting along-side their mum, kept playing with her doll, ignoring the consternation all around her.

It was a family classic and the tape had gone patchy from being overplayed. Every aunt and uncle who came into the house had to see it. "Wait'll your children see it," his dad would say to Neil, chuckling heartily. And Neil would wave him off with a grin, wondering whether, if he ever had a son, he would know as little about him as his own dad. He pressed the fast-forward button and watched his speeded-up family whizzing around the beach, performing their part for the camera. He pressed the play button on a happier shot of himself, dribbling a football, with his two older brothers making exaggerated dives in the sand, pretending that they couldn't get the ball off him. His mum was cheering him on. Neiley Nook, the baby of the family, kicked the ball into the goal with mounds of sand as goalposts. Grinning, he raised his two skinny arms in celebration and turned to face the camera. Neil pressed the freeze-frame button. That happy, carefree child was him. What if they could see their little boy now? What if they knew then what that little boy would want to do with that little body when he got bigger? Maybe it would've been better if the big wave had drowned him, then his memory would have been crystallized in all those innocent snapshots that adorned the mantelpiece.

Neil began to feel drowsy. Through the half-sleep, another holiday memory from the same summer forged its way into his thoughts.

"Daddy! Neil's fallen into the water!" Kate roared.

The five-year-old Neil splashed and floundered. He had slipped off the pier in Portsalon. Paul and Joe were fishing at the end of the short pier, Kate and Jackie were listening to a guy playing the guitar, and his mum and dad were sunbathing on the pier wall.

"Swim, Neil! Swim!" came Kate's shrill cry.

His dad plunged into the crystal-clear water and wrapped his arms around the drowning boy. He swam to the pier steps, and Neil thought he was going to suffocate from the hug he gave him. There were tears in his dad's eyes as he held his bristly jaw against Neil's face and whispered that he could never do without his Mister Happy. And all the way back to their holiday cottage, Neil was allowed to sit on his lap and hold the steering wheel.

———————

"Neil."

"Hmmm." His mum shook him again. "Neil, wake up, there's someone on the phone for you."

Neil opened his eyes blearily. "Who?" he muttered sleepily.

"I don't know…Some man," his mum replied, picking his clothes up off the floor. Neil tensed. The events of the previous night came flooding back. Then he relaxed. It was more than likely another rugby club Alicadoo asking him to sign with their club for the forthcoming season.

"Should I get him to call back?" his mum asked, lingering by the bedroom door.

"Nah, I'll get up."

Neil jumped out of bed and grimaced when he saw his reflection in the mirror. He looked shattered. Maybe he was still drunk, he thought, as he ran down the stairs in his boxer shorts.

"Hello?" he answered the phone huskily.

"Good afternoon," said a cheerful, businesslike voice.

"Afternoon," Neil replied warily.

"Guess who?"

"Huh?"

"You don't know who this is?"

"Haven't a clue."

"And, Gary, you told me that you were twenty."

Neil froze.

"Know who it is now?" Sugar said with a little chuckle.

"Yeah," Neil said, doing his best to sound unfriendly, wondering how the hell he had got his number.

"You dropped your ID card in my car." The older man seemed to have read his thoughts. Neil sighed inwardly, conscious now that the kitchen door was open and his mum could hear every word.

"Could you mail it out to me, please?"

"Mail it? But I could drive out that way after work and meet you if you like," Sugar suggested.

"What's the last date for applying?" Neil asked.

"You can't talk?" Sugar was obviously familiar with these situations.

"No, not really."

"Okay, listen, you've got my number, give me a ring later."

"Right."

"All the best, Neil."

"All the best." Neil put the phone down, closed his eyes in anguish, and cursed himself for being so careless. He had visions of Sugar calling around to the house and asking his dad if he could take his son out on a date. Oh Jesus, why had he gone into town?

"Who was that, Neil?" his mum called.

"Just someone about some job I applied for," he said, joining her in the kitchen.

"How did last night go?" His mum was making brown bread, her back turned to him.

"Fine," he said, taking the carton of orange juice from the fridge.

"What time did you get home at?"

"Not too late, around one."

"Put that in a glass!" his mum snapped without looking around.

Neil shook his head and smiled. "How d'you know I was drinking out of the carton?"

"I know what you're like."

You probably do too, Neil thought. *You probably even suspect who that was on the phone.* Gulping his orange juice, he stared at his mum, in her floppy blue tracksuit and her white sneakers. What would she say if he told her where he had been the night before? Nothing, more than likely. She'd probably just wear her knees out praying to save his soul.

"And someone left an empty milk bottle in the fridge last night."

"Must've been the fairies," Neil said, unable to contain a self-mocking laugh.

His mum looked around at him. "Go and put some clothes on."

"Is Jackie here?" Neil asked.

His mum snorted derisively. "I've missed the last bus home," she said in what was supposed to be an imitation of Jackie. "I don't know how Michelle puts up with her, imposing on her and her flatmate like that all the time," she added with a sigh.

Neil furrowed his brow. Surely his mum didn't really believe that Jackie stayed with Michelle. Of course not, it was just more of her hiding from the truth.

"What's the job?" his mum asked.

"What?"

"The man on the phone."

"Ah, it was just some office job Gary heard about," Neil blustered, feeling his face redden.

The doorbell rang, saving him from more lies. He slipped into his sweats while his mum answered the door.

"Oh hello, Gary, hello, Trish."

Neil cursed under his breath when he heard his mum bringing the two lovebirds into the hallway and telling them he wasn't dressed yet.

"Nothing we haven't seen already," Gary replied, and Trish giggled.

"Neil!" his mum called, laughing.

Grinning, Neil went out into the hallway and greeted Gary and Trish with his best glad-to-see-you face.

"Oh, he's made himself decent," his mum said.

"No cheapo thrills for Trish in this house," Neil said, wondering what the reaction would have been if he said no cheapo thrills for Gary.

"Where did you get to last night?" Gary said, and Neil glared at him, flashing his eyes toward his mum, who was lingering at the kitchen door. She smiled at Neil before she went back into the kitchen.

"You missed a great party at Tara's," Trish added.

"Ah, I was out of my brains," Neil said, motioning the pair of them into the living room.

Gary and Trish gave him a blow-by-blow account of the late night party in Tara's mansion. Who got off with whom. How many beers they drank. Who locked themselves in the parents' bedroom with the waterbed for over an hour. How Mick Toner let off a fire extinguisher in the kitchen. Who was smoking joints...Neil smiled as they described scenes he seemed to have experienced a million times, scenes he never felt part of. He wished he could tell Gary and Trish about his own night. Instead he told them he had puked his guts up and gone to Becky's house to recover, aware that he was rapidly becoming one of Dublin's most compulsive liars.

"Right, get your act together," Gary said, standing up and rubbing his hands together, "we're going to Brittas Bay."

"Tom's got his mum's car," Trish explained.

"MacDaniels after," Gary added, again rubbing his hands together.

Neil hesitated.

"C'mon, you can't say you're studying." Gary grabbed hold of Neil's arm and dragged him toward the door.

"I'm wrecked," Neil protested.

"We're all wrecked," Gary replied.

"There's room for Becky as well, if she wants to come," Trish added.

Neil thought quickly. "No, see, the thing is, we said we'd meet some friends of hers."

"Ah, we're not good enough for him anymore," Gary joked, relinquishing his grip on Neil's arm. But Neil could see his pal looked slightly peeved. *Give him a taste of how I felt for so long*, Neil thought, keeping his fake grin cemented onto his face.

Trish looked at her watch. "C'mon, Gary, we better hurry if we're going."

"Well, tell your new friends we were asking for them," Gary said as a parting shot.

"Sorry, your names are?" Neil shouted after them when they reached the gate. Gary held his middle finger up in the air.

Neil closed the door and dashed upstairs for a shower. It was time to head to Becky's.

As always, they went upstairs to Becky's cluttered bedroom. Neil lay across her bed on his side, propping his head up with his elbow and letting his feet dangle over the edge. She continued to pack her rucksack while he gave her a detailed account of his exploits the previous night. There was a slight hint of I-told-you-so in her nods as he informed her that the crowd in the pub, for the most part, was exactly like the crowd you'd find in any city-center pub. She told him not to worry about Sugar Daddy, insisting that if he was that mad about him, he was hardly going to jeopardize his chances by saying anything out of place.

"So how did your own night go?" he asked eventually, remembering Becky's date with Brian.

She turned and beamed at him. "Great. I followed your

advice and treated him just like he was a friend. No heavy stuff at all."

Neil had warned Becky not to behave the way Yvonne Lawlor had behaved with him, telling her that it would scare any bloke away.

"He's really upset that I'm going," she added in delight.

"Course he is."

"All I have to do now is forget about him," she sighed.

Neil smiled. He sat up straight when Becky's mother came into the bedroom carrying an assortment of Becky's clothes. They exchanged a friendly greeting. But Neil always felt awkward with her. Like his own mother, she didn't understand his relationship with her daughter.

After her mother left the room, Becky surprised him. "A couple of the slags in my class know I'm having an affair," she told him.

Neil didn't know what to say.

"We were spotted by Tara what's-her-face and a friend of hers, and as luck would have it, her friend just happened to live on the same road as Brian," she muttered, rolling her eyes up in resignation.

But the arrival of two of Becky's friends prevented Neil from saying anything. He grinned in embarrassment as the two girls started to discuss their sex lives in front of him. Even Becky looked slightly embarrassed. A couple of veiled, giggly references were made to the size of various bloke's sex organs. Blokes that he knew. It crossed his mind that maybe Becky had told her friends that he was gay and that was why they were treating him like one of the girls. Then he remembered that the conversation had been equally crazy on the other occasions that he had met them. When the pair of them started to discuss the art of giving blow jobs, he began to feel uncomfortable, made up some feeble excuse, and left the house.

The afternoon sun glared down on Booterstown Avenue. Neil started to wish he had gone to Brittas Bay with the others. He reached the church, checked that no one was looking, then ducked inside. Silence. The church was empty. He shivered slightly in the coolness. Goose pimples rose on his bare arms. Why was he here? He walked up the center aisle and looked at the tabernacle. Anyone home? he felt like shouting. Long time, no see. *Compose yourself, will you. Kneel down and say a prayer. Like what? Please God, give me seven straight A's on my finals? Or, please God, just make me straight? Make me happy? That's it, as a birthday present, make me Mister Happy again. Turn back the clock, make me twelve years old again.*

chapter five

The night of his birthday, Neil avoided all his friends and went for dinner in Liam's apartment in Rathmines. He knew it would cause a hassle, especially after all the birthday cards he received, and the ultra hip shirt that Gary and Trish gave him, but he wasn't in the mood for pretense. Tonight was a special night. A night for honesty.

The summer evening buzz in Rathmines fascinated him. This was student town. Carefree bicycles with two, sometimes even three, people on board whizzed past him, blatantly ignoring traffic lights and one-way signs. Music blared out of shops and passing cars. Old world three-story houses sat next to tacky fast-food restaurants with glaring neon signs. Each street corner seemed to have its own slick twenty-four hour shop with bored-looking assistants sitting at computerized cash registers. Plastic bags filled with rubbish sat in little clusters at gateways, and every doorway had columns of anonymous door-bells. Empty beer cans, chip bags, cash withdrawal slips, and burger wrappers littered the pavements. But the people here looked and behaved differently to the people he knew in Blackrock. These were country kids, who seemed to specialize in wearing clothes and hairstyles that were a couple of years out of date. Country kids whose hard-pressed parents probably fretted and worried about them. Neil liked the way they didn't seem to care about their appearance, unlike his own friends, who spent hours in front of the mirror before they'd even venture out to the shops.

He stopped outside a record shop to listen to the song his mum had sung at Kate's wedding.

Now the harbor light is calling
This will be our last good-bye

The clear female voice left a lump in his throat, just like his mum's rendition had done when he was thirteen. She had ruffled his hair when she came down off the stage, but she must have noticed the glistening in his sensitive eyes. It had been the same that morning when she had given him the watch for his birthday. He had smelled her familiar perfume as she leaned forward hesitantly and kissed his cheek. Then she put her arms around him and gave him a tentative hug. His eyes were definitely glistening as he grinned awkwardly and thanked her. "You don't look a day over sixteen," she said jokingly, and inside him, the volcano was rumbling, bursting to tell her the secret that had mounted the invisible barriers between them. But, as always, he mumbled an excuse and made a hasty retreat upstairs to the safety of his bedroom.

The high standard of Liam's spaghetti Bolognese surprised Neil, and after a few glasses of red wine a warm feeling glowed inside him. All his anxieties were replaced by a pleasant vagueness.

"Try it, Neil," Jackie insisted, handing him the joint that Liam had rolled carefully. Neil hesitated; he had taken a few pulls from a joint at a house party once, and he still had a vivid recollection of the half-hour he spent leaning over a toilet bowl afterward. Ever since, the smell of the stuff had been enough to make him nauseous.

"Go on, it's your birthday," Liam said, smiling. Both he and Jackie were wearing odd shoes for the occasion. Neil put the joint to his mouth and pretended to take a drag. He leaned back on the tatty sofa bed as he exhaled, hoping that the others wouldn't notice the absence of smoke.

"Good, isn't it?" Jackie enthused.

"Cool," Neil said in his hippie drawl, bringing a burst of drunken laughter from his dinner companions, especially Jackie. Neil knew she was delighted that he had come for dinner, and he was delighted himself when Liam and Jackie gave him the tape of Sinead O'Connor's *Am I Not Your Girl?* to add to his collection of birthday presents. Kate and Dan had given him a rugby ball autographed by the Irish team.

"A fucking rugby ball?" Jackie exclaimed.

Liam was smiling, his eyes glassy.

"You'd swear I was still fourteen," Neil replied with a laugh.

"What did Kate ever see in that dork?" Jackie sighed.

But the best present of all was the four hundred dollars he got in the mail that morning from his two brothers in New York, together with a note telling him to buy a plane ticket and come over for the summer. His mum had been quick to discourage this possibility, pointing out that New York was far too dangerous a place for someone his age.

"You should definitely go," Jackie insisted when he told her. She couldn't understand Neil's reluctance. But later, he would tell her about the beautiful sixteen-year-old boy who, unknowingly, dictated the pattern of his life. He would tell her about how his brothers had promised to fix him up with some randy New York women, and he would explain to her that he could never tell his two brothers of his fear of this situation. They wouldn't want to hear it.

Am I not your girl?
Am I not your girl?

Sinead's evocative vocals flowed out of Liam's boom box.

Neil didn't feel nervous when he broke his news. Maybe the story gets easier with each telling, he thought as Jackie, tears streaming down her face, embraced him and kissed his cheek. Liam draped his arm around his shoulder, the way an older brother would.

"Oh, Neil," Jackie sobbed, hugging him again, "I'm so sorry."

"It's not that bad, is it?" Neil said, smiling at the pair of them.

"No, it's just, I knew something was wrong," Jackie said, holding his face with her tiny hands, her bangles falling down out over the sleeve of her blouse. "I should've said something to you."

"You won't be able to lift your arms soon with all those bangles," Neil said, attempting to force a laugh from Jackie and Liam. He wasn't in the mood for a heavy soul-searching session. It struck him though, that her reaction was what he would expect if he had said he had cancer.

"I love you, Neil," Jackie muttered in his ear, and Neil had to struggle to hold back his own tears.

"Listen, Neil," Liam spoke in his slow stoned voice, "I just want you to know, it makes no difference to me, man . . . that you're like, gay."

Neil nodded. He tried to imagine what Liam's reaction would be if he made a pass at him. He'd probably just laugh. Liam was okay, and Neil had known that there would be no problem in telling him.

Neil told them about his sortie into the gay scene. They laughed when he told them about Uncle Sugar, but he didn't tell them that he had seen the same Sugar's car parked down the road from the house one night. Nor did he tell them about Ian, afraid that they might consider his blind love a bit pathetic. Inevitably, the question of telling their mum and dad cropped up.

"I don't think it'd be a good idea," Liam said with a smile, and Neil agreed wholeheartedly with him.

"Well, I think you should tell them," Jackie insisted. "After all, you are their son, and they'll just have to accept you the way you are."

"Can you just imagine Mum?" Neil sighed.

"She'll just have to learn to live with it, won't she?"

"I think it's Neil's decision." Liam's was the voice of reason.

It was Jackie's idea to go into the gay bar. And once they arrived at the pub, Neil was glad that they were with him. There was no nervousness this time.

"It's a weird place!" Jackie exclaimed.

"No weirder than where we normally go," Liam said in his drawl.

To Neil, the pub looked incredibly ordinary in comparison with his first night. He felt as if he was in his local place. Liam bought the drinks and Neil felt like a tour guide as he showed them around. Waves of electronic rave music, with its pumping drums, staccato, computerized vocals, and space-age noises, reverberated off the walls. Despite Jackie's attempts to appear relaxed, Neil could sense her unease. On one occasion, he caught her staring at him. It was the same stare his mum often gave him. The "What's wrong with you, Neil?" stare. He knew that she wanted him to grab her by the arm and reveal that it was all an elaborate hoax, that he wasn't gay, that her little brother was just like everyone else.

Then the incredible happened. Neil spotted Redser, a bloke who had been two years ahead of him at school. Neil remembered him as a quiet, scruffy sort of bloke, who always moped around the school corridors with a glum look on his face. He was anything but that now. He was holding court at a small table before two guys around the same age as him. His face was animated, he gesticulated wildly while he explained something to his amused listeners, each of whom had their stools tilted forward to huddle in closer to the speaker. Redser was wearing a trendy red waist-jacket, a green silk shirt, and his hair was gelled back stylishly, nothing like the nondescript hairstyle he had at school. Then their eyes met. Redser nodded in recognition but Neil automatically averted his eyes. *Oh Jesus,* he thought, *what now?* He considered walking on, pretending he hadn't seen the guy, but Jackie put an abrupt end to that possibility.

"Redser!" she exclaimed, holding her arms out and embracing the surprised-looking, red-haired giant. "I didn't know you were gay!" Jackie was too hyper to consider the embarrassment she may have been causing. But Neil also sensed her relief at spotting a familiar face.

"I'm not Gay, I'm Redser," Redser replied deadpan, making his two pals laugh.

"A Blackrock reunion," Redser joked, smiling at Neil.

"If Donno could see us now," Neil tried to sound relaxed, but inside he was a cauldron of anxiety.

"He'd probably give his left testicle to be in here with us," Redser said with a laugh.

"Spare me the thought," Neil grinned, conscious that Redser's pals were giving him a good look-over.

"Let's have some introductions!" Redser said, clapping his hands, obviously delighted with the new arrivals from his hometown. Stools were organized before Redser did the introductions. And Neil made sure he was sitting between Jackie and Liam.

"This is Dave," Redser announced, pointing to the smiling pudgy-faced bloke with the closely cropped brown hair. Dave smiled and gave them all a nod.

"And this is Daphne," Redser patted the head of the skinny, ultra-camp bloke with the pale complexion.

"Hi," Daphne said in a high-pitched, effeminate voice, waving to the three newcomers.

"Daphne!" Jackie shrieked with mirth, a mirth that Neil knew was false.

"It's Eddie really," Daphne protested indignantly in his deepest voice, and this brought a burst of laughter from Redser and Dave.

Neil couldn't help staring at Daphne. He was such an effeminate-looking bloke, not just physically, but in mannerisms, facial expressions, and speech. And that awful clipped accent couldn't possibly be the way he really spoke. This put-on gay accent annoyed Neil. Why couldn't he behave like an individual, instead of mimicking pouting stereotyped clones from some American soap? How did he ever get through school, Neil wondered, and what did his parents make of him? But Neil's thoughts were interrupted by Jackie announcing to the assembly that today was her younger brother's birthday. This precipitated a flurry of embarrassing pecks on the cheek from Redser and his pals, all of which, of course, were encouraged by Jackie.

"Eighteen!" Daphne exclaimed theatrically. "Oooh, I'd give anything to be eighteen again."

"The only time you'll see eighteen again is on the back of a bus," Dave jeered.

"Bitch!" Daphne pouted, clicking his tongue and throwing his head back in an exaggerated display of feigned disgust. Both Liam and Jackie were in stitches. Still feeling uneasy, Neil forced a grin onto his face. Daphne flashed him a quick look, as though wondering why he wasn't laughing like the others. But Daphne was obviously relishing his new audience, especially Jackie.

"I just love the bangles!" he shrieked, clasping hold of Jackie's arm and raising it up for inspection.

"Snap," Liam said, shaking his arm and rattling his own bangles.

"Rhythm is a dancer," Daphne replied like a shot, pointing at Liam as he plonked his foot up on the edge of Jackie's stool and rolled up the leg of his cream-colored, baggy trousers. He wasn't going to be outdone easily.

"George," he sighed, closing his eyes and pointing to the narrow strips of leather encircling his skinny ankle.

"Who's George?" Jackie asked, much to Daphne's delight.

"Have you got a week to spare, dear?" he replied, clasping Jackie's arm and again throwing his head back dramatically. Daphne began to elaborate on his latest tragic romance but Neil's attention drifted. His eyes had rested upon a new arrival. A dark-haired guy, dressed in faded jeans and a white T-shirt, drinking alone near the door. He couldn't believe it; at last he had spotted someone attractive. But what now, he thought. Was it just like in Hollies? "Where've I seen you before? What school d'you go to? D'you have a light please?" Or worse still, "D'you come here often?" Surely you didn't have to go through those awful chat-up routines in here. Again he was shaken out of his daydream by Jackie.

"D'you fancy any of them?" she whispered, shooting looks over in the direction of Redser and his two pals.

"Spare me," Neil sighed, conscious that his face had gone bright pink. Whatever about telling his sister that he was gay; it was a little peculiar having her ask him which fellows he fancied. Especially when he knew that her interest was forced. Attack was the best form of defense, he decided. "I mean, apart from Liam, how many blokes in this pub do *you* fancy?"

Jackie pursed her lips. "Hmm, one or two."

"Well, it's the same for me," Neil whispered.

Jackie looked at him, almost in disbelief. "Which ones?"

"What?" Neil asked.

"Which ones d'you fancy?"

Neil shook his head slowly and sighed. "You're worse than Cilla Black."

Jackie laughed and then she leaned over to kiss his cheek. Their eyes met for the briefest of moments and his sister's confused look saddened Neil. Even she didn't understand how he really felt. Then Neil nodded casually toward the door. Maybe it was time to try and make her understand.

"What age would you say that bloke is?" he asked in a low voice.

"Which one?"

"White T-shirt, near the door."

Jackie focused. "God, he's gorgeous!"

"Ssssh, will you?" Neil gasped.

"He is," Jackie insisted.

"What age?" Neil muttered out of the side of his mouth.

"I don't know, twenty-two, twenty-three. Neiley Nook, d'you have the hots?" she smiled anxiously.

Neil faked a weary sigh and threw his eyes up toward the ceiling.

"You do," Jackie teased.

"Don't be stupid," Neil muttered.

"I tell you, don't they have lovely manners, those Byrne sisters, whispering in company like that," Daphne exclaimed, and Neil sensed that Daphne was miffed because he didn't have everyone's undivided attention. When he heard Jackie begin to speak, he immediately clamped his hand over her mouth. He knew his sister well enough to realize her intentions. Jackie struggled to free herself.

"Oh lovely," Daphne cooed, "washing the family's dirty laundry in public."

Even though her speech was muffled, Jackie still managed to point over toward the door. Bemused, the others turned to look.

"Jackie, I'm warning you," Neil hissed, relinquishing his grip.

"The bloke in the white T-shirt," Jackie gasped. "Neil thinks he's gorgeous."

Mortified, Neil lowered his head into his hands.

"He's new," Dave announced eventually.

Neil peeped out between his fingers and spotted Dave and Redser holding hands beneath the table.

"Let me at him!" Daphne moaned, brushing the back of his hand across his forehead as he rose to his feet. "I'm in love!"

Redser grabbed hold of Daphne and pushed him back into his seat. "We'll have to chain you down," he said, smiling.

Daphne arched his back and spread his arms wide. "Is that a promise, dear?" he gasped, bringing a ripple of laughter from the others. When Neil glanced back toward the door, his look was met by the guy in the white T-shirt. Neil felt his face color, and he averted his gaze shyly when he thought he saw the guy winking at him. Daphne was holding court yet again, telling them all about Jason, the love of his life before George.

"Jason was adorable, but oh, his feet!" Daphne pegged his fingers to his nose and crunched his face up. "I tell you, sisters, Saddam would've beaten those hunky Americans if he had just one pair of Jason's socks in his artillery!" he added.

A couple of minutes passed before Neil glanced toward the door again. Another wink. Maybe he was imagining it, Neil thought. After all he'd had a lot to drink. He sneaked another look. Wink. There was no mistaking it that time, it was definitely him. What now?

Conversation was buzzing at the table. Redser had somehow managed to knock Daphne off the stage, and was telling Jackie and Liam that he and Dave had been going out together for two years. Jackie's eyes nearly popped out when Dave told them that his older brother was also gay. Redser went on to explain that no other pub in Dublin had such a mix of backgrounds, that none of the usual silly social divides mattered here. He pointed to people: he's a banker, she's a solicitor, he's a janitor, she's a teacher, he's a barman, she's an actress, he's a politician, she's a bus driver, he's a butcher. His list went on and on to Jackie's and Liam's amazement.

"And the rest of us are government artists," Daphne said, managing to interject.

"Government whats?" Jackie asked.

"Drawing the dole." Daphne got his laugh, but Neil felt too light-headed to listen. He felt the funny sensation inside, the one he experienced every time he saw Ian. He'd have to return White T-Shirt's wink. He looked down at his feet, but his practice winks were interrupted by Jackie's nudge.

"Neil, your man over there's trying to attract your attention."

Neil felt his heart surge. It must be White T-Shirt. What would he say to him? But the tingle of excitement disappeared abruptly when he saw who Jackie was pointing to. The one and only Uncle Sugar, sporting a new haircut, was waving Neil's ID card in the air.

"Oh God!" Neil muttered under his breath.

"Is that Uncle Sugar?" Jackie asked in puzzled amusement.

"Hmm," Neil nodded.

Everyone turned to look at the older man who Jackie had described earlier.

"Oooh, he's so cuddly," Daphne purred, making Liam splutter into his pint of Guinness. Neil stood up and struggled his way through the packed crowd. Sugar looked uncomfortable, realizing that he was the focus of their conversation.

"Sorry I didn't phone you."

"That's okay, Neil, no problem."

"I've been up to my eyeballs," Neil added weakly, struggling to smother a grin when he saw the sad attempt at a trendy haircut close-up. It was shaved over the ears, exactly the way Neil's hair was cut, but the style didn't suit gray hair.

"Happy birthday."

"Thanks."

"You're legal now," Sugar added, pointing to his drink. Neil nodded nonchalantly.

"I see you've made a few friends."

"Yeah," Neil muttered, detecting a hint of envy in the older man's tone. He wanted to tell him that he saw his car driving past his house, assure him that he understood, that he did the same sort of thing himself, but that there was no point in him falling in love, that it wouldn't be reciprocated. Instead, he took his ID card and escaped from Sugar's company as politely as he could.

On his way back to the table, he sneaked a look toward the door. His heart sank. White T-Shirt was gone. He scoured the pub, but there was no sign of him. *Oh God*, Neil sighed inwardly, *he probably thought I was chatting Sugar up and left in disgust.* Disconsolately, he rejoined the others.

A friendly lesbian couple came over to their table and while they chatted with Redser, Dave, and Daphne, Neil could sense Jackie recoiling in horror. The two girls were quick to sense her discomfort and after they moved off to the back of the pub, Jackie admitted to Neil that she didn't mind gay blokes but that lesbians gave her the creeps. Neil didn't bother to argue with her, realizing that if he wasn't gay, he'd probably have the same reaction to gay blokes.

"Here's the ladies," Dave said, nodding toward two transvestites who had just paraded into the pub.

"The clit-teasers," Redser smiled.

Jackie's and Liam's eyes were wide in amazement. But Neil was surprised at how indifferent he felt to the new arrivals. No one else in the pub was even batting an eyelid.

"Love the mascara, Gladys," Daphne said, touching the taller of the two as they passed the table.

"Thank you," Gladys replied in a husky voice, shyly flicking the silky brown wig back from his eyes. He was about six-foot-five, his face was caked with makeup, and he wore a saffron low-neck blouse, a pink mini, black fishnet tights, and red stilettos. With that height, those shoulders, and those bulging leg muscles you could've been an international second-row forward, Neil felt like saying. And he grinned to himself as he imagined the gentle giant trundling out in front of fifty thousand spectators at Lansdowne Road with his green jersey flopping down over his pink mini. All the horrified rugby fans would choke on their cigar smoke and, no doubt, the likes of Neil's brother-in-law would lead the chorus of hisses. Gladys's companion, Penelope, was more the scrum-half build. A shorter, slighter man, sporting a neat tweed pinafore, sensible brown shoes, a smattering of makeup, and a short blond wig. Like Laurel and Hardy, the pair of them ambled their way up to the crowded bar.

"Oh God!" Jackie wheezed. She couldn't contain herself any longer.

"Now, now, sister," Daphne tut-tutted.

"Did you ever see anything like it!" she exclaimed to Liam, who was now controlling his smile, aware that he and Jackie were alone in their reaction.

Daphne was wagging his finger. "Live and let live."

"Both of them are married," Redser told them.

"To each other?" the near-hysterical Jackie gasped.

"Don't they wish," Daphne sighed, while Redser shook his head.

"With kids," Dave added.

"Oh God!" Jackie wiped the tears from her face.

"You haven't seen me in my little black number," Daphne said, almost giving Jackie a relapse.

"But, aren't they gay?" she spluttered.

"No, they're boring heteros like you and Liam," Daphne replied, smiling as he hit Jackie's arm. "Only joking, sister."

Gladys and Penelope were now chatting to Uncle Sugar. Neil was trying to imagine what the reaction in his local pub would be if Gladys and Penelope strolled in, dressed in full regalia. The whole place would grind to a halt. And they'd more than likely be flung out.

Daphne hid his face in his hands when the bright lights came on to signal closing time. "Oh my God, I feel naked!" he squealed hysterically. The dash for the exit had begun. Neil noticed how old Daphne looked for his age. Too many late nights, he presumed.

"Let's go clubbing," Redser said, and Neil was delighted when Jackie and Liam agreed. The guy in the white T-shirt might be there.

The upstairs part of the nightclub was just like a large sitting room. Comfortable armchairs lined the walls, the floor was carpeted, oil paintings hung on the walls, and a big mirror adorned the wall over the fireplace. Downstairs was a different matter. Steep stone steps led into a low-ceilinged cavern-like dungeon, complete with dark and mysterious alcoves, a mirrored dance floor, pounding dance music, a melee of frenzied dancers, and a bar manned by a barman who could have passed as Daphne's sister.

"It's so sleazy!" Jackie exclaimed, putting her martini down on one of the many upturned beer kegs that served as tables.

"Sister, what d'you think of the music?" Daphne, who hadn't budged from Jackie's side, asked.

"It's loud!" Jackie roared, causing two nearby snoggers to come up for air.

Neil, Liam, Redser, and Dave stood around in a circle chatting. The boys over here, the girls over there, Redser joked. Neil felt his bottom being pinched, but by the time he looked around, the culprit had melted into the throng. Then two blokes with shaved heads, one of whom was Dave's brother, came over, their arms draped around each other's shoulders. Dave broke away from the group to chat to them.

"What d'you think?" Neil asked Liam.

Liam smiled and nodded approvingly. "Best music I've heard in a long time."

It was true, Neil thought, they were already playing remixes of tracks that were considered brand new in Hollies. But he was too busy keeping his eyes peeled for white T-shirts to concentrate on conversation. When Dave rejoined them, Redser started to sing:

"That brother of mine is so butch," Dave said, imitating Daphne's clipped accent.

"Bitch!" came Daphne's reply from five yards away.

"Rhino ears," Dave retorted.

Nearby, Jackie and Daphne clung onto each other, both squealing with laughter. Another one of Daphne's high-camp jokes, Neil presumed, thinking how irritating Daphne and his type would get after a while. It was all right for Jackie; this was all a novelty for her, she wouldn't have any long-term association with the place. She would get married just like the rest of his friends. But for him it was different; this was his life. He'd have to come in here on his own if he really wanted to meet someone.

The thought depressed him. The club made him feel so uncomfortable. Watching the confident, stylish dancers on the small dance floor, he wondered how many had AIDS. Strutting time bombs. He was mad coming in here. But what else was there? San Francisco? No way, everyone would guess. And anyway, it's AIDS city. *Hot Press* maybe? White T-shirt first and then *Hot Press*, he decided. The next suitable ad he saw, he'd give a public pay phone number and tell them to ring at a specified time. The pay phone in Stillorgan, that was far enough away from his house, he thought; he'd cycle down there tomorrow and get the number.

This cheered Neil up and he didn't object when Jackie and Daphne dragged him out onto the dance floor. Although, for some reason, he kept facing Jackie as they danced, trying to give the impression that she was his girl-friend. Years and years of social conditioning, he presumed.

Daphne emitted a high-pitched screech when the first piano notes of the Sister Sledge dance remix tinkled through the nightclub. There was a skirmish as people rushed to the dance floor. Every dancer held their hands up in the air in preparation, almost in adulation.

We are family
I've got all my sisters with me

The rhythmic drums pumped into action, a signal for the wild dancing to begin. Neil was reminded of voodoo dancers. Hypnotic, trancelike gyrations all around him. Faces distorted beneath the flickering lights, images blurred in the mirrors, lost in the music. Jackie's hair flayed everywhere. Daphne kept bouncing up to him and bumping his chest off Neil's. Not unlike rugby training, Neil thought in amusement, but he winced as he imagined what the reaction of his rugby teammates would be if they could see him now.

And for the first time in his life, Neil relaxed and joined in the rhythm of the crazy dance. All his normal self-consciousness left him. There was nothing to worry about here. Nobody cared. He felt himself being submerged into the sexual sea of graceful movement. A dizzy tangle of arms, legs, torsos, hips, backsides, and pelvic thrusts, swirling all around him. Happy faces, desolate faces, drunken faces, faces of every age, swept past him in the timeless frenzy.

He was shaken out of his trance by Jackie, who was pointing across the dance floor, her face distorted in hysterical laughter. Daphne and the six-foot-five Gladys were slow dancing. Neil nearly choked. A full foot shorter than his partner, Daphne had his arms wrapped around the giant's waist and his head buried into his bosom. It looked just like a mother hugging her prodigal son. Sort of sweet, in a funny kind of way.

After the sweaty dance had finished, Neil walked down to the bathrooms at the back of the nightclub. He tried not to look at the couples snogging in the smoky darkness. Then a tall bloke with huge ears, who was leaning against the door of the gents' rest room, blew him a kiss. The light was off inside the rest room and Neil could see shadows moving around in the murkiness. Ignoring the man's less-than-subtle advances, Neil ducked into the ladies' rest room and locked himself in a cubicle. What a squalid dump, he thought, God knows what he was walking on. What would his mum and dad say if they could see him now?

In mid-leak, he nearly died with embarrassment when he heard the announcement coming over the PA system. "Happy birthday to Neiley Nook Byrne, who's eighteen today," the dj read out in amusement. The Beatles' "Birthday" then started to blare around the nightclub. Neil wanted the toilet bowl to open up and swallow him.

When he saw the look on Jackie's face, he felt like strangling her. She clasped his arm in delight and handed him the free bottle of birthday champagne. Everyone seemed to be watching as he tilted the bottle and drank from the neck. When he stopped for air, a burly bearded bloke of about forty walked up to him and rested his hand on Neil's shoulder. Neil grinned at him, thinking that he was going to wish him happy birthday.

"I wish that bottle was my dick," he said with a leer before retreating back to his pals. Neil felt repulsed. Jackie pretended that she hadn't heard, but Neil knew by the look on her face that she had. He wished he had thought of a clever put-down. But this incident spoiled the remainder of his night. And Neil felt uneasy when he realized that the bearded bloke and his pals were watching him.

When they were leaving the nightclub, a tired-looking Daphne came over to Neil. "I'll do some research on

White T-Shirt," he whispered confidentially. Neil just smiled, he was too exhausted to say anything. All he could think of was his bed for the night, the dingy sofa in Liam's flat. The bearded guy made some comment when Neil passed him, and Neil simply ignored him. But he was glad that he was with a group, especially glad that Gladys the Giant was leaving the club with them. One whack of his handbag would put the bearded slimeball into orbit.

Outside on the pavement, the group stood chatting in the gray dawn light, waiting for Daphne, who was resting on the nightclub steps to muster up the energy to walk to a taxi line. Neil kept hopping nervously from one foot to the other, anxiously keeping a lookout for people he knew. Then Gladys spoke to him for the first time. "Happy birthday, sweetie," he said, stooping down awkwardly to peck Neil on the cheek.

"Thanks." Neil felt himself blushing. His world was going crazy.

"Tell me, is my makeup a mess?" Gladys asked, stooping down to Neil's level again. Neil tried to act casually while he examined the giant's face.

"Nah, it's not too bad," he lied. The makeup looked comical, it was smudged so badly. And dawn's bristle was beginning to spike its way through the mushy brown paste.

"Let's see." Jackie arrived at Neil's side. "Gladys, it's a

mess!" she shrieked after her cursory examination. "You can't rely on these men," she added, pushing Neil away.

Gladys opened his large handbag and produced his emergency makeup kit. While Jackie was reapplying his makeup, a police car prowled slowly past. Before Neil had time to hide behind Gladys, he saw Penelope and the police officer driving the car exchange friendly waves.

"They look after us," Penelope explained. Neil was flabbergasted.

"I love a man in uniform," Daphne muttered weakly from the steps. Neil glanced around and was surprised at how wretched Daphne looked. His frail body seemed to lie in a crumpled heap like a puppet without its strings. All normal sprightliness had disappeared. Daphne met Neil's stare and Neil averted his eyes in embarrassment. In that momentary encounter Neil had seen a frightened, almost pleading, look in Daphne's dark eyes.

Soon after, a taxi swung around the corner, and Redser jumped out onto the road to flag it down.

"We'll take this poor fellow home with us," Gladys said, draping his huge arm around Daphne and tenderly lifting him to his feet. To Neil's surprise the taxi driver didn't bat an eyelid as the strange cortege of passengers piled into the backseat.

After they had said their good-byes to Dave and Redser, Neil, Jackie, and Liam walked arm-in-arm down Baggot

Street, with the two lads swinging Jackie up into the air. Then another thought occurred to him; his dad would be going to work on the very same street in a matter of hours in order to earn the money to keep Jackie and himself in the lifestyle they had become accustomed to.

"C'mon, Gladys, will you hurry up?" Jackie shouted to Neil.

"Be quiet, you, Penelope," came Neil's Daphne imitation.

"*We are family, I've got all my sisters with me,*" Liam sang, and Neil and Jackie soon joined in. Their impromptu singsong attracted some funny looks from the few passersby. The rising sun was now beginning to crawl slowly up into the sky, coloring the pavements and the buildings with its crimson rays. Milk trucks and bread vans whirred past them. Birds fluttered and squawked overhead. A single magpie alighted on a nearby tree. Probably the only magpie in Dublin that's up and about, Neil thought, but he was too tired to point it out to the others and maybe share the sorrow. Although he did search in vain for the magpie's soul mate.

———————

Gary's mother and another neighbor, Mrs. Burke, were having coffee with his mum when Neil arrived home the following morning. The throbbing nightclub music was still ringing in his ears.

"Here's the wandering minstrel now," Mrs. Burke said, and Neil gave the visitors his fake grin.

"How did last night go?" his mum asked.

"Great," Neil said, wondering how his mum's friends would react if he told them about the sleazy nightclub. That'd wipe those nosy smiles off their faces. Then, of course, the moment he left the room, the inquisition would begin. "Where was he last night, Catherine? He stayed in Jackie's friend's flat. Michelle?" "That's right." The two neighborhood gossips would exchange doubtful glances. "He has a new girlfriend, hasn't he?" Gary's mum would remark innocently, all the time aware of Becky's entanglement with a married man. And, of course, his mum would play along, delighted that everyone thought Becky was her little boy's girlfriend, but of course she knew the truth. She must know, Neil thought for the millionth time that month, she's my mother and mothers know these things.

"Show us the new watch," Mrs. Kelly grabbed hold of Neil's wrist, and she and Mrs. Burke expressed their approval.

"Oh, the real McCoy."

"Looks very expensive."

"That man phoned for you again, Neil," his mum said.

Neil looked puzzled.

"About the summer job."

"Oh yeah," Neil poured himself a glass of water, turning his back on the ladies to conceal his unease.

"Has he got a job?" Mrs. Kelly asked, cocking her thumb toward Neil.

"Your Gary fixed it up for him," his mum told her.

"Gary did?" Mrs. Kelly nearly choked on her cream bun.

Neil closed his eyes in anguish. He could feel Mrs. Kelly's puzzled eyes burning into his back. Of course she was puzzled. Gary hadn't got a summer job for himself, so what was he doing fixing his pals up with jobs? He'd have to get hold of Gary and arrange some story, Neil thought, resolving to put an end to his litany of lies.

"When did he ring?" he asked, deliberately steering the conversation away from Gary.

"This morning," his mum replied.

"He must really want you," Mrs. Burke added.

You said it, Mrs. B., Neil thought. *You said it, babe.*

"You better phone him before he gives the job to someone else," his mum said. "And remember to be polite."

Neil was going to phone him, all right, but he was going to be anything but polite.

"What type of job is it, Neil?" Mrs. Kelly asked.

"Ah, just an office job," he muttered, sliding toward the door.

"So you're alone here for the summer then," Mrs. Kelly added, stalling his escape.

"Yeah," Neil said, lingering at the door, presuming that she was referring to Jackie's departure to Amsterdam.

"Isn't she one of the McGanns from off Booterstown Avenue?"

Neil hesitated for a moment. His mum was purposely avoiding his searching look.

"Becky?" he said eventually.

Mrs. Kelly nodded, her steely eyes unflinching, her lips set in a doubting sneer. Neil imagined her in a Nazi uniform. *Sieg heil! Salute Frau Goose-Step Kelly. Why do you want to know these things, Frau Goose-Step? Know what you are? You're a vulture, feeding off the pain of an emotionally crippled boy. Is it just because I'm going to get better final grades than your son? Or because I got on the rugby team and he didn't? Or simply because I'm better looking than he is?*

"Well, she lives just off Booterstown Avenue, so I presume that makes her one of the McGanns who live off Booterstown Avenue," Neil said. His mum and Mrs. Burke laughed, but Frau Goose-Step Kelly was not amused. Neil ducked out of the room before she had time to continue her inquisition.

Upstairs, in the sanctuary of his bedroom, Neil scrutinized the personal ads in *Hot Press* while "Am I Not Your Girl?" blared from his boom box. *Bizarre incorporated*, he thought, reading through the ads. He remembered how he used to laugh at them in school with the others, while privately, of course, they fascinated and excited him. "Older man looking for younger guy."

"Definitely Uncle Sugar," he muttered aloud. Then he saw it. "Gay guy, 22, good-looking, own pad, looking to meet similar age or younger. Interests include theater, cinema, music, sports, and long evenings of passion." He printed his reply and signed it "Ian." The phone number in Stillorgan was all he needed now.

Downstairs, the front door closed, signaling the end of his mum's coffee morning. A minute later his bedroom door opened and his mum came in.

"Any dirty clothes? I'm going to start the wash."

"Yeah, could you put this shirt in?" Neil said, wincing from the whiff of smoke as he pulled his shirt over his head.

"Who's Ian?" His mum was twisting her head around to read his *Hot Press* reply.

"Mum, that's private!" Neil snapped, snatching the letter quickly and shoving it into his pocket.

His mum smiled as she checked the pockets of his shirt. Neil sighed with relief. She obviously hadn't had time to read the contents of his letter.

"Shaft? What's that?" she asked, reading from a scrap of paper she had found in his shirt pocket. Neil felt his face turning bright crimson.

"Ah, it's just a place Jackie, Liam, and I went to last night," he replied, trying his best to sound casual.

"What is it? A film?"

"Nah, a nightclub."

"I've never heard of it." His mum furrowed her brow. "Is it on Leeson Street?"

"Yeah," Neil said, bending down to take a white T-shirt from his drawer. He couldn't let his mum see his face; she'd know immediately that he was lying. "I'm sure they change the names of those nightclubs once a week."

"And you're the fellow who wonders why he's always short of money."

"It was my birthday, Mum."

"I'm only kidding you," she said, leaving the nightclub entrance receipt down on his table. "Well, did you have a good night?"

"Yeah, great."

"A couple of people phoned for you."

"Who?"

"Oh the usual, Gary and Tom and Yvonne and . . . Oh I can't remember the rest." His mum retreated toward the door. "You'll have to get a private secretary to take your messages for you," she added, and then her attention turned to the music. "That's nice singing, who is it?"

"Sinead O'Connor."

"Oh." His mum rolled her eyes up toward the ceiling

and clicked her tongue. "It's a pity she doesn't stick to the singing," she sighed, leaving the room.

Neil examined the entrance slip to Shaft. No mention of what type of nightclub it was. Relief. He'd have to warn Jackie, though, just in case. He lay down on his bed, curled up on his side, and fell asleep.

At lunchtime, Kate came over with Danny and Annie. Marian Finucane was doing an item on her radio show about gay people in Ireland. It was on in the background as they ate their lunch. Neil pretended to be engrossed in the newspaper.

"You'd feel sorry for them," Kate said after a gay man had phoned in and talked about the loneliness he experienced growing up in a country town during the seventies and how he went to England after his secret became known.

"They bring a lot of it upon themselves," his mum replied.

Neil crossed the kitchen and picked Annie up, he didn't want Kate or his mum to see his bright crimson face.

"Ah, that's unfair, Mum," Kate replied.

"No, I mean, we've always had homosexuals, and they've been fine people, contributing to the art and what-have-you. But they didn't make such a big fuss out of it like they do these days," his mum said.

Neil felt the volcano inside him rumbling. Little Annie

gave him a funny look when she saw him contort his face in exasperation. She was imitating him, thinking that it was a game.

"Annie-moo," he said, tickling the girl, much to her delight.

"No, Annie-moo," came her squealed reply.

"Don't be annoying Uncle Neil now," Kate instructed.

"She's fine," Neil said, keeping his back turned on Kate and his mum.

"Where's Danny?" Kate asked, leaning down to take a look under the kitchen table.

"In the living room," Neil told her. "He wanted to watch the cartoons."

"Anything for some peace," Kate sighed.

Another caller came on the radio, an elderly man. He opened by saying that he was sick of homosexuals hijacking the airwaves, glamorizing their lifestyle for young, impressionable people. It was an unnatural way of life, he insisted, and active gay people like the earlier caller were deservedly discriminated against. Marian Finucane argued with little success. The elderly man finished by saying that he didn't believe that anyone was born homosexual, that they just acquired those tendencies as a result of evil propaganda.

"Oh, I'm tired of listening to all that stuff," his mum sighed, switching the radio off.

"I better check that Danny isn't wrecking the living room," Neil said, leaving the kitchen. He went straight upstairs to his parents' room and phoned the radio hotline.

The girl who answered the phone told him they were flooded with calls and that it was unlikely that they'd be able to put him on air. But as soon as Neil said he was gay, she changed her tune. He felt his heart pounding while he waited to go on the air. His palms were sticky, his armpits were soaking, and his anger was abating slightly now as the realization that he was going to be talking on national radio began to sink in. *They're going to put distortion on your voice*, he told himself. *There's no need to worry.* But he still couldn't stop his hands from shaking. Marian Finucane introduced him as a young gay person living in south Dublin, who didn't want to be identified for obvious reasons. When the presenter gave him his cue, Neil kept his audience waiting for a couple of seconds before he found his voice.

"I just want to say, in reply to that last caller, that I've…eh, that I've known my sexual orientation since I was ten or eleven." Neil coughed to clear his throat. "I didn't even know what being gay meant then, but I do know that I've always found boys more attractive than girls…So all his talk about evil propaganda is just rubbish…People like him will just have to accept that there are other human beings who are different. And I can

128

assure him that it's not a glamorous lifestyle. In fact it's quite the opposite. It's a very lonely existence..." Neil stopped. His voice had begun to waver slightly. The presenter coaxed him along gently. Neil knew that every listener would be glued to their radios now; this was high-quality radio.

"I mean, so many people in this country purport to follow Christ's teachings...But the thing to remember is that Christ surrounded himself with the social outcasts of his time...And anyway, if this is supposed to be a Christian country, then why have I thought of killing myself so many times, simply because I'm...I'm..."

Neil was too choked with emotion to finish. All the years of pain seemed to swell inside his throat, blocking his words. He sat on the edge of his parents' bed and stared at the phone in his hand, with Marian Finucane's voice inquiring if he was still on the line. He wanted to empty his mum's jar of headache tablets, swallow the lot of them, and announce it on the airwaves. Now see what you've done to me. Then the program went into a commercial break.

Neil went into his own bedroom, switched on his radio, and listened to the flood of callers expressing their support for him. One elderly female caller said she wished he was her son. Another lady from Longford said the whole country should hang its head in shame, that we were supposed to be a nation who cherished its children, but in her experience, there was nothing further from the truth when it came to gay people. "My own son died of AIDS," she then announced in a hushed tone, struggling to retain her composure. "He was a lovely, gentle boy…"

Again Marian Finucane had to use all her skill to coax the story from the caller, a story the caller so obviously wanted to tell.

"When he was nineteen, he went to a dance in the town…And he came home with blood all over his face…"

There was another delay as the lady struggled to control her heartbroken voice. She continued her story bravely, her sentences punctuated with sobs.

"He told me that he had just got into a fight, that it was nothing to worry about…But soon after that he went to live in San Francisco. He took twenty years of my life with him that day he left, Marian. It broke my heart. You see he was my only child, and his father had died a few years before. Anyway, for five years, he phoned me every Sunday night without fail. I can't tell you how much I looked forward to those phone calls. He sounded so happy there. Until October two years ago, I'll never forget it. I hadn't heard from him for a month and I was worried stiff. You see, he didn't have a phone where I could call him. But this windy October night, he phoned and I knew immediately that something was wrong. His voice sounded different. He told me that he was coming home. Of course I was delighted. But then he said those words that I'll take to the grave with me. 'Mum,' he says, 'Mum, I'm dying…'"

The sobs began in earnest and a record was put on. Neil felt the teardrops trickling down past his chin and dripping onto his pillow. By the time the music had finished the lady caller had recovered her composure.

"After he died, a fellow who was in school with him told me of all the jeering and torment my son had suffered at school and around the town. And I never knew about it. All those years he had kept it hidden. But the saddest thing of all was that I never even knew that he was gay until he came back from San Francisco. He was my only child, but still he felt he couldn't tell me. And he was such a lovely, gentle boy. He wouldn't have harmed a flea. I loved him so much. But they crucified him, Marian, they crucified him…"

She broke down for the final time. Neil covered his face with his hands. He felt dizzy. If that story didn't change people's attitudes, nothing would. He tried to visualize the lady's face, but he kept seeing his mother's. Would his mum have gone on the radio and told the same story about him? She probably would, that was the thing. After he was dead and gone, when she realized that it wasn't such a big deal after all. Maybe Jackie was right, maybe he should tell his parents before it was too late.

The rest of the show was a blur. Suddenly the whole country seemed to support the gay cause. Each one of them in turn stated their disgust at the treatment of the Longford caller's son. But their liberal professions made Neil skeptical. He couldn't help wondering how many of them had been a party to a similar lynch mob in their day. How many of them would be so liberal if it were their own son or daughter who was gay? Very few, most likely. He tried to think how he would react himself if he was heterosexual and one of his own children told him that he or she was gay. But it was an impossible situation to imagine.

That night Neil went over to Andrea's house to watch a movie. Gary, of course, had heard the Marian Finucane Show, and when he began to tell them all about it, it was a relief to Neil that the room was dimly lit. He felt like he could've lit a cigarette off his face. The fact that Gary had heard the show didn't surprise Neil. His pal seemed to have a built-in radar for detecting shows with a gay theme. Films like *Sebastiane* and *Edward II* had fascinated him, and many were the breaks in school he had held court, elaborating to his school pals about how much the films had disgusted him. "Two men kissing! Ah, it's fuckin' disgusting!" He would spit the words out, and of course all his classmates, including Neil, would voice their agreement. When Neil had told Becky about Gary's fascination, she had insisted that he was more than likely a closet case. But, as he had done during those breaks, Neil remained silent and pretended that he hadn't heard the radio show that day.

"I feel so sorry for that mother," Trish said after Gary had told them about the caller from Longford.

"The problem is," Gary shook his head knowledgeably, "all homosexuals are promiscuous."

The volcano inside Neil rumbled into life again. He had trouble lighting up his cigarette, his hands were trembling so much.

"It's true, they are," Gary insisted, looking over at Neil. Neil shrugged. Why did he always have to maintain this calm exterior? Why was Gary looking at him?

"You should know, Gary," Andrea said, and the others laughed.

Gary ignored the comment. "I mean, when you think of it, a man's sex drive is higher than a woman's."

This brought a volley of protest from the girls. But Gary was undaunted. "So if you put two men together for sex…" He whistled as he shook his head. "You're talking Richter scale."

The others laughed loudly.

"I mean, let's face it, that bloke from Longford didn't catch AIDS from knitting handbags."

Again, the others whooped with laughter.

Neil bit his tongue and waited for Gary to tell them all about the caller who had distortion put on his voice. Gary didn't disappoint him. He told them that he didn't believe that anyone could know that they were gay at ten years of age.

"I think that old fella had a point though; a lot of it is caused by propaganda," Gary continued, draping his arm around Trish's shoulder as though to prove his manhood. "And there's nothing worse than all those bloody intellectual queers, making it all sound so natural."

Neil wanted to cry out loud. His insides were shuddering with helplessness.

"Jesus, Gary, you're a bigger bigot than I thought you were," Andrea said with a laugh. Knowing that he wouldn't be able to contain himself much longer, Neil excused himself and went upstairs to the bathroom. He stood over the hand basin and splashed cold water onto his face. Gary's comments had hurt him, but still he couldn't say anything. He looked at himself in the mirror and started to cry.

After he had washed his face again, Neil went downstairs and told the others that he wasn't feeling well.

"He's lovesick," Gary teased.

Yeah, I am, Neil thought as he grinned at his pal. *And I'm now going to walk my promiscuous way home past my loved one's house. Jealous, are you?*

"Aren't you going to stay for the movie?" Andrea asked.

"Nah, I'll pass," Neil replied, holding his stomach. *Fuck the lot of you*, he thought. *Sitting here passing judgment on something you know nothing about. Someday I'll shake you out of your smugness…Someday.*

Neil caught a bus into town. Soft drizzling rain drifted through the narrow cobblestoned lanes. None of the first night nerves bothered him now; he was feeling too empty inside to care. Tears of self-pity welled up in his eyes. Why was he so lonely? He stood at the end of the gloomy road and watched the pub door across the road for a while. Strangers desperate for love, filing in singly and in pairs. Arriving late under cover of darkness. Lost souls.

Go home and go to bed, Neil, the voice in his head told him. *Everything will be all right in the morning. Even if the guy in the white T-shirt is in there you'd be terrible company tonight. Better you don't meet him.*

A couple, their arms draped around each other's shoulders, looked at him as they passed, and Neil met their stares defiantly.

Lights on Capel Street bridge were red. Headlights blurred in the drizzle. Snarling engines waiting. Cross now? Maybe wait for the rush of traffic, then step off the pavement. The screech of brakes. A scream. A hollow thud, followed by deafening silence. Blood on the road. Report on the news, maybe. An appreciation of the late

Neil Byrne in the *Blackrock Annual* written by his closest pal, Gary Kelly. *Oh God, spare me. Cross now while it's safe. Pull the baseball cap down over your face. I don't care if anyone sees me. Oh yes, you do.* Inside now. Upstairs. No sign of White T-Shirt. No sign of Redser and his pals. Rain has kept everyone at home. Not even a video playing.

"Pint of Budweiser please."

You should know my order by now, Poncehead. Imagine if you said that aloud. Barred from a gay bar. Marvelous. Oh fuck, here comes Uncle Sugar.

"How're you, Neil?"

Return the cheery smile. God, the state of the hair!

"You're becoming a bit of a regular."

Look who's talking. Stop fooling yourself, Neiley Nook, you're glad to see him and he knows it. Let him rabbit on a while and then steer the conversation toward his little bachelor pad. "What videos d'you have, old-timer?" *That'd be a good opener.* "I'm horny as hell!" *That'd be sure to give poor old Sugar a heart attack. Jesus, look at him, yapping away like an excited schoolkid. Of course he's excited, he knows that in fifteen minutes you and he will be driving to Clontarf in his sex machine.*

"You look like a little lost boy with your hair wet."

Tell him that you took your cap off in the hope of catching pneumonia. Tell him how empty you feel tonight. Wouldn't he just love to become a confidante?

"Neil, sorry about the phone calls, I didn't realize they'd cause you such hassle."

Grin politely. *Just don't do it again, Sugar, or you're dead meat. And don't be driving past my house late at night hoping for a chance meeting. It's pathetic, I should know. Oh great, bulging wallet's out and he's buying another round. A belated birthday drink, he says. Feeling better now, maybe this world isn't so bad after all. The headlines. Radio star feels merry after two pints. More like, gay radio star feels randy after two pints. But, Sugar, perhaps you should know, if that guy in the T-shirt walks through that door, you're history.*

"You're certainly knocking them back tonight." Uncle Sugar's wallet reemerged.

Yeah, what d'you expect? I have to get drunk to face your sad little pad. Cut the crap, Sugar, let's go out to your car, before I start to cry. I'm in a mess, Sugar, can't you see? You're the only one in the whole world who's in love with me. Sad, isn't it? Worse than that, it's pathetic.

"I love the watch, is it new?"

Any excuse for a grope. Fondle my skinny wrist, tickle my hand, I don't care, it feels nice. Wish I could fall in love with you, Sugar, it would save so much hassle. But I couldn't, not in a million years. Life is funny, isn't it?

"D'you fancy coming back for a cup of coffee?"

Phew, thought you'd never ask. But not so fast, agree reluctantly. There are roles to be acted out here, games to be played.

Maybe I'll play the game Trish played with Gary when they first met. Coy and shy and the oh-I'm-so-innocent face. Ah fuck, can't be bothered. A little nod. Okay, I wouldn't mind a cuppa. Look at the face on him, he can't believe it. Poor old Sugar, he's going to burst a blood vessel. Finish the pints and let's hit the road.

———————

Sugar slipped another tape into the VCR and sat back in his armchair.

Oh Jesus, he's looking over again. Pull your T-shirt right down over your weapon. There, he won't see much now. "Hey, Sugar, d'you hear about the sexy bullfighter? He died on the horn." *Ha, ha, ha, very funny, aren't I? Would you look at the collection of pornos he has? No wonder he looks worn out. What does he do? Sit in here every night? Forget about Sugar and concentrate on the action. Oh God, it's amazing.*

"D'you want a hand there, Neil?"

Would you fuck off. No, don't say it, just throw him a disdainful look and shake your head. Set the ground rules. You keep to yourself, Sugar, and I'll keep to myself.

"There's some tissues there."

Sleazeball, would you just go and pull yourself and stop gawking over here? Is there anything sacred anymore? My God, look at what they're doing! Elastic limbs! And that guy looks a little like Ian! Oh Jesus, tissue quick!

Now what? Don't look over at Sugar. God, his sound effects are repulsive. Feel dirty now. And guilty. All those video stars have mums and dads, brothers and sisters. How in the name of God do they perform in front of cameras? They all look stoned. Twosomes, threesomes, foursomes. Jesus, it's disgusting really. And depressing. What the hell am I doing here? Sounds like Sugar's reached his climax. Finish the coffee, one smoke, and then tell him he's bringing you home. You don't belong to this under-world. No, you'll have a big wedding in Blackrock one day. And at your stag party, a male kiss-o-gram will burst into the pub and sit you down on his knee. "Everyone knows about you, Neil," he'll say, and all the lads will be doubled over in hysterics.

"Fancy another cup of coffee?"

Shake your head. Listless now. Maybe everybody does know. Gary kept looking at you when he was talking about the radio show.

"You can stay the night here if you want."

Shake your head again. Could think of nothing worse, Sugar. Stand up as you put your jacket on. Subtle hint. Oh God, the noise he's making chewing that biscuit. That's what comes of living alone. No mammy to say, "Stop eating with your mouth open, Sugar." That must be his mammy in that photo on top of the telly. All the time watching her son, the king of porn. And that must be Sugar there, at his confirma-tion. In short trousers! The state of the outfit. But he wasn't a bad-looking kid, whatever happened him since.

"There's a great view of the sea out this window during the daytime."

Look out the window into the blackness. How interesting. C'mon, Sugar, let's get the show on the road. Oh no, don't tell me he's going to try and get romantic again. Get your hand off my shoulder, you disgusting old pervert. Never know what I'd catch off you. Yuck, he hasn't even washed his hands!

"D'you want another biscuit?"

Have some candy, children. Shake your head and shrug his hand off your shoulder. Wouldn't eat one if you paid me.

"Right, let's hit the road."

———————

Everyone had gone to bed when Neil got home. He told his parents he was in, slipped one of the family home videos into the VCR, and lay across the sofa. He fast-forwarded to the part he wanted to watch. Himself at twelve years of age, sitting proudly on his new BMX bike, about to head off with Gary and Tom for a ride. The grinning faces, looking as innocent as the day they were born, cushioned from the confusing world that awaited them. No one could ever have guessed what would happen that summer in Donegal when Gary had gone on holidays with Neil's family. He and Neil had to share a bed. And before they fell asleep, Gary started to play nighttime games. "Pretend it's a girl who's touching you. See how still you can lie. Stop giggling. Now you do it to me." Innocent excitement under the sheets. The next day both boys blushed whenever they saw each other. The encounter was never mentioned again. Sometimes Neil wondered if it had ever happened at all.

The living room door opened and his dad stuck his head in.

"Ah, just the man I want to see," his dad said, tucking his dressing gown in underneath him as he sat down on the arm of a chair. "What're you watching?" he added, glancing around at the television.

"Ah, just some of the old videos," Neil replied, sitting up and flicking the TV off, thinking of the quagmire he would have been in if he had taken Uncle Sugar up on his offer of a loan of some videos.

"I was talking to Charlie Dunne, you know the pal of mine who owns the civil engineering firm?"

Neil nodded, knowing exactly what was coming next.

"Yeah, well, he says he can fix you up with a bit of summer work."

"Oh, great." Neil tried to infuse his voice with interest.

"It'll give you a taste of what you're going into."

Neil rolled his tongue around his mouth, struggling to resist the bait. His dad was always doing things like this, making plans for him that he knew were contrary to

Neil's wishes. It was his way of provoking the conflict that he wanted resolved. In typical family fashion, a cloak of silence had fallen over the matter since the day Neil broke the news about wanting to study art. But it was constantly bubbling beneath the surface, detectable in the worried glances he sometimes caught his mum and dad sneaking in his direction when he was eating or watching the TV.

"And it'll give you a few bucks to put toward your college fees."

"Yeah," Neil answered, chewing the nail of his index finger nonchalantly.

"Oh, Becky-what's-her-name phoned for you earlier."

"Did she?" Neil's face perked up.

"I think she said she'd phone again, you better ask your mother."

Neil shifted uncomfortably when his dad turned and stared at him. "Tell me, are you and Becky an item?"

Neil felt his face redden. His dad had never asked such a direct question about his love life before this. But the no-go zone was obviously being breached at his mum's behest. The pair of them had probably spent the whole evening agonizing over their son's unusual romance.

"Well, we were before she went to France." Neil tried to sound jocular in his reply.

"Well, just take one bit of advice from your old fella... Never mess around with a girl's heartstrings." His dad tried to make it sound like he was being lighthearted. Neil clenched his fist in frustration. It was all so ridiculous. What a day for his dad to pick to start advising him on how to treat the fairer sex. Did he really know that little about his son?

"Hmm." Neil nodded.

His dad rubbed his chin thoughtfully. "Is everything okay, Neil?" he asked with uncustomary tenderness.

"Yeah," Neil said stiffly, maintaining his calm exterior. Inside he felt a strong urge to reveal all, gush it out onto his dad's shoulder. Be his little boy again.

"It's just..." His dad lowered his embarrassed gaze. "Your mother and myself, we've noticed that you haven't been in the best of form recently."

Neil swallowed the lump in his throat. "I think it must be the exams and all that," he stammered, a slight waver in his voice. Now he really wanted to clasp his arms around his dad and cry his heart out.

His dad stood up and ruffled Neil's hair. "They're done now, no point in worrying about them anymore." Neil could sense the tone of victory and relief in his dad's voice. He could go back up to bed now and report to his wife that he was right after all, that it was the exams. But she would know better.

"Oh, and some other friend of yours phoned as well."

"Who?"

"Someone called Eddie."

"Eddie?" Neil wrinkled his nose in puzzlement.

"Well he asked to speak to Jackie then, so you better ask her who it was."

Then it dawned on Neil who it was. The one and only Daphne. No wonder his dad's voice had a slight hint of bemusement.

"Is Jackie in bed?" Neil asked, steering the conversation away from Daphne.

"Ah, she's been in bed for hours, she was exhausted," his dad said, going toward the door. "She has a long journey ahead of her tomorrow."

Neil felt a sharp dart of pain. The events of the day had pushed his sister's imminent departure from his thoughts.

"Time you were hitting the hay yourself, isn't it?" his dad added, glancing at his watch.

"Yeah, I was just about to go."

"'Night then."

"'Night, Dad."

As soon as his dad left the room, Neil closed his eyes and threw his head back in anguish. Things were getting complicated.

chapter six

As they drove up to the airport terminal, the enormous dark outline of an airplane loomed overhead, making a deafening roar as it soared into the night sky. Neil leaned out of the car window to watch the red flashing taillights grow smaller and smaller in the distance. Alongside him in the backseat, Jackie was making her hundredth last minute check of her hand luggage.

"Passport, tickets, money…" she muttered.

"Hairbrush," his dad joked.

"Ssssh!" Jackie hissed, and Neil's dad caught his eye in the mirror and winked conspiratorially.

"Well, if you've forgotten anything, it's too late to go

back for it now." Their mum was the voice of reason. Jackie gave another panicky squeal as their dad turned the car into the short-term parking lot.

Neil smiled when he spotted Liam, lurking behind a pillar, way off down at the other end of the lengthy departures concourse. He was smoking a cigarette, his scruffy rucksack leaning against a video games machine. As planned, Neil pretended he had to go to the bathroom so he could give Liam the ticket Jackie had had for safekeeping.

"Thanks, man," Liam beamed, flicking his long hair back from his face and slipping the plane ticket into the top pocket of his faded denim jacket.

Neil grinned. "Your name is dirt in our house."

"Do they know I'm here?" Liam winced, his eyes open wide.

"Of course they do, but they're pretending they don't," Neil said and Liam smiled.

"How're you feeling, man?" Liam asked.

"Okay," Neil answered and saw Liam eyeing him thoughtfully. There was something soothing, almost Christlike about his hair, his beard, his smile, that left Neil feeling totally at ease. Maybe Liam was the one to talk to. But, of course, he was going away, like everyone else who meant anything to him. Deserting him for his crisis summer.

"Fancy a pint?" Liam asked, handing Neil a cigarette.

"We'd never have time," Neil said, leaning forward to catch the flame of Liam's lighter.

"Course we will," Liam drawled, slinging his rucksack up onto his back and loping gazelle-style past the lines of people waiting to check in their luggage and into the bar.

Jackie came rushing in before the froth had settled on their pints. She shrieked with nervous laughter when she spotted the pair of them.

"Give us a swig of that," she said, taking a long gulp out of Liam's pint.

"Where's the old pair?" Neil asked.

"Brendan, if I don't get a cup of coffee soon, I'll pass out," Jackie said, doing an exaggerated imitation of their mum.

"You'll have time for one," Liam said, going up to the bar to get a pint for Jackie. Neil and Jackie were alone. Jackie slipped the silver chain that was hanging around her neck out from beneath her T-shirt.

"Look what she gave me," she giggled, holding the miraculous medal out for Neil to inspect.

"Holy Josephine."

Jackie leaned forward and cupped Neil's hands in her own. "See ya in September then, Gladys."

"Yeah." Neil lowered his gaze.

"We'll be going to college together," she enthused, squeezing his hands in delight. "It'll be brilliant."

But Neil was subdued.

Jackie moved closer so their faces were almost touching. She waited for the latest announcement over the PA system to finish before she spoke.

"What's wrong, Gladys?" she asked, lifting his chin tenderly.

Neil's eyes were moist when he met her gaze. "Gonna miss ya, Penelope," he said in his American drawl.

She wrapped her arms around him and hugged him tightly. "Look after yourself, Neil," she whispered.

The tears were streaming down their cheeks when Liam returned to the table. He sat down awkwardly beside them. Neil wiped his face with a tissue before he made his way to the rest room.

He smiled to himself after he locked the cubicle door. Every time he came to the airport, he seemed to cry. Like at Christmas when his brothers Paul and Joe came home from New York. Neil and his dad went to collect them. The place was crazy. Christmas decorations and *Welcome Home* banners hung everywhere. Crowds and crowds of people were swarming around, waiting for the new arrivals. When a plane would land, the emigrants flooded through the arrivals gates, where they were practically assaulted by shrieking relatives and friends. Emotions were highly charged. But beneath the delirious joy lay the poignancy of the return to foreign lands. Neil had tried his utmost to hold back his tears, but when he spotted Paul and Joe sauntering through the nothing-to-declare customs gate, he found it impossible to contain himself. It was obvious that neither of his brothers, nor his father, were going to express their feelings openly. As always in the family, the real emotions were hidden behind jokes and banter. So Neil had pretended that he wanted to go to the bathroom.

Before she headed through the departures gate, Jackie slipped one of her love bangles onto Neil's wrist. Neil noticed his mum smiling. But when he caught her eye, she looked away and pretended that she hadn't noticed the little exchange. Jackie gave them all one last hug before she left to join her two imaginary female friends from college. Neil couldn't bear to watch her going, so he strolled over to the window overlooking the runways. A huge, brightly lit 747 was taking off in the darkness outside. The roar of the engines shook the building as the plane lifted off up into the blackness. It reminded Neil of the time, years ago, when his dad brought Gary and him out to the airport for plane spotting. They were about nine or ten years old at the time. And Gary was so excited by the planes, that out of the blue, he had turned to Neil and blurted out that the two of them would always remain friends, no matter what. Neil remembered that he had simply grinned at the time, embarrassed by his pal's openness. But Gary had tugged him by the sleeve and insisted that they pledge their everlasting friendship. And they did. It was one of those touching moments that Neil would always remember, but he doubted that Gary would.

While they drove down Capel Street, Neil had difficulty concentrating on his parents' conversation. His dad had missed the turning, so they were going to have to drive right past the gay pub. Neil's imagination went into overdrive. There was going to be a traffic jam right outside the pub, and Daphne and a couple of his high-camp friends would be crossing the road at the very time they arrived. Daphne would knock on the car window and ask him, in his inimitable way, to join him for a drink. "Sister, won't you come in for a little bev, and let me tell you all about the hunk I met last night." And knowing Daphne, he would probably invite his mum and dad in as well.

"You'll be glad to hear Charlie says you needn't wear a suit," his dad said, wakening Neil from his daydream.

"Huh?" Neil was lost.

"For the job," his dad added.

"Oh, great." Neil tried to sound enthusiastic but, inside, he was sighing with relief. There was no traffic congestion outside the pub. Then, his heart missed a beat. There was the unmistakable figure of Uncle Sugar hopping out of his car. Neil lay down flat on the backseat.

"You'll have to get a decent pair of shoes and…" His

mum turned around, "What's wrong with you, love?"

"Just feeling a bit tired," he said, grinning up at her.

She wrinkled her brow. "You'll have to start going to bed earlier."

"He'll be going to bed early all right when he starts going to work," his dad added with a chuckle.

Later that night, Neil had just climbed into bed when he heard the soft purr of a car engine outside. He dashed over to the window and peeped out in time to glimpse Uncle Sugar's BMW crawling slowly away off down the road.

———————

"I think they're fine, Neil."

Neil said nothing.

"Don't you like them?"

Neil shook his head.

Again, his mum turned apologetically to the shoe shop assistant with the slicked-back hair. The willing young assistant came forth with yet another pair of shoes from the storeroom, stooped down on his haunches, and held Neil's ankle gently as he slipped them on. *Is he gay or what?* Neil wondered, struggling to control his mounting hard-on. Heaven for a foot fetishist. Such a friendly young man, his mum had said during one of his many wiggly bummed sorties into the storeroom. The enjoyment of watching his athletic physique compensated slightly for the embarrassment of going shopping with his mum. "I don't want you buying a pair of Doc Martens," she had said, "not if I'm paying for them." And she had insisted on being there to oversee his selection. He had been tempted to throw a tantrum and announce that he'd buy his own shoes, but years of holding himself back had come to his wallet's rescue. A steely calmness under pressure, his rugby trainer had called it. Little did he know. But it felt funny being in town with his mum again after a gap of so many years. He was glad he had come, though; it was worth it just to watch her try to hide her happy expression as she fussed over him.

Eventually, they came to a compromise. A sensible pair of black shoes, the type that Penelope probably wore when he was in his man mode. But they did have a little frayed-end flap hanging over the laces, and this stylish feature won Neil over to the otherwise dorkish clodhoppers. The assistant grinned delightedly, more from relief than anything else, Neil suspected. His shop was in a mess, just for one measly sale. *We might meet again*, Neil thought, giving him a seductive little wink as he left the ravaged shop.

With the shoe box tucked beneath his arm, Neil held on to his mum's shoulder while they descended on the steep escalator into the bowels of St. Stephen's Green

Shopping Center. The huge glitzy clock ticked toward midday. Hoards of shoppers passed them on the upward-bound escalator.

"You're so vain." His mum slapped his hand playfully when she caught him admiring himself in the sidewall mirror.

"At least I've got something to look at," he replied.

"Cheeky brat," his mum smiled.

But then, Neil's heart froze. Daphne was approaching on the up escalator. No sly glances in the mirror for Daphne. No; he stood facing the sidewall mirror, preening himself, oblivious to the looks of amusement he was attracting. He had an AIDS Action collection box tucked under his arm. There was no escape. The moment of meeting was almost upon them.

Oh Jesus, please don't let him see me, pleaded Neil. *Please, please, please, I'll never have another bad thought in my life if you just let him float on past.* His mum gave him a funny look, wondering why he was ducking down behind her.

"Sister! Sister!" Everyone in the shopping center must have heard the shriek. Neil didn't budge. All around him, heads turned to look at the strange-looking individual rattling the collection box across the escalator wall.

"Sister! Sister! Help the cause!"

"Who's that?" his mum asked.

"Some nut," Neil muttered, turning his head slightly to

give Daphne an icy glare. Daphne understood immediately. He clasped his hand to his mouth comically before proceeding on his journey as though nothing had happened. All the subtlety of a double-decker bus, Neil thought.

"He seemed to know you," his mum looked puzzled.

"Never seen him before in my life," Neil "Judas" Byrne replied.

"Very peculiar-looking fellow," his mum added in typical understatement.

Before they left the shopping center, his mum tossed a pound coin in another AIDS Action collection box, bringing a loud "thank you" from the young man collecting, who was also eyeing up Neil.

———————

The summer evening's crowds of teenagers had gathered in clusters outside Stillorgan Bowling Alley, around McDonald's, on the shopping center wall, and outside the cinema. Openly drinking cans of beer, the gangs engaged in a seemingly endless banter, a banter that Neil had never felt part of. He watched them from the pay phone booth while he waited for his unknown caller to phone. But his thoughts were elsewhere. Was he being watched? Did the vice squad place the ad in the personals column? A carefully laid trap. The phone booth was under surveillance. It would all happen in an instant. The screech of tires. Burly undercover detectives swarming everywhere. Dragged from the phone booth. Bundled unceremoniously into the back of an unmarked car. "A pervert," one of the detectives would say by way of explanation to the swelling crowd of nosy onlookers. "That's Neil Byrne, isn't it?" he'd hear someone shriek. And he'd see all the leering faces pressed against the car window as they drove away.

Neil's heart skipped a beat when he spotted Ian cycling up to the crowd on the shopping center wall. His beloved had to scrape his runners along the ground to stop his brakeless bike. Then a girl ran over to him and hugged him before he even had time to dismount, making Neil's heart sink. One of the gang handed Ian a can of beer, and the golden boy took a furtive look around him before he put the can to his lips. *Oh, to be that can.* Neil sighed, parting his lips slightly. Another two fellows from Ian's class arrived and Neil was delighted to see the girl give them each a hug as well.

Bleep-bleep, bleep-bleep. The phone started to ring. The receiver nearly slipped from Neil's grasp, his palms were so sweaty.

"Hello?" He felt dizzy as he spoke.

"Is that Ian?"

"Yeah."

Then there was a pause. Neil smiled to himself, the ludicrousness of the situation occurred to him. Here he was, holding the receiver in his left hand, hoping to forge romantic links with a complete stranger, while across the street, the passion of his life was pretending he was drunk, unaware of being watched from the nearby phone booth.

"I got your letter," the cautious voice muttered.

"Well, obviously," Neil said.

But the caller wasn't amused. "D'you want to meet?" he asked in a flat voice. This guy is quick, Neil thought, smiling as he watched his beloved grab a baseball cap off one of his pals and toss it frisbee-style into the shopping center parking lot.

After further careful non-revelations, they finally arranged to meet on the steps of Trinity College chapel in an hour's time. Details of each other's appearance were exchanged and the show was on the road. The meeting point was Neil's suggestion, but the irony was lost on his compatriot in shady romance, whose sole concern seemed to be to discover whether Neil was part of a gang intent on beating him up. Neil stepped out of the phone booth and waited for the burly detectives to grab him. "Excuse me, sir, could you accompany us down to the station please."

"Of course I can. Men in uniform!" he'd shriek in his best Daphne imitation. "My fantasy come true!" He allowed himself a small, self-mocking smile when he reached the bus stop unhindered.

Neil strolled over to the chapel steps and sat down, donning his red baseball cap and resting the newspaper on his knees, as agreed. The cobblestoned grounds of Trinity were swarming with camera-clicking tourists and Neil bowed his head anytime he noticed a camera lens pointed in his direction. He could picture himself on the cover of some tabloid, with the headline reading: *Trinity's Gay Meat Rack Exposed! Steps of Chapel to Be Blessed by Archbishop!* An appearance on *The Late Late Show* would follow during which he would be heralded as Ireland's first gay teenager.

A light breeze ruffled the colorful roses lining the pathways. Students engrossed in conversation wheeled their bicycles past him. Their relaxed and happy faces, as well as the beauty of the surroundings, made Neil wish that he had applied to Trinity instead of UCD. The big clock over the archway ticked past eight o'clock. Gay guy, twenty-two, good-looking, own pad, was late. Neil was surprised at how relaxed he felt now. A Japanese woman smiled at him when she and her husband passed to get a closer look at the chapel. Neil smiled to himself, remembering what his mum had said to him at breakfast that morning. "You were talking in your sleep last night, Neil."

Of course, at first, he had nearly suffered heart failure, wondering what dark secrets he had unwittingly divulged. But his mind was set at ease when his mum went on to remark that it sounded like he was speaking Japanese. In his relief, Neil had pulled his eyes into slits and spoken in a Japanese accent. His mum had laughed. "You better not behave like that when you start your job."

Ever since the midnight chat with his dad, Neil had submerged his darker moods and tried to make his mum laugh as often as possible. He had also reconciled himself to taking the job in the engineering firm, which he was due to start the following morning. With Jackie gone, domestic harmony was essential. It lessened the constant glare of parental attention somewhat.

Neil braced himself. Gay guy, twenty-two-ish, not-so-good-looking, own pad probably rat-infested, was approaching. Shifty-eyed and scruffy, he shuffled toward the chapel with his hands jammed into the pockets of his dirty combat jacket. Good-looking he was not, Neil decided, watching Mister Scruff draw closer. Another few paranoid glances over his shoulder followed before he slouched over to the steps and sat down about four or five feet away from Neil. *Lucky he's downwind*, Neil thought, guessing that the heavy combat jacket did the guy's armpits no favors.

"You Ian?" Mister Scruff hissed out of the side of his mouth.

"Sorry?" Neil was thinking quickly. This guy was definitely a psycho. And even if he wasn't a psycho, sex was the name of the game, and sex with this guy was a no-no.

"Is your name Ian?" came another gruff hiss, his clandestine behavior reminding Neil of a drug pusher he had once seen in some TV detective series.

"No, why d'you ask?" Neil replied, changing his accent somewhat. Mister Scruff glanced at the newspaper on Neil's lap, and then stared at Neil's red baseball cap dubiously. His deep-set eyes were filled with anxiety and his hands were trembling. Neil smiled cheerfully, in the hope of appeasing the guy's anxiety. But Mister Scruff mumbled something about mistaken identity before he stood up and slouched away aimlessly across the campus. Neil drew a deep breath before he headed off in the opposite direction. New tabloid headlines: *Gay Meat Rack Stinks of Double-Cross! Archbishop Admonishes Double-Crossers!* He was being a bastard, he knew, but it was for the best.

When he arrived at the pub, Bono and B.B. King were up on the screens and "When Love Comes to Town" was blaring from the video jukebox. *This is getting to be a bit of a habit, lads, people are going to talk*, Neil thought, before his eyes went on a white T-shirt seeking mission.

"Hello, stranger!"

Daphne. Neil shook his head slowly and sighed, conscious that heads were turning to look at him. He grinned affably as he joined Daphne, Dave, and Redser.

"Oh, you lucky boy!" Daphne exclaimed in his shrill voice.

"Jesus, who gave him the fresh batteries?" Neil sighed, bringing sighs of agreement from Redser and Dave.

"White T-shirt thinks you're so cute!" Daphne continued, again loud enough for half the pub to hear. "He thinks you look so innocent, like a little lost waif."

Neil laughed, but his heart was dancing and his face was reddening.

"And he says he loves the way you blush!" Daphne clasped his hands to Neil's face, which turned a brighter shade of crimson.

"Well, you're enough to make anyone blush," Redser said.

"Be quiet, you, golden knickers," Daphne retorted.

"At least I wear knickers," Redser replied.

"Sticks and stones may break my bones, but whips and chains excite me," came Daphne's response.

Neil was scouring the pub for White T-shirt.

"He's not here." Daphne read his intentions. "You'll have to wait until Saturday night."

"I think you've got yourself a personal secretary," Redser said.

"Shane," Daphne announced, pointing at Neil.

"Huh?" Neil looked to Redser and Dave in puzzlement.

"The guy's name," Daphne explained.

"Shane what?"

"Oh, come on now, Neil dear, I didn't get his life story."

"It wasn't for the want of trying," Dave remarked.

"Be quiet, you, you silver-tongued rascal," Daphne pouted.

Tiring of Daphne's campiness, Neil glanced up at an overhead screen in time to get a close-up of B.B. King's tonsils.

But I've seen love conquer
The great divide

The gritty vocals cast their spell on Neil, giving him that light-headed feeling of invincibility that rock music sometimes did.

Neil bought himself a pint and listened to Daphne giving an in-depth account of his latest one-night stand.

"I'd like to spank your bottom, he says," Daphne told them. Redser and Dave exchanged amused looks. But Neil's thoughts were elsewhere. He wondered what impression Shane was going to have of him after meeting Daphne. God love him, but Daphne wasn't the sort of bloke you could introduce to your mother. *Shane.* He had never thought about the name before, but now it sounded like one of the sexiest names in the world. Even as sexy as *Ian.*

"And when we got back to his apartment," Daphne shrieked, his eyes bulging comically, his hands gesticulating wildly, "what do I see lying in the middle of the big double bed, but a slipper!"

Neil smiled when Daphne clasped his hands to his mouth exactly the way Jackie often did.

"Oh my God, I nearly passed out!" Daphne gasped.

"Did he put you over his knee or not?" Redser was smiling.

"Well, the horny little devil suggested it, but I told him where to get off."

"And we believe you!" Dave jeered.

"I should hope so, sister," Daphne replied.

"Show us your red bum," Redser said teasingly.

Daphne turned to Neil, and Neil noticed a slight hint of a blush behind that pale complexion. "Is that red-haired rogue a friend of yours?" he asked, cocking his thumb toward Redser.

"It's a wonder he's even able to sit down," Redser remarked.

"Central heating," Dave added.

"Bitches!" Daphne pouted.

"Oh my God, look!" Daphne shrieked, pointing up at one of the video screens. Every head turned to see Annie Lennox starting to sing "Every Time We Say Good-Bye." All conversation hushed in reverence.

"George's song," Daphne whispered, and Neil noticed that Daphne's eyes had begun to water ever so slightly. Out of politeness, Neil averted his eyes and listened to the hauntingly sad lyrics. He imagined himself singing the song to Ian. He'd be sitting at the piano in the living room at home and the moist-eyed Ian would be reclining delicately on the sofa.

When you're near
There's such an air of spring about it
I can hear a lark somewhere
Begin to sing about it.

"Oh, please don't go, Neil," Ian would plead, "I couldn't live without you."

"Sorry, Ian, you had your chance, got to go, there's a new love in my life."

Neil's fantasy was interrupted by Uncle Sugar's arrival. He gulped down the remainder of his pint and bade farewell to Daphne and the lads, using his early morning start as his excuse. Then he grabbed his jacket and made a hasty exit, pretending not to hear Sugar call his name.

Moonlight on the streets. Symbolic? Of course it is, you're meeting Shane on Saturday! Better splash on the Paco Rabanne and spray those armpits. Keep singing, heart. How will I survive until then? A little skip to celebrate. Even the gloomy road looks romantic. Wait…Listen—those footsteps close behind you. Keep walking. Quick look around. Three shadows, getting closer. Run maybe? Legs feel too wobbly. "Faggot!" *one of them hisses. Oh Jesus!* "Fuckin' queer!" *Dizzy with fear now. Plead with them. Tell them you were in there with a friend, that you're not gay. Jesus, help me. A thump in the ribs. A kick. Searing pain. Stumbling now. Another kick. Taste blood. On the ground. Cover your head. More kicks. Vicious ones. Losing consciousness.* "Faggot! Queer!" *Spewing hatred. Please stop.* "Faggot! Fuckin' queer!" *Going to die. Oh Jesus, please don't let me die!… Someone shouting…Sound of feet running away…A voice… Jesus? Is that you?… Jesus?…*

"Oh sweet Jesus!"

It's Uncle Sugar. Kneeling over you. He's crying. Tears flooding down his cheeks. Blood on his hands.

"Oh Jesus! Someone call an ambulance!"

Want to sleep now.

"Neil…Neil, can you hear me? Don't go asleep."

Too weak to stay awake…You hold me, Uncle Sugar… What you always wanted…Oh God, my head is burning… Cloudy now… "Mum, I did the dishes and cleaned my room. I'm going out to play now"… "Tell your mother that you love her"… "Don't kiss me when my friends are looking"… "Go 'way out of that, Neiley Nook"… "Ah Mum, you're tossing my hair now"… "Mind yourself out there"… "Bye, Mum."

Bless yourself with the holy water before you go… "I love you, Mum"… "And I love you too, little man…God bless…"

An ambulance siren. Faraway voices talking. Someone holding something over my mouth. My head is so hot. Someone holding my hand. Sugar? Lifting me now. Putting me into the ambulance. A sharp needle prick and up to the clouds I go…

chapter seven

Neil blinked a number of times before he opened his eyes fully. Bright sunlight streamed through the open window, and the sweet aroma of fresh flowers filled his nostrils. Then his mum's and Jackie's blurred faces appeared above him, and he realized that it was his mum who was holding his hand.

"Neil, can you hear us?" his mum whispered.

But the steel wiring on Neil's jaw made speech impossible.

"Just blink once if you can hear us, Neil." Jackie's voice was a fusion of joy and anxiety.

Neil blinked, and his mother and his sister hugged each other. A nurse appeared at his bedside and busied herself adjusting the many drips that were attached to various part of Neil's body. Three doctors rushed into the ward and amidst the flurry of activity his mum leaned forward and kissed Neil's cheek softly.

"God bless you, love," she whispered.

"Neil, you were in a coma for three days," he heard Jackie say, while the nurse tried to usher her and his mum out of the room. Three days! Neil sighed to himself. On the third day, he rose again. How many hard-ons did he have? He had read somewhere that the average was seven a night. He imagined the gaggle of nurses gathered around his bed. One of them lifts the sheets. "Look at this one! Not bad. Pint of milk there at least." All of them giggling. Three days! What had happened in his absence? But his thoughts were interrupted when a needle appeared above him. Before he fell asleep again, he noticed the huge collection of flowers and cards surrounding his bed.

———————

Neil was sitting up, propped by a stack of pillows. From his new vantage point, he noticed that the little wisp of a nurse was smiling while Daphne made his presence felt in the ward.

"I hope this isn't some sort of sexual contraption," Daphne whispered, pointing to the snoozing elderly man sharing the semiprivate ward with Neil. The poor fellow had both his legs up in traction. The nurse had told them that he had fallen off a wall and broken both his legs.

"Tie me up, tie me down," Dave said.

"Humpty Dumpty, the trapeze artist." As always Daphne went one better, and the nurse was struggling to smother her laughter. But he was secretly relieved that Humpty Dumpty was asleep. Apart from Neil's own embarrassment, a dose of Daphne would probably have set Humpty's recovery back by a couple of months.

"I think that metal brace suits you…" Daphne was saying. "It's you, Neil. It gives him that hunky Arnie Schwarzenegger look, doesn't it?" He turned to Dave for backup. Dave nodded dutifully, a broad smile creasing his face.

"Before you leave here, Neil dear, you might ask that nice nurse over there if I could maybe take a loan of it," Daphne added, feeling his jaw for size. "Just for the occasional night of passion."

The nurse was laughing noiselessly; only the tremor of her shoulders gave her away.

"She might loan you her uniform as well," Dave suggested.

Daphne pirouetted stylishly. "Would you, dear?"

The nurse, who was supposed to be preparing Neil's medicine, went into convulsions, giggling uncontrollably. Neil's own laughter made his entire body ache.

"I think virgin white would suit me, don't you?"

But when Daphne turned to face the window, Neil noticed how drawn and haggard his face actually was. No wonder he always raced out of the pub as soon as the bright lights came on.

Just then, Gary, Trish, Tom, and Andrea sauntered into the ward, carrying gifts for the patient. Neil closed his eyes in anguish and braced himself. The nightmare scenario was upon him.

"A wig, a pair of stockings, suspenders, a little touch of eyeliner, and Bob's your auntie," Daphne added, arching his back and spreading his arms like a glorious swan. But Daphne noticed that Neil wasn't laughing and he tracked Neil's line of vision. All the theatricality drained from his stance when he spotted the incredulous stares of the new arrivals.

Without the assistance of their silent host, awkward introductions were performed between the two groups of friends. Daphne became uncharacteristically quiet, and this both pleased and annoyed Neil. Pleased because his subsequent embarrassing explanations were being minimized, but annoyed that Daphne should have to feel so inhibited. Gary stood there, mouth agape, looking Daphne up and down, and Neil could see that Daphne was pretending not to notice this sneering attention. Probably so used to resentment, Neil thought, picturing Daphne standing alone in a schoolyard, with a thousand Garys gathered in a circle around him, spitting at him and taunting him.

Daphne and Dave made their exit within minutes, and the others huddled around Neil while he grabbed a pencil and scratched a lie on an envelope. *They're friends of Jackie's*, he wrote.

"They're friends of Jackie's?" Trish read, holding Neil's arm gently. Neil "Judas" Byrne nodded, and he could see the warm glows of relief. Their pal Neil wasn't a weirdo after all.

"Backs to the wall, boys," Gary joked with a laugh.

"Gary!" Trish slapped his arm.

"What a bender!" Gary gasped.

Neil noticed the nurse frowning as she left the ward. He also saw that Tom and Andrea weren't amused by Gary's comments. He tried his best to register a look of disdain on his battered face.

"Where did it happen, Neil?" Andrea asked.

Trish leaned over to read Neil's scribbled reply. "Town?" Neil nodded.

"Where in town?" Gary asked.

Again, Trish did the reading. "Near Trinity."

"What were you doing in town?" Gary asked, and Neil forced a painful grin on to his face as he threw his eyes skyward.

"Don't be so nosy, Gary," Trish snapped.

"We should organize a posse," Gary continued, "and go in and beat the crap out of the fuckers who did this."

Neil smiled. Sometimes his well-meaning pal's stupidity knew no limits. The others were quick to point out the impracticalities of the suggestion.

"Where's your new watch?" Trish asked when she noticed that Neil was wearing his old one. They all expressed their disgust when Neil informed them that it had been smashed to pieces during the attack.

After this, his pals got on to more familiar territory. Who got off with who in Hollies the previous night… Neil tried to yawn but the jaw scaffolding prevented him. He was relieved when the nurse returned to announce the end of visiting hours.

The nurse had introduced herself as Mairead and she came from somewhere in Tipperary. Neil was becoming aware of the inordinate amount of time she spent by his bedside. On a couple of occasions he had woken during the night to find her watching him. At meal times, her eyes would melt as she patiently spooned the food into his mouth. It was obvious that the poor thing was falling in love. Years of wrangling out of similar situations had familiarized Neil with the signs, and he had developed a faultless early-warning radar for detecting any forms of feminine interest. But there was no running from this one. He just hoped she didn't turn out to be a psycho. She told him that he was lucky to escape with five broken ribs, a broken jaw, a smashed nose, severe concussion, and extensive bruising, stating recent deaths in Dublin as testimony to this fact. She held up a mirror for him to witness the extent of his facial injuries. He looked like a mess: two puffy multicolored shiners, a bandaged nose, and something metallic propping up his jaw.

"It's a miracle you didn't lose any teeth," Mairead said and Neil attempted a toothy grin.

"You'll be back and as good-looking as ever in a few weeks," she added, and Neil noticed a slight flush in her cheeks and a shy flicker of her hazel eyes. God, she was the type of girl he'd marry, he thought, if he were the marrying type. "D'you want the curtains drawn? Have you got enough pillows? Would you like me to read to you? D'you want more food? D'you want me to bring you in some of my tapes?" She was a little treasure, and he was only going to end up hurting her.

Neil had started to pray again since landing in hospital. Not conventional prayers, just talk to reestablish links. It was the least he could do, he decided, because he had definitely called on Jesus the night of the attack, and Jesus had responded in the shape of good old Uncle Sugar. Two outcasts that Jesus would never turn his back on.

Neil wasn't sure if it was the effect of the drugs or not,

but sometimes he was sure he experienced lucid moments of spirituality during these chats, just as he had felt during his younger, more innocent days. But no spiritual high could have compared with the sensation he experienced when Shane walked into the ward that Saturday evening. Kate and Dan and the two kids were in the ward, and Neil was sure that they could hear his heart thumping.

Oh Jesus, thanks for sending me an angel, he thought. He wanted to scream, he wanted to cry, he wanted to laugh, he wanted the whole world to celebrate this moment, but most of all, he wanted to hear Shane speak.

"Never seen you looking better," he said to Neil, after Dan had got the introductions out of the way. Neil attempted a grin. Suddenly he had fallen in love with the Belfast accent. Dan started to quiz Shane, while Kate was busy trying to stop her two kids from charming candy off Humpty Dumpty.

"I've just finished a law degree," Shane was telling Neil's inquisitive brother-in-law, making Neil wish he had applied to do law.

"Where d'you do it?" Dan asked.

"Trinity."

"I thought you might've done it at Queens."

Neil caught Shane's attention and rolled his eyes, making Shane smile. "I'm a UCD man myself...Commerce," Dan continued. "I'm in industry now."

Shane nodded politely. Neil felt like strangling his brother-in-law.

"I suppose you're thinking of going on to become a lawyer," Dan went on.

Shane shrugged his shoulders. "Ach, I haven't really decided yet."

"Good money in that line," Dan said, rubbing his hands together. "So, tell me, how do you two know one another?"

An awkward pause followed. Dan looked questioningly from Shane to Neil. But Shane was quick to spot an escape route. "Look at the wee man," he said, pointing at Danny, who was fiddling with Humpty's full bedpan. Dan had to dash across the room to prevent a disaster, much to Neil and Shane's amusement. The three-year-old's misbehavior signaled the end of the family visit.

And Neil and Shane were left alone. Alone, that is, except for the watchful eyes of Humpty Dumpty. Neil's hand was trembling as he wrote "Thanks for visiting" on his notebook. Shane smiled and wrote "Don't mention it" beneath Neil's note. Neil grinned and scribbled "Do you come here often?" underneath Shane's tiny printed comment.

"There's no need to be rude," Shane whispered, and Neil felt a dart of pain shoot through him as he laughed. But it was a pain he would've gladly suffered again and again. Then, his heart skipped a beat when the fuzziness in his head cleared and he saw that Shane was holding the pen with his left hand.

"Left-handers make the best lovers," Shane grinned after Neil had pointed at his writing hand. This simple remark turned Neil's heart inside out.

"Here, I brought something for you," Shane said, handing Neil a cassette tape. It was a struggle for Neil to read the tiny writing listing the music Shane had compiled. Beethoven, Mozart, Puccini, Bach, Chopin; it was all classical music, music that Neil had ignored up until now, mainly because of his dad's strenuous efforts to get him interested in it. But now he was converted. The moment he got out of hospital, he was going to turn his dad's collection upside down.

"They're some of my favorites," Shane added casually. "Hope you like them."

But Neil was too happy to concentrate properly. His faith in mankind was restored. The world was a wonderful place. It was as though they had known each other all their lives. As they chatted, they had great fun developing their own language of winks, nods, and hand signals to save Neil from writing everything down. Poor old Humpty was left shaking his head in confusion, and this only encouraged them to complicate their signals even further. It reminded Neil of the signals they used on the rugby team. A half hour flew past before nurse Mairead came in to announce the end of visiting time. Before he left, Shane wrote on the piece of paper and told Neil to read it after he had left. Neil waited until Mairead had left the room before he unfolded the piece of paper. His heart was in his mouth and his hands were shaking as he read the tiny print.

"Hope you let me get a word in the next time we meet."

Neil's burst of nervous laughter attracted a peculiar, almost suspicious, look from Humpty. But Neil didn't care, his heart was on fire. He spent the next hour trying to imitate Shane's handwriting while he listened to his new tape. Outside, the burning evening sun was sinking low into the red sky. Neil sank back onto his pillows and tried to remember a time when he had ever felt so happy.

Later that night, his brothers, Paul and Joe, phoned from New York, and Mairead had to act as intermediary, imparting the details of Neil's scribbled notes across the Atlantic. At one stage during the bizarre exchanges, Humpty farted in his sleep, and Neil insisted that the shy nurse tell his two brothers about the nocturnal fragrances he had to endure. However, Mairead was even more embarrassed when they started to warn her about how randy their little brother was. But Neil could sense that Mairead was enjoying her involvement in the family's transatlantic conversation; it was the sort of desperate straw he had clutched at himself so many times over the years. Those days were over now. A minor panic attack gripped when he realized that he couldn't visualize Shane's face. What did his nose look like? What color were his eyes? What shape was his mouth? It was all a blur. If he had Shane's phone number, he would have called and asked him to describe himself. The thought amused him. He'd probably get reported for making obscene phone calls. Neil lay his head down on the soft pillow and closed his eyes to the sound of Mozart.

At lunchtime the following day, two men in business suits arrived at the ward. Neil barely paid them any attention, presuming that they were Humpty's visitors. When they stood alongside his bed, he assumed they were doctors or maybe even police detectives. But doctors or detectives would hardly be bringing him a box of chocolates.

"How are you?" the taller man asked.

Neil very nearly swallowed his tongue. Gladys and Penelope were amused by his amazement.

"Our civvies," Penelope said, holding on to the lapels of his dark jacket.

"Should see what we've got on underneath," Gladys whispered, aware of Humpty's straining ears. Every inch of Neil's body ached as he laughed.

Daphne had told them about his hospitalization. He had also told them about Shane. Neil shook his head and smiled; the entire city probably knew about him by this stage. Soon after, some visitors came in to see Humpty, making conversation a little easier. Neil was fascinated when the two men began to talk about their family lives. Both had very differing experiences. Penelope's wife had left him and had taken their two children to live in England. Gladys's wife on the other hand was very supportive. She even advised the pair of them on their makeup before they hit the town. It was a struggle for Neil to conceal his amusement at the thought of the two of them being fussed over by Gladys's wife.

"My children saw me one night," Gladys told him, pursing his lips into a sigh. Neil looked up at the giant questioningly.

"But they didn't recognize me," Gladys smiled. "It was wonderful; they thought I was a friend of the missus."

"You were wearing the evening dress, weren't you?" Penelope asked without the slightest glimmer of amusement.

"Yes, the blue one," Gladys replied in a soft voice.

"That looks really nice on you," Penelope assured him.

"Thank you." Gladys blushed slightly.

Neil pinched himself beneath the sheets. He couldn't believe it; the pair of them were slipping into their tranny mold, but what was funniest was that they didn't seem to even notice the subtle change in their behavior. The woman in them was bursting for release. A little well-earned lunchtime thrill. The more they discussed their hidden passion, the more uncomfortable-looking their drab suits seemed to become.

Neil's dad arrived and Neil shivered with fear as Gladys and Penelope introduced themselves. *Relax, Neil, how could he possibly suspect*, he told himself. Maybe there's a hem on display, or worse still, maybe there's little traces of nail varnish or mascara showing. But he needn't have worried, Gladys and Penelope became ordinary businessmen in an instant.

"So, how come you gents have the misfortune of knowing this young tearaway?" his dad asked presently, causing Neil to cross his fingers anxiously.

"Well, it's a little bit embarrassing really," Penelope said.

Neil stiffened with fright. His dad glanced from Penelope to Gladys. Neil braced himself, waiting helplessly for the end of family life as he knew it. Maybe he should cause a disturbance. Try and roll out of the bed. Or toss his Walkman across the room and clock Humpty. But he needn't have worried; Gladys and Penelope had prepared themselves for this scenario.

"This man here was your son's rescuer," Penelope said, pointing to the embarrassed Gladys.

Neil's dad looked puzzled.

"In the road," Penelope explained.

"Really?" his dad's eyes brightened, and he immediately extended his arm and shook Gladys's hand warmly.

"I just happened to be passing," Gladys mumbled.

"I can't tell you how indebted I am to you," his dad added, and Neil saw tears well up in his dad's eyes. Gladys bowed his head in discomfort. But his dad's uncustomary display of affection also had Neil blinking to keep his own eyes clear.

"It was very brave of you," his dad continued. "So many other people would've just walked on by."

Neil couldn't help smiling while he sat back and watched as Gladys reluctantly stole poor old Uncle Sugar's limelight.

After Gladys and Penelope had left, Neil's dad spent the remainder of his visit trying to think of ways of repaying Gladys the rescuer. *Get him a few new dresses*, Neil felt like scribbling on his notebook, *and a couple of good strong girdles*. He tried to concentrate on his dad's tales about what was happening at home, all the neighbors and all his aunts and uncles who sent their regards, but his thoughts kept drifting back to Gladys and Penelope. He pictured them, shifting uncomfortably at their office desks in their claustrophobic business suits, furtively slipping their hands beneath their polyester shirts to touch those silk blouses, and more than likely sneaking out to the toilet every so often for a quick twirl in the cubicle. What an impossible existence. And he thought his own life was difficult.

"Right...so we'll see you this evening then," his dad said, standing up.

Neil nodded to his dad and grinned.

His dad delayed at the bedside awkwardly. "Okay then . . . eh, d'you want us to bring you in anything?"

Neil crinkled up his nose in thought. Then he slipped his new classical tape from his Walkman and smiled as he watched the look of surprise form on his dad's face.

"Making some musically educated friends at last," his dad said, squinting to read Shane's tiny writing.

Neil winked at his dad, who gave him a thumbs-up gesture before he left the ward. It was just as well he couldn't speak, Neil reflected, because he knew that if he started to talk about Shane, his dad would've quickly realized that he was far more than just a musically educated friend.

The ball is flashed out along the well-drilled back line until it reaches Neil's safe hands. He ducks inside his opposite number's despairing tackle. The race is on. Thirty yards to the line. The entire west stand rises to its feet. Shrill schoolboy voices ring in Neil's ears, a sea of blue and white urging him on. He skips past the fullback's last-gasp attempt at an ankle trip. The noise reaches a deafening crescendo. He is in the clear. Fifteen yards to go. Suddenly, everything seems to switch to slow motion, the pandemonium fades, he is on his own, effortlessly gliding toward that try-line. Ten yards to go. Clouds skid silently across the sky, his jersey flaps in the spring breeze. Five yards to go. His steel cleats sink into the carefully manicured grass. Seagulls circle overhead. What if he just kicks the ball? Or what if he just stops? But he doesn't, no, he does what any good Rock winger would do. He reaches the line and touches the ball down victoriously. The cacophony of noise returns, and Neil grins as his teammates rush to congratulate him. One of the forwards pats him on the bottom, rugby-buddy style. Pity he's so ugly. Another clasps his arm around his neck and kisses him. The opposition hangs their heads disconsolately. One of them is so cute looking, Neil wants to go over and apologize for scoring. Then his brother-in-law vaults the perimeter railings and charges over to lift him off his feet in a bear hug and swing him around joyfully. Now he notices the thousands of delighted faces in the stands and on the terraces. All cheering him. He sees Gary and Tom with their crazy hats and their cheerleader megaphones. He sees his mum and dad and his Uncle Frank. He sees Father Donno with his arms raised in triumph. He blushes in embarrassment. The sea of blue and white are singing his name.

> There's only one Neil Byrne
> One Neil Byrne
> Only one Neil Byrne

But his grin fades when he sees Yvonne Lawlor taking over as cheerleader. Her leering face seems to expand and contort as she leads the new chant.

> Neil Byrne is queer
> Neil Byrne is queer
> Eee-yyy-adio
> Neil Byrne is queer

All the bright schoolboy faces are demonic now. Up in the west stand, Gary and Trish are clutching each other in hysterics. Everything goes foggy. He can't see if his mum and dad are joining in the deafening Lansdowne Road chant.

> Neil Byrne is queer
> Neil Byrne is queer
> Eee-yyy-adio
> Neil Byrne is queer

His teammates move away from him, nudging one another, exchanging nods and winks. He searches for a friendly face, but there is none. He stands alone.

"Neil."

The clouds of sleep retreated.

"Neil." His mum was shaking him from his slumbers.

"Hah?" Neil woke with a start.

His mum smiled. "You were talking in your sleep again."

Neil rubbed his stiff jaw, hoping that his sleep talk was indecipherable. He glanced out his bedroom window and saw that it was still bright. But what day was it? The book he had been reading lay on the sheet beside him. And not for the first time during his two-week convalescence, he felt completely disoriented.

"There's someone else here to see you."

He sat up and rubbed his eyes. "Who?"

"A fellow called Shane."

The words trickled out like honey. Neil's heart started to thump. His head started to swirl. A warm glow filled his insides. When his mum asked who Shane was, he wanted to tell her how madly in love he was and how his life had changed since they had met. Instead, as prearranged, he told her they had met on the Cooperation North weekend he spent in Belfast during the school term.

"What's this?" Shane smiled as he picked up the teddy bear sitting on top of the chest of drawers.

"Blame my mum," Neil muttered, blushing profusely, and Shane ruffled his hair.

"A fresh listen," Shane said, leaving a tape down on the bedside table.

Neil grinned and held out his hands seductively, his eyes speaking louder than words. Shane took hold of his hands and leaned forward. They kissed for the first time. Neil's lips tingled and any lingering shadows of sadness melted from his heart. His misty-eyed lover caressed his chest gently. Time seemed to stand still. Like a sleepy, golden storm. No forced kisses in Hollies could compare. The hand tickled as it crossed his stomach. Lost in a dizzy haze, he felt the hand slip beneath the sheets and gently cup the mounting bulge, squeezing ever so delicately. Outside the birds sang on the tree house, the glorious sun emerged from behind a cloud, rejoicing the kisses, deep and warm. Then they heard footsteps. Hastily, the hand was withdrawn and their lips uncoupled.

Both of them were blushing when his mum handed them the glasses of Coke. Neil sensed his mum's slight bafflement. He wondered if the scent of stolen kisses still lingered in the air. Maybe it was all a dream, a blissful mirage in his emotional desert. Maybe he was still in a coma. Or maybe he had been given a momentary glimpse of heaven.

An avalanche of get-well cards poured in through the mailbox during the next week. But the visits from Shane ensured his speedy recovery. Neil even managed to look disappointed when his dad told him that his pal Charlie Dunne had to give the office job to someone else.

Neil's dad was pleasantly surprised by his son's sudden interest in his vast collection of classical records. Every day, when Neil's dad arrived home from work, Neil had to face a barrage of questions on the latest composers he had discovered. But Neil could tell that his dad enjoyed being pestered. It gave them a common interest, breaking down the invisible barriers that had arisen between them over the past few years, barriers that his dad could never understand. Neil also knew that his dad secretly enjoyed it when he got enthusiastic about anything. He would sit back and smile while he listened to the words tumble from his son's mouth, so fast that they almost tripped over one another. Often, the pair of them would be so engrossed in their listening that they wouldn't hear the calls for dinner, and then Neil's mum would come into the room. She'd stand there with her hands on her hips, shaking her head slowly in mock annoyance, wagging her finger at Neil, who would be sitting on the floor with his legs tucked beneath him, and then at her husband, who would be squatting down alongside his son. "How many times do I have to call you two? Your dinner is frozen!"

But Neil could see that the new development pleased her more than anyone. All his loneliness seemed to have disappeared. Her little boy was Mister Happy again.

A minor heat wave hit the country and Neil took to sitting out in the back garden. The wiring had been removed from his jaw, his bruises were fading, and he wanted to replace them with a suntan. One afternoon, he was trying to kick a football through the tire hanging from the tree house, when Shane dropped by. Neil laughed when he saw his cycling gear. "Sexy," he whispered, pointing to the cycling shorts.

"Job requirements," Shane told him.

"What?" Neil was puzzled.

"Bicycle courier," Shane explained.

"You!" Neil spluttered.

"Speedy deliveries, that's our motto."

Neil laughed. "You need a law degree to do that?"

"Helps with the compo claims," Shane replied, removing his cycling helmet. Neil smiled as he watched Shane awkwardly attempting to kick the ball through the tire. He hadn't an ounce of soccer talent. Each time they met, he learned something new. He felt a bit like a magpie, gathering up all these snippets of information to pore over that night. But it was so difficult to extract all the details he wanted. Maybe it was all the years of living in fear that made Belfast people hold their cards so close to their chests.

"Love the tree house," Shane said, sitting down beside Neil.

"Don't look now, but we have company at ten o'clock." Neil had spotted Gary's mother watching them from her bedroom window next door.

"Huh?"

"The neighborhood watch is at her gun turret," Neil whispered, staring down at his runners, a wide grin on his face.

"Should I kiss you?" Shane teased.

"Piss off."

"Just a little cuddle?"

"You do, and I move to America."

"She'd probably enjoy watching us."

"She'd have us burned at the stake."

"She'd fit right in in Belfast," Shane said as he jumped to his feet and began to climb up into the tree house.

Neil turned to watch him. "The first time I went up into that tree house, I couldn't get down again."

"When was this? Last year?"

"How d'you guess?"

"I can see into the future." Shane was sheltering the

sun from his eyes, looking out across the neighborhood gardens.

"What d'you see there?" Neil called.

"I see a wee fellow called Neil…and, *mein Gott*! He's burning at a stake!"

"What did he do to deserve that?"

"He was caught molesting an older man."

"The dirty pervert."

"Yo! Byrner!" Gary shouted.

Neil's heart missed a beat. Gary and Trish were strolling up the garden path. How much of the conversation had they heard? Then they spotted Shane, and Neil smiled to himself as he saw them raising their eyebrows in unison. *Like lovers, our eyebrows will always rhyme.* Shane swung down from the tree house Tarzan-style, and Neil thought quickly as he performed the awkward introductions, telling Gary and Trish that he had met Shane in the hospital.

"What were you in for?" Gary asked, slapping Shane's shoulder in his friendly way.

"Can you not tell?" Shane opened his eyes wide in mock surprise. Gary was smiling as he and Trish shook their heads.

"Mental instability," Shane told them in a mischievous voice.

"Well, you'd want to be nuts to pal around with this spacer," Gary joked, pointing at Neil.

"Here, Neil, we got you these," said Trish, handing Neil a cheap pair of mirrored sunglasses.

"Tack-y," Neil said, putting the sunglasses on and grinning at everyone. "But I like them."

"You look like Tom Cruise," Trish smiled.

"Tom who?" Neil joked.

"Great for hiding red eyes," laughed Gary.

As soon as Shane headed back to work, Gary delivered the verdict, "Dead-on bloke."

"One of the best," Neil nodded in agreement.

"Good-looking bloke too; saw you giving him the eye," Gary teased Trish.

Oh God, how obvious can he get, Neil thought. If anyone was giving Shane the glad eye, it was Gary. He wondered if Trish ever noticed these things. She probably did, but chose to ignore them. And in about thirty years time, with four or five kids in tow, Gary would break the news to her, and go on the scene. And all the younger crowd would probably call him Uncle Sugar…

Neil sighed and turned his attention back to the conversation. *What are they talking about now? I don't believe it; they're planning what everyone's going to do the night the final grades come out. And they're not due out for a month. Sad. Nothing better to talk about, and they're the ones who feel sorry for you. Your hospitalization has been the highlight of their summer so far. Fake the pain in the head routine.*

Better go now, folks, I need a lie-down.

Neil needed to get his daily fix of Shane. He felt like a drug addict. Hearing his voice on the phone was a small fix, but seeing him was a major fix. Then, inexplicably, three days passed without contact and Neil began to suffer withdrawal symptoms. His parents noticed his edginess. Anytime the phone rang, his heart leaped. But it sank down below his knees again when it wasn't Shane. He rang Shane's house and left numerous messages with the girl who lived in the flat below. He could tell that she was getting fed up with him begging her to pin messages to Shane's door. The one phone in the house was in the hallway, and Shane had warned him that he often didn't receive his phone messages. He began to imagine things. His obsession had been knocked down. He was lying immobile in some hospital bed. Maybe he had gone back to Belfast; maybe someone in his family had died. Maybe he himself had died. Or worse than that, he had met someone new. By the third night, Saturday night, Neil couldn't take it anymore. Against his mother's wishes, he cycled into town. His hand was trembling when he pressed Shane's doorbell. There was no answer. He chose another bell at random and rang it. A girl with long straggling hair opened the door. She told Neil she had seen Shane going out with some friends about half an hour before.

"Try Hartigans," she suggested when she saw the look of intense disappointment that clouded Neil's face.

But all his worries disappeared as soon as he spotted Shane. He was sitting in a corner of the crowded pub with another guy and two girls. Neil stood watching the four of them chatting. They were all around Shane's age. College friends, he presumed. *But why didn't he phone me?* Neil wondered. *Better go home now, you've seen him, you've had your fix. C'mon, will you? You can't stand there staring. He'll get the message that you called to the flat and he'll phone you tomorrow. I have to talk to him. Don't be silly, you'll embarrass him in front of his friends. They're all about five years older than you. I could say that I work with him, my bike's outside the door, isn't it? Wake up, dopey, the barman's asking you what age you are. Show him your ID. How embarrassing, everyone's looking at you.*

"Made it by the skin of your teeth," the barman jokes, handing back his ID.

Better order a drink. "Soda water and lime please."

Last of the big spenders. More like last of the big benders. Light up a cigarette and try to look relaxed. Feel like an undercover agent. No, you feel like a dork, everyone thinks you're here alone. Well, you are, aren't you? Why doesn't he see me? Because he's engrossed in conversation with his friends, like everyone else in the pub. Anyway, even if he does see you, he'll probably just ignore you. No, he won't. I'm going to wait over here till he goes to the Jacks, then I can talk to him on his own. You could be waiting. I don't mind. And what are you going to say to him? Are you going to tell him about the hours you spent waiting by the phone? How you've been afraid to leave the house in case you missed his call? If you did, he'd just think you're pathetic, and he'd be right. Oh God, he's seen me! He's waving me over. And he's smiling, he's delighted to see me. His friends are looking around now. He's calling me over.

"This is Neil, the kid brother of an old girlfriend of mine," Shane told his friends, patting Neil's back as he squeezed in beside him.

"Shane the heartbreaker," the girl sitting on the other side of Shane said with a forced laugh.

"An amicable split-up," Shane turned to Neil. "Wasn't it?"

"He treated mah sister fine," Neil said in his American drawl. The others laughed. Everything was fine again. He could tell that Shane's pals liked him, especially the two girls.

He had guessed right, they were college friends of Shane's. One of the girls and the other guy were a couple, who were heading off to work in London soon. The second girl, Geraldine, obviously had romantic designs on Shane. She kept grabbing hold of his arm, but she didn't realize who Shane was playing footsie with under the table. The drink took effect quickly on Neil, and he blurted out that Becky was coming home for the weekend, bringing inquisitive looks from the others.

"She's my girlfriend," Neil told them, and very nearly cried out when Shane pressed his mountain boot down firmly upon his runner.

"She's au pairing in France," he explained.

"I hope you treat her better than Shane treats his women," Geraldine joked, but Neil could tell that she was being deadly serious. Her expression reminded him of the confused look he had often seen on Yvonne Lawlor's face. But, in his excitement, Neil was making a lot of stupid comments, and he could tell that Shane was embarrassed by him.

At closing time, Shane and his three friends went nightclubbing on Leeson Street. Neil headed off home, despite the girls' attempts to entice him into the nightclub. He wanted to scream as he cycled off. It had been impossible to speak privately with Shane. He thought that Shane might have wrangled some way of sneaking him into his flat, but the awful thing was that he could tell that Shane didn't even want him coming to the nightclub. He felt worse now than he had earlier. It was foolish coming into town. He wanted to get knocked down, nothing serious, just enough to get back into hospital again and then Shane would be back the way he was. And when he got out of hospital, he'd behave more maturely;

he'd read up about law and he'd impress Shane's friends with his comments. There'd be no more childish remarks from him. If only he could turn back time.

An empty beer can narrowly missed his head as he cycled past Sachs Hotel in Donnybrook. His bike wobbled precariously when he looked around and saw three drunk blokes laughing at him.

"Wankers!" he shouted when he was safely out of reach. The drunks roared abuse after him. Cycling through the night like this reminded him of his Saturday nights of old. Rather than go to Hollies he used to head off aimlessly on his bike, just so his parents wouldn't think he had nowhere to go. It was a strange time of night. The streets would be deserted. Everyone seemed to be packed into the pubs. He would hear the clamor as he cycled past. Sometimes he went to the cinema, but on one occasion he plucked up the courage to go into a pub in Milltown. And while he sat there sipping his pint, he kept looking at the door and then at his watch, to give the impression that he was waiting for someone. He vividly remembered one couple who was sitting across the lounge from him. Both were in their forties, and they had probably paid a baby-sitter so that they could get out for a drink together. During an hour or so of watching them, he didn't see them exchange one word, friendly or otherwise. It was sad, he thought, but at least they had each other to be bored with. Then, three local couples around his own age squeezed in beside him. He soon became conscious that he was the main focus of their whispered conversation, so he gulped back the remainder of his pint and left. It was times like that that finally drove him onto the gay scene. But they were a thing of the past now.

He reached Hollywood Nights, stopped his bike on the opposite side of the road, pulled the peak of his baseball cap down to cover his face, and watched the swarms piling into the nightclub. He recognized a number of them. But still he felt no temptation to join them. He took Becky's letter from his pocket and read it again. Her impending weekend home cheered him up. Then his heart froze. He had forgotten to tell Shane about his free house. A burst of adrenaline pumped through his weary limbs as he turned his bike around and began to pedal furiously. He had to get to Leeson Street before they switched nightclubs.

The drunks were nowhere to be seen when he sped through Donnybrook. On he pedaled, past all the familiar buildings, over the little bridge, and right into the teeming nightlife. Hoards of wild revelers packed the street now. People were shouting and screaming, car horns hooted, drunks staggered on the pavements, police cars cruised down the street, and taxis double-parked. Neil stopped to lock his bike to a set of railings. A decrepit old woman was begging on the pavement. All the nightclubbers ignored her as they passed. But Neil could see flickers of embarrassment cross some of their faces. Maybe, like him, they saw their mothers in the poor woman. He must be a poet, he thought; that was the sort of thing poets thought about. Another problem soon presented itself though. The thick-necked bouncers insisted that he was too young for their nightclub. It took him a couple of minutes to convince them that he wasn't going to stay in the club, that he only wanted to get an urgent message to his brother. Such was his insistence that some of the other nightclubbers began to plead his case for him and the bouncers eventually relented.

He strolled into the dimly lit cauldron of pumping dance music, ignoring the waitress's attempts to get him to buy wine, inspecting faces. A sharp dagger of pain stabbed right through him when he saw them kissing. They seemed to be glued to each other, Shane and Geraldine, lost to the world in a snug overlooking the dance floor. A bottle of wine sat in an ice bucket on the table in front of them. Minutes passed. Neil wanted the ground to open up and swallow him. His life was in tatters. But then his heart surged. The kissers surfaced for air and Shane spotted him. He was coming over.

"What's up?" Shane had to shout over the music.

Neil struggled to prevent his voice from wavering.

"Forgot to tell you," he said, forcing his lips into a smile. "I've got a free house tomorrow."

"A what?" Shane stumbled, moving his ear closer to Neil's mouth.

"A free house…My parents are going to a wedding in Limerick. They won't be back till late."

"Ach, great, I'll come by," Shane beamed, clapping Neil on the back.

"Any time in the afternoon." Neil was struggling to contain himself. He wanted to fling his arms around his Adonis. Instead he returned Geraldine's friendly wave. Their conversation was cut short by the arrival of some other drunk college friends of Shane. Neil sidled away unnoticed.

His heart was singing as he skipped up the steep steps out of the dungeon nightclub. The bouncers gave him a vacant stare when he tapped them on the shoulder and announced his departure. The old lady grabbed hold of his hand when he gave her his last fiver.

"God bless you, love," she whispered in a husky voice.

"That's okay," he said with a grin, moving away from her before she had time to kiss him. A fiver! Even for a poet, he was mad! But what the hell. His bike seemed to find its own effortless way home. What did it matter that Shane was kissing Geraldine, he thought. Sure, hadn't he bonked the brains out of Yvonne Lawlor last March? It was silly worrying about it. Things like that didn't really matter.

———————

Bright sunlight streamed through his bedroom window the following morning. Birds were singing, the foghorn sounded way out at sea, a dog was barking somewhere, and church bells rang in the distance. It seemed as though all the lazy Sunday morning sounds were celebrating the arrival of the special day. He was curled up blissfully in bed, resisting all temptations to caress his morning glory, when his mum came into the room.

"What time were you in at last night?" she asked, feigning annoyance.

"Early enough." His voice was husky from all the previous night's cigarettes.

"You want your head examined, going out on your bike at that hour," she added, prodding him gently.

"I only went down to Andrea's house," he lied.

"Well, you know what the doctor said."

Neil groaned. "Are you going now?"

"No, I don't think I'll go, love," his mum said, sitting down on the side of his bed and tenderly pushing his hair back off his forehead.

"Why not?" Neil asked.

"Ah, it wouldn't be fair to leave you, so your father's going to go down on his own."

Neil had to struggle to control his mounting panic. "Don't be silly, I'll be all right," he assured her. All his plans were in jeopardy.

"Ah, no, I couldn't leave you here on your own," she sighed.

Neil thought quickly. "Gary and Trish and a few of the others are coming over later," he said, avoiding his mum's concerned gaze.

"Oh, are they?" his mum's frown eased.

"Yeah, we're going to watch videos. So you needn't worry, I won't be on my own."

"Are you sure you'll be all right, love?"

"Mum," he drawled, cocking his head sideways and looking at her as though she were a simpleton.

"Well, I'm going to prepare some food for you," she said, standing up, "and I want you to eat it."

"Cross my heart and hope to die," he promised, making the shape of a cross on his bare chest.

"And don't forget to go to Mass," she added as a parting shot.

Neil raised both his arms toward the ceiling, threw his head back, and closed his eyes in silent celebration.

———————

Neil stood at the doorway, waving to his mum and dad as they reversed out of the driveway. Clenching his fists in jubilation, he watched the car drive off out of sight. It was time for action stations. He got the vacuum cleaner out and gave his bedroom a quick run-over, tidied away all his scattered clothes, hid the teddy bear at the back of his sock drawer, and put clean sheets on his bed. Then he vacuumed the living room and the hallway, removed all the photos of himself as a child from the mantelpiece, took his dad's classical records out of the cabinet and left them stacked neatly on the floor beside the record player. He couldn't wait to witness Shane's reaction when he saw them. He smiled as he placed a bottle of his dad's homemade wine strategically on the table. Uncle Sugar had taught him something after all. Get them drunk and have your wicked way.

After lunch, Gary and Trish called and he told them that he had to go into the hospital for a check-up.

"On a Sunday?" Gary was surprised.

"Hospitals don't close on Sundays," Neil replied with a laugh.

"There's a free concert in Blackrock Park," Trish said.

"I'll try and get down there later," Neil said, feeling a little guilty at the way he was treating his friends.

"Mick Toner's band is playing," Gary said.

"Oh God," Neil laughed. "All-ticket, I presume."

"There's a rumor that Sinead O'Connor might be making a surprise appearance," Gary said.

"Fuck off," Neil grinned in disbelief.

"And the Hothouse Flowers," Trish added.

"Are you serious?" Neil's eyes lit up. He knew Trish never spoofed.

"That's the word on the street," Gary added.

"I'll definitely make an appearance then," Neil assured them, deciding that he'd drag Shane down to the park with him. Why not join all the rest of the happy couples?

"We'll be in the usual place," Trish said before she and Gary said good-bye.

At four o'clock there was still no sign of Shane. Neil phoned telephone inquiries to check that there was nothing wrong with his phone. His hands were shaking when he eventually phoned Shane's house. The girl living downstairs answered. She plodded slowly up the stairs and rapped on his door a number of times. Then Neil heard the footsteps clomping down the stairs again.

"He's gone out," she announced in a weary voice and hung up before Neil even had time to thank her. But it didn't matter, his Adonis was obviously in transit on his hunky mountain bike. He switched off the black-and-white afternoon matinee and stood by the living room window. A couple of the local kids were playing soccer in the road. Neil wanted to join them but couldn't leave the telephone unattended. Five o'clock came and went. After he changed his T-shirt for the third time, Neil phoned Shane's house again. The phone rang and rang. Then, the dreamy Belfast accent answered.

"Hello?"

"Hi, it's me."

"Ach, how's the man?" Shane sounded badly hungover.

"Why aren't you out here?" Neil tried his best to sound jocular.

"What?" Shane was puzzled.

"My free house."

There was a pause before Shane answered. "Ach, Jesus, I completely forgot!" he exclaimed, and Neil felt like screaming.

"Well, it's not too late, they won't be back for another five or six hours."

Neil felt crushed when Shane explained that he had already made arrangements for the evening, but he felt worse still when Shane said that he was going up to Belfast in the morning and wouldn't be back down to Dublin until Friday.

Neil wheeled his bicycle through the outskirts of the large crowd that sprawled on the hillside around the lake in Blackrock Park. It was a natural amphitheater. A young four-piece rock band was playing on the small man-made concrete island in the middle of the lake. Everyone seemed to be shirtless as they basked in the last of the day's hazy sunshine. Then, the entire crowd did the wave to a passing city-bound DART, practically drowning out the band. A couple of drunk young guys lowered their shorts and bared their backsides to the amused train passengers. Across the bay, the hill of Howth shimmered in the heat haze. Yachts bobbed up and down on the frothy sea.

As the crowd settled down again, he spotted Gary, Trish, Tom, Andrea, and a couple of others, languishing in the usual spot, way over on the other side of the park. Like Neil, they were all wearing shades and baseball caps. Then Trish poured some beer onto Gary's bare chest and the pair of them started to wrestle playfully on the grass. Watching them, Neil realized he had no desire to join them. It'd be just like the spare prick days all over again. A girl laughed and shook her head drunkenly when he asked her if Sinead O'Connor or the Hothouse Flowers had made an appearance. Neil fidgeted with the bangle on his wrist while he glanced over at the crowd gathered outside the public rest rooms. He wondered if Bushy Mustache was on duty. Certainly having a bumper day if he was, he thought, as he wheeled his bicycle back toward the road.

When he got home, Neil opened the bottle of home-made wine, wincing when the bitter-tasting liquid touched his palate. Rocket fuel, Gary had once called it. Now he wished he had gone over and joined Gary and the others. In keeping with his mood, he put on Kate's Leonard Cohen tape. He wanted to feel depressed. All the gentle lyrics of love and despair seemed to have been written especially for him. Gazing out into the back garden, he drank slowly and methodically, aware of the tingling sensation that was weaving its way through him. Speaking aloud, he reenacted his telephone conversation over and over again, and the more he had to drink, the more favorable Shane's responses became. By the time he had finished the bottle, his Adonis was sitting alongside him. He began to worry about his sanity. "Oh Jesus," he muttered, "I'm out of my face."

He went upstairs to get his address book. There was only one person in the world that he could speak to now.

"Bonjour," Becky answered in her dreadful French accent, and Neil burst out laughing.

"Neil!" Becky exclaimed.

"Bonjour, madame," he spluttered.

"You're locked!" she screamed into the phone. But he could hear the delight in her voice.

"I've been stood up," he slurred.

"What?"

"He never showed up."

"Northern Joe?"

"Yep."

"Is that why you rang me?" she gasped incredulously.

"Well, yeah…And I just wanted to tell you that I was thinking about you."

Becky's voice softened. "Ah, Neil, you're so sweet."

Neil swallowed the lump in his throat. "Can't wait to see you," he muttered, blinking back the tears of self-pity. Why was his life in such a mess?

"Can't wait to see you," she whispered tenderly, and the tears started to flow freely. But while he told her about his afternoon of waiting in vain, he realized that maybe things weren't as bad as he thought. Becky assured him that he had a long way to go before he matched her for time spent waiting by phones. She even jokingly suggested that he join her in France, that that would put the skids under Northern Joe. After that, the conversation became livelier. Becky told him that she had been to London to see her brother Jimmy, and that Jimmy had invited Neil over to stay with him and Jamie.

"You told him?" Neil gasped.

"Don't worry, Jimmy won't say a word," she assured him.

Speaking to Becky had cheered Neil up. He took her advice and headed up to Hollywood Nights. There was no point sitting in and moping.

Neil's head was swirling when he walked into the crowded dance hall. The revolving lights were blurred, and the heavy pumping dance music sounded almost distant. Everyone there seemed sunburned. He pretended not to notice Mal and Tony beckoning him to join them at the bar. Tonight was a night to be with his real friends. The bottle of wine inside him ensured that he didn't feel like a spare prick. Andrea hugged him and pecked him on the cheek. Trish did likewise. Gary bought him a pint, and Tom proceeded to describe how the bass player in Mick Toner's band had been thrown into the lake. Besides that, they said, he hadn't missed much, neither Sinead O'Connor nor the Hothouse Flowers had made their anticipated appearance.

"If you ask me, it was all a Mick Toner rumor," Tom said.

"But why did they throw your man in the lake?" asked Neil.

"Because he was brutal," Gary laughed.

Neil laughed too as they described again how a couple of drunk guys crossed the narrow bridge onto the man-made island. The crowd went hysterical when they grabbed hold of the surprised bass guitarist and flung him into the shallow water. Neil knew that it was because of him that none of them was going out onto the dance floor. Besides the sympathy factor, it was so rare that he joined them these days, that he could tell they were making a special effort to make him feel welcome.

Neither couple was even holding hands. Then Yvonne Lawlor came up to him and kissed his cheek.

"Sorry to hear about your accident," she said, and Neil could tell she was genuinely concerned.

Neil thanked her for her get-well card, but he wanted to tell her that her blouse was the same sexy color as his tranny friend Gladys's.

"I'm back in business now," he grinned, grabbing hold of Yvonne's arm and dragging her out onto the dance floor. Within minutes, they were French kissing, much to the bemusement of Neil's friends. Mal and Tony looked like they were in shock. Neil's jaw ached when Yvonne became more passionate in her warm, moist kisses. But try as she might, she did nothing for him. He felt like such a fraud. He knew he was doing it just to be like Shane. But then, the cavalry arrived in an unexpected shape. A fight had broken out at the other side of the nightclub. Shrieks of panic rang out and the chaotic dance floor cleared instantly. The music stopped and the full lights came on.

"Some northside knackers!" he heard someone mutter in the crowd that had gathered in a circle to watch. Neil felt nauseated when he saw two tough-looking types with cropped hair kicking another younger guy, who was lying on the ground with his hands clenched over his head. All the memories of his own assault came flooding back. Out of the corner of his eye he was relieved to see that the bouncers were moving swiftly toward the fracas.

"Jolly Good Fights," Yvonne muttered the rhyming slang nickname for the nightclub. But Neil's attention was focused elsewhere. He had spotted Ian on the peripheries of the fight. Then he recognized the bloke on the ground; it was one of his pals. Alarm bells rang in his head when he saw a third, toothbrush-headed hard-chaw shoving Ian roughly to the ground. He let go of Yvonne's hand and surged forward. Everything changed to slow motion. He heard Gary's shout of warning in the background, he saw a boot land on the blond head, he felt his insides steel up with intense fury. All the years of rugby tackling came into play as he launched himself and flattened Ian's assailant. The crowd of onlookers cheered, and Neil glimpsed the momentary look of surprise on his victim's face. Then he felt an arm grab him roughly around the neck. The bouncers had arrived.

After the hard-chaws were driven away in a police car, Neil set off home with Ian and his pal. Despite all the protests from the crowd, the three of them had been thrown out, much to Neil's delight.

"Feel the lump," Ian said, stopping outside the nightclub and inclining his head toward Neil. A shiver ran down Neil's spine as he caressed the soft hair.

"D'you feel it?" Ian asked, grinning at him.

God, look at his eyes. Can't speak. Just let the world freeze on its axis now.

"Don't know what you're complaining about," Ian's pal said before Neil had time to answer. "You only got one kick."

One kick too many, Neil wanted to say. *If you were a real pal of Ian's, you would've put your face between that boot and his perfect skull, because let's face it, another well-aimed kick might've straightened that nose of yours out. Hush now, everyone, my beloved's about to speak.*

"Sorry to hear about you being beaten up," Ian said, flicking his hair back ever so delicately.

What am I supposed to say? Aw shucks, it was nuttin', kid. We macho men are forever getting in these scrapes; you know yourself.

"I would've visited you, but I didn't know which hospital you were in."

Neil wanted to howl up at the black night sky. *Go on, risk one little peck on that smooth cheek. Blame it on the drink if he creates a scene. Thanks, Ian, that's very thoughtful of you. Thoughtful? That's the kind of word grannies use. Shucks, Ian, that's sure hip cool of you, dude.*

"Hey, Byrner!" The spell was broken by Gary's raucous shout.

"Wait for us!" Andrea shrieked.

Gary, Trish, Tom, and Andrea had decided to leave the

nightclub in solidarity with them and were running toward them.

"Didn't think you'd be safe with these two knackers," Gary said to Neil, punching both Ian's and his pal's shoulders.

"Save your aggression for the rugby pitch." Tom was mimicking Donno, wagging his finger at the two grinning lads. All the way home, Neil found it difficult to conceal his despondency. They discussed the dance hall incident again and again, but his ears only heard one voice.

Neil was disappointed to find that his mum and dad were not home yet. It was childish, he knew, but it was nice just to know that they were both asleep upstairs. He put on the fairground video, which had been filmed years before on a sunny Sunday afternoon in Bray. "Daredevil Neil Byrne riding the merry-go-round," his dad's voice announced. And there he was, at five years of age, clinging on to the little horse for dear life. Jackie sat up confidently on the horse alongside him, but none of her comforting words could lessen his fear. In the background, the rest of the family was smiling and waving to them as they passed. Round and round the dizzy merry-go-round went, up and down the horses bobbed, with all the happy mums and dads waving to their children. And all the children, except him, seemed to be smiling and waving back. Round and round he went, the passing world a blur of happy faces.

He was woken by his mum's light tap on his shoulder. Beaming affectionately, his dad leaned over and tussled his son's hair. In that drowsy moment of half-sleep, he wanted to tell them. Whisper all those secrets he kept hidden from them, nestled in the depths of his heart like dark storm clouds lurking beneath a rainbow.

"I'll tell you one thing now, Neil, if you want us to come to your wedding, make sure you get a decent band," his dad said, smiling as he held his fingers to his ears.

"They were dreadful," his mum agreed, stooping down to switch off the blank TV screen.

Neil listened while they told him about the wedding, knowing that the moment for revelations had slipped away.

"Another thing, Neil," his dad said before Neil headed up to bed, "your mother and I have been discussing what you want to do in college."

Neil looked over at his mum uncertainly, but she winked to him reassuringly.

"And we think that…Well, if you want to study art, then you should…Like, there's no point in doing something that you don't want to do."

Neil felt like hugging the pair of them. But instead, he blushed, stared down at his sneakers, and muttered his thanks.

"I'm sure Father Donnelly would give you all the teaching practice you wanted in Blackrock," his mum added.

Would she say that if she knew the truth about him? Neil wondered. And would his dad be smiling so benevolently at him? Doubt it. There are some things they probably never want to hear.

chapter eight

The weekend arrived. Becky sat in the corner of the pub, holding court with Neil, Shane, Redser, Dave, Dave's brother, and Dave's brother's boyfriend, gathered around her, listening to her stories about France. Neil smiled to himself; Becky was in her element with gay blokes. A fag hag, she had jokingly referred to herself as earlier on their way into town.

"If I see one more dirty nappy in my life, I'll scream," Becky said. "I'm warning you boys, use condoms, you don't ever want to have screaming brats."

"It's a pity Daphne isn't here," Neil said after the laughter had subsided. Becky's drunken gesticulations had reminded him of Daphne.

"Yeah, I've heard so much about him, I'm disappointed that he didn't come in to see me," Becky added, almost having to shout to be heard over the driving dance music.

Neil noticed Redser and Dave exchanging somber looks every time Daphne's name was mentioned. But he was more worried about Shane's revelation earlier in the evening when he and Becky had met him in Hartigans. Everything had being going fine until Becky, for the umpteenth time, leaned over to inspect Neil's fading bruises. She placed her hands on either side of his head and then, after her inspection was completed, kissed him on the lips. This seemed to work as the catalyst for Shane to casually let it slip that Geraldine had spent the week in Belfast with him. Outwardly, Neil had pretended to be unaffected by the remark, but inside, he was in turmoil. Even Shane's explanation about giving his parents the right impression didn't appease his disquiet. He reasoned with himself that this apparent jealousy was a good sign. At least it showed that he was interested. But the incident signaled Shane's switch to double vodkas, and his subsequent drunken behavior surprised Neil. He became loud and aggressive and began to make cutting comments that seemed totally out of character. Neil presumed that Becky couldn't help noticing the unease the incident had created.

"Your elderly friend is here," Redser said, nudging

Neil out of his daydream. Uncle Sugar was making his way up to the bar.

"My one and only Sugar!" Neil cried, and he saw Becky frown when Shane told him to calm down and stop behaving like a kid.

Neil ignored him. He jumped up and hurried across the bar to intercept Sugar. Grinning, Neil wrapped his arms around the surprised older man.

"Never said thanks," Neil muttered. He felt very guilty about not contacting Sugar since the ill-fated night. But secretly, he knew that his uncustomary display of affection was designed to annoy Shane. Uncle Sugar was momentarily overcome. Then he reached into his jacket pocket and took Neil's watch out. "I found this in the road."

While Neil was thanking him again, Becky arrived by his side. "Becky, this is a very special friend of mine," he said, realizing that he had forgotten Sugar's real name.

"Jack," Sugar smiled, extending his hand for Becky to shake.

"I've heard so much about you," Becky told Sugar.

"All lies, I hope," Sugar smiled with embarrassment.

"Of course," she said, touching the sleeve of Sugar's jacket.

"What's this girl drinking?" Sugar asked, reaching for his wallet.

"No way," Neil pushed Sugar's wallet back into his pocket. "I'm getting you this one."

Sugar knew better than to object. The determined, "try scoring" glint in Neil's eyes seemed to amuse him slightly. Up at the bar, Neil sneaked a look at Shane, who was slumped forward in his seat, his chin resting in his hands and an intensely bored look on his face. "He loves me, he loves me not," Neil muttered, tearing a beer mat to shreds.

"This fellow looks great again, doesn't he?" Sugar said when Neil returned with the drinks.

"Ah, he's a little pet," Becky said, cuddling Neil.

"You'd easily know I just bought you a drink," Neil grinned.

Later, when Shane came over and announced he was going home, Uncle Sugar insisted on giving them all a lift, saying that he didn't want Neil walking up any cobblestoned roads again. The four of them piled into the sleek car and headed off across town.

"So, what d'you think of the pub?" Sugar asked Becky, who was sitting in the front passenger seat, cheerfully rummaging through his collection of tapes.

"Massive," Becky purred, and Neil giggled, realizing that she was doing her Yvonne Lawlor imitation. Shane let out a little snort of derision beside him.

"What's the matter?" Neil whispered, but it suddenly

dawned on him how left out of things Shane must have felt. After all, he and Becky hadn't stopped nattering all night, and naturally they had all their inside jokes, their inside phrases, and private moments that Shane could never be part of.

But Shane didn't answer. Instead he leaned across the back seat and kissed Neil, something he had never done in public before. Neil noticed the exchange of amused glances between Becky and Sugar. He got embarrassed and pushed his drunken boyfriend away.

"What's up with you?" Neil tried to sound jocular.

"I'm just getting sick of that place," Shane said in a loud voice. In the mirror, Sugar's eyebrows lifted in surprise.

"I mean, let's face it, it's a dump…I've never seen so many psychologically fucked-up people gathered in one place…And I thought Belfast was bad!" Shane laughed sardonically.

There was an awkward silence in the car as Sugar did an illegal right turn at Trinity College. A number of young blokes at bus stops glanced at the car in admiration. And now that he wasn't alone with Sugar, Neil didn't feel the usual compulsion to lower his head and avoid their looks.

"And another thing; I've never heard such bitching as I've heard in that dump," Shane went on.

"Ah, it's not that bad," Neil said, trying to lighten the tone.

"Oh Jesus, typical naive Neil," Shane sighed. "Everyone in there is lovely really." And, he added sarcastically in what was supposed to be an impersonation of Neil, "What a riveting collection of kind and interesting people."

"I don't think that," Neil protested weakly, aware that Becky's fuse was close to explosion point.

"All they can talk about are their dicks," Shane growled.

Neil rested his hand on Shane's sleeve but it was abruptly shrugged away. He wanted Shane to stop; after all it was Sugar's second home that he was criticizing.

"Maybe that's where the term *dickhead* comes from," Sugar muttered, and both Neil and Becky laughed. Shane didn't speak again until they reached Leeson Street. Without a word of good-bye, he hopped out of the car and slammed the door. As soon as the car drove off, Sugar and Becky burst out laughing. But Neil was sorry that he had joined in the ridicule of Shane. It was cruel, he decided; he'd have to call him in the morning and apologize.

Sugar dropped them to Neil's house, and despite Becky's strenuous attempts to lure him inside for coffee, Sugar refused. Even Neil couldn't persuade him.

"I'm sure you two have plenty to chat about," Sugar said before he drove off. Neil couldn't understand it; if he got an opportunity to get inside Ian's house, he'd be in like a shot. Maybe Sugar's passion for him had waned because of Shane. Deep down inside, he felt a twinge of disappointment, realizing that he liked being admired by the older man. Then he put himself in Sugar's shoes and imagined how embarrassing it would be to meet a friend's parents if they were the same age as you.

Just as Neil was pouring two glasses of his dad's home-made wine, his mum wandered into the living room in her dressing gown. A warm glow lit up her face as soon as she spotted Becky.

"I thought I heard you coming in," she said, smiling at Becky.

"Hiya, Mrs. Byrne," Becky did her best to speak clearly.

"How's the au pairing going?"

"Oh, don't talk to me," Becky moaned.

"Don't mind her, she loves it," Neil said, pushing the ashtray behind the armchair. His mum sniffed. "I don't smell something burning, do I?"

"That's my cigarette," Becky lied, and Neil spotted the faintest flicker of a smile cross his mum's face.

"Mum, look," he said, holding his wrist up in the air to display his watch. The loudness of his voice brought a wince of surprise to his mum's face.

"I got my watch back," he added slowly, concentrating on every syllable this time.

"Oh, did you?" His mum was delighted as she took hold of his wrist to inspect the watch. Then she furrowed her brow. "That's not your watch," she said.

Neil pulled his hand away and took a closer look at the watch. "Isn't it?"

"It looks like it all right, but it's definitely not the one I bought for you," his mum insisted. "They must have got it mixed up."

Neil shook his head slowly. Uncle Sugar and his heart of gold.

"Listen, I'm exhausted, I'll say good night," his mum said, backing away toward the door.

"'Night, Mrs. Byrne," Becky said.

"When are you coming home again, Becky?"

"The end of summer."

"Well, look after yourself now."

"'Night, mum."

"Don't you stay up all night," she said to Neil.

"We're going up to bed now in a minute, but I doubt that we'll get much sleep," Neil said, nudging Becky.

"Dream on," Becky retorted.

His mum smiled. "I don't know where we got him from," she sighed before leaving the room.

Becky smiled when Neil explained about the watch.

"That man's an angel," she whispered.

"I can't keep it," Neil insisted. But he knew that he would have to. Uncle Sugar would never accept it back. He would definitely have to call him and thank him. But he had more important things to talk about now. He had waited eagerly to ask Becky this question.

"Well, what d'you think of him?" he asked, turning to face her.

She leaned back in her armchair, dipped her finger into her wine, and stirred it around slowly. "He's very good-looking, all right."

Neil was delighted. "Ignore his behavior tonight, that's the first time I've ever seen him pissed."

Becky just nodded noncommittally. Neil refilled the wine glasses and proceeded to reiterate all the good times Shane and himself had had together, though Becky already knew the details from his numerous letters.

"This stuff is dynamite!" Becky laughed, holding her glass up. Neil laughed, but he was disappointed at her obvious attempt to change the subject.

They began to talk about the other events of the night, but the shadow of Shane lurked constantly below the surface. Eventually there was no more they could say about Uncle Sugar or Gladys and Penelope or any of the others they had met in the pub. They were on to their second bottle of wine, and Becky seemed to have to force her jaws open as she spoke.

"I'm sorry, Neil," she said, her blurred eyes struggling to focus on him, "but I don't like him." Then, by way of apology, she held both her hands up in the air drunkenly.

"I know that," Neil replied calmly, hiding his despondency.

"I wish I could say that I do. But I don't. Sorry to have to say that. But you know I can't lie to you," she mumbled.

"But what is it you don't like about him?" Neil asked.

Becky swayed as she leaned forward to pour another two glasses of wine. "For one…He has zilch sense of humor."

"Yes, he has," Neil protested.

"Well…" she continued, "he keeps it well hidden then …"

"That's unfair, you hardly know him."

Becky mustered her thoughts together. "I just don't want to see you hurt, Neil."

Neil said nothing.

"I mean, who's this Geraldine one? You said you saw them kissing, didn't you?"

"That doesn't mean anything. Sure, I chewed the face off Yvonne Lawlor last Sunday, didn't I?"

"Yeah, but you didn't invite Yvonne Lawlor to stay in your house for a week, did you?"

Neil had difficulty focusing on Becky's face. "She's gone to Portugal for two weeks," he said, recalling the delight he had felt when Shane told him.

"So you'll do for two weeks then," Becky countered cruelly.

"Thanks a lot." Neil was angry.

"I'm sorry…" Becky draped her arms around his neck, but Neil shrugged them away. Then she dipped her finger into her wine and eyed him carefully.

"If he does swing both ways…avoid him like the plague."

"What're you on about?"

"My brother Jimmy once had a bad experience with a bi," Becky went on. "He said that they were usually emotionally immature—that they couldn't stay in relationships for long—and that they treat their various partners like shit."

Neil felt crushed.

"Anyway, you're not in love with him, Neil."

"I am." Neil's voice was barely audible.

Becky sighed. "You're not, he's only a replacement for Ian."

"If only it were that simple," he replied, wishing his world wasn't so mixed-up. Why couldn't he just have an ordinary romance like Tom and Andrea? Or even Gary and Trish. Why did he always have to keep everything so hidden? Why was he born this way? It'd be better if he'd never been born.

Becky hugged him when she saw the tears rolling down his cheeks. She kept squeezing him tightly and insisting that she had only said what she had said because she loved him.

But even Becky couldn't understand how he really felt. No one ever would. They'd always just see him as the grinning idiot who liked to keep himself to himself. They'd never realize how much he had to offer. They wouldn't want to. And not for the first time that summer, he wished some mad scientist somewhere would press a button and end it all gracefully.

―――――――――

The colored barbeque lights seemed to be dancing around in tiny little circles. Neil was lying flat out on a hay bale, staring up at the starry night sky, listening to John Lennon's soul-baring lyrics. Somewhere near him, Gary was telling a joke. "Did you hear about the queer whale? He put his mouth over the submarine's periscope and sucked out all the seamen." And Shane joined Mal and Tony in whoops of laughter.

He doesn't want to be seen sitting with me, Neil thought. *And if I was standing with them, you can bet that Gary would've been staring at me when he told that joke, watching for my reaction. "Will you just relax and enjoy your secret admission to the rhyming couplets?" Secret my eye. Our arrival was greeted by raised eyebrows; don't think I didn't notice.* "Who's your hunky friend?" Yvonne Lawlor asked. "Bit of all right," her pal Carmel said. *But of course they were suspicious and I felt like shouting, "Oh girls, I've got to hand it to you, you're so per-fucking-ceptive."*

Hey, you've got to hide your love away

You said it, John, you said it. All the fun of the fair, but still I don't feel a part of it. Oh shit, I wish I hadn't drunk so much. There's Tara's father, standing on the porch of his mansion, watching all his daughter's friends with disdain. Probably wondering why the hell he should have to spend his hard-earned cash on these gobshites. The hassles of having a socialite daughter who's turned eighteen. Wait till her wedding day.

Loud, drunken yelps and cheers rose from the crowd when Mick Toner tossed another hay bale onto the crackling bonfire. Neil sat up and focused on the glowing faces, drinking their free beer and chomping their free hamburgers, all watching the flames spark and shoot up into the blackness.

Why should any of them want to hurt me? Mick Toner is mad. I could tell him. "Hey, Mick, I'm gay and you're mad, so let's be pals." Knowing Mick, he'd probably just say, give us a smoke and it's a deal. But Mal and Tony, they'd pick me up like a bale of hay and toss me onto the bonfire. And I wouldn't cry or scream as the flames rose up all around me. No, I'd just stare out at them all like good old Joan of Arc or whoever, and my sad eyes would haunt them for the rest of their lives. Po-faced Shane is flashing a dirty look in my direction. The pull-yourself-together big brother look. But still he keeps his respectable distance. Nice friendly grin for everyone. That's it, Neil, can't rock the boat, can we? I'm gay! Imagine if you screamed it out in your best Daphne imitation. Tara's happy jolly birthday barbeque would grind to an abrupt halt. Snogging couples would surface for air. Give them all something to really talk about. They'd probably just say, "Tell us something we don't already know, Neil." There must be others here the same as me. Maybe they'd all come out. "Yeah, funny you should say that, Neil, so am I." And we'd all join hands and dance "A Ring around the Rosy" around the bonfire.

Hey, you've got to hide your love away

The colored lights are whizzing around in circles now. Stomach is swirling. Drunken howls as the swimmers plunge into the floodlit swimming pool. Well-fed bodies tucking their bulky knees up into their chests to do cannonballs, drenching the shrieking onlookers. *Maybe you should join them. Sober you up. Yeah, maybe I'd drown. Floating round and round, facedown, staring at the silent blue-tiled underwater world. Wonder how long would pass before any of them'd notice me. "Hey, look at Neil, he's drowning and we're all enjoying ourselves. God, that's a laugh, isn't it?"*

Neil leaned forward, opened his legs, and felt his fragile insides heave violently. It was as though a volcano was erupting inside him. Torrent after torrent of spewy liquid kept gushing up from the darkest recesses of his stomach, spreading like molten lava across the neatly clipped grass. Sweat dampened his forehead, his head was spinning, his whole body shivered, and he wished that he was at home tucked up in his bed with his mum holding a damp sponge to his forehead like she had done when he was a kid.

"You all right, Byrner?" Mal asked with uncustomary tenderness, draping his arm around Neil's shoulder.

"He's puked his ring up!"

That's it, Gary, tell the world.

"You'll be okay, Neil," Trish said, wiping his face with a tissue after the volcano had eventually subsided.

"Nothing like a good puke," Gary laughed.

Hands lifting me up now. Mal looks concerned. Maybe I've misjudged him all these years. But don't think my bleary eyes don't spot your judging looks as I head off with good old Shane, who's going to end it with me soon. Why don't you say all those things to my face? "Who's Byrner's friend?" "Yeah,

228

who's the granddad?" "Pair of bum boys if you ask me," someone will no doubt say, and you'll all laugh your cruel laughs and feel superior.

And the things you say about me will make you all so glad that you're together, all safely the same. So you think, anyway. Ah, c'mon, stop staring at us and get back to the things you do. Shoot those cans, shout till your tonsils rattle, talk about the upcoming festival, kiss your rhyming couplet, and tell them the great things you're going to do. How you're going to go to college, and after that you're going to get a job in the financial center or wherever, and then you're going to buy a flashy car with electric windows and a big house with a swimming pool, just like Tara's mansion. A big world where there'll be no room for embarrassing friends like me...

But you're all going to end up in your semi-Ds, pretending to be happy with your little electric lawn mowers and your dishwashers, and your smart timer-lights to trick the burglars. Bored out of your brains. And when it's all over, we'll all end up in our wooden boxes, rotting deep in the soil. All so fucking crazy and predictable. So why should you look down on me? Wish I didn't feel so low.

On our first proper date, Shane and I went to a restaurant for a meal. It felt so funny, finding something that every other couple seems to do without even thinking so nerve-wracking. Anyway, there we were, sitting facing each other at the small table, pretending to be relaxed, when Shane spotted a girl he *knew from college. He waved over to her but she just looked right through him, and when he kept trying to attract her attention, she turned her back on him like he wasn't there. Talk about being put in your place. Of course, we made excuses, like maybe she didn't see you waving, or maybe it was a case of mistaken identity. But her look said it all. We accept you and all that but just don't try and raise your heads above a respectable level, please.*

After the meal, we sort of drifted back toward Shane's flat and sat there babbling away like two nervous kids for over an hour, doing our own little bit for cross-border relations, until he finally plucked up the courage to cross the room and place his hands on my shoulders.

A special moment. But it all seems so vague now.

chapter nine

The hordes of kids stopped playing when they saw the taxi driving up their quiet Coolock cul-de-sac. Their scruffy faces pressed up against the windows as Shane paid the taxi driver.

"The welcoming committee," Neil muttered, climbing out of the taxi.

"Who're ya lookin' for?" a young lad in a tracksuit asked them.

"God," Shane replied calmly.

A couple of young girls shrieked with laughter.

"Fuck off," the embarrassed young lad muttered.

Neil glanced at the door numbers on the cluttered row of terraced houses. He caught Shane's arm and pointed to

Daphne's house, which was beside a graffiti-sprayed pedestrian road. The throng of kids followed them.

"Are youse a pair of pig's ears?" a grinning girl of about eleven asked when she saw them entering Daphne's postage-stamp front garden.

"What did you say?" Shane asked.

"Are ya bent?" The girl was playing to her gallery of friends.

"That's for us to know and you to find out," Shane replied calmly.

"Wha'?" The young girl was taken aback.

"There's no rumor in the truth," Shane added, smiling.

"You're fuckin' scats, you are," the girl said, bringing another burst of sniggers from her pals. Neil smiled, realizing that only a short time ago, a comment like that would've caused him untold embarrassment.

"Are ya in the IRA?" the young lad asked Shane.

"Who told you?" Shane said, emphasizing his Belfast accent.

"Fuck off," the young lad muttered again, eyeing him warily.

Once Neil pressed the doorbell, the kids dispersed. While they waited, they noticed one particular piece of graffiti in the road. "Eddie O'Reilly Is Bent" was daubed in white paint on the wall facing Daphne's house.

A fat bustling woman opened the door. "You've come

to see Eddie?" she said before either of them got a chance to speak. "C'mon on in, don't be standin' there," she added, ushering them into the tiny hallway. A young girl of about eight sat on the stairs, filling in a coloring book. She dropped her eyes shyly when Neil smiled at her.

"He's not feelin' the best today," Daphne's mother said, opening the living room door. "Now, Eddie love," she announced in a loud but tender voice, "some of yer friends here to see ya."

Neil and Shane exchanged a tentative glance as they followed her into the room. Daphne's mother straightened out her son's pillows and helped him to sit up. Neil noticed a large picture of the Sacred Heart and a crucifix hanging over Daphne's bed, which was tucked into the corner of the snug living room. Just like in his own house, all the furniture seemed to revolve around the television. Numerous family photos and other trinkets lined the mantelpiece.

"I'll leave ya alone," Daphne's mother said, going out and closing the door.

"Hello, sisters," Daphne said in a croaky voice, struggling to muster some life into his bones. Neil couldn't stop staring at the emaciated face, the eyes sunk deep into the head, the mouth that looked like an old witch's mouth, and the nose whose length was accentuated by the hollow cheeks. He reminded Neil of the pictures in their history books of Holocaust victims.

"How's the man?" Shane said, leaning over to kiss Daphne's cheek. Neil felt himself retch as he followed suit. A musty smell of death lingered in the air. He noticed that Daphne's skeletonlike fingers were clutching a set of rosary beads.

"Give me a cigarette before I scream," Daphne said, forcing a smile onto his face. Neil's hands were shaking as he lit the cigarette.

"Mother doesn't allow me to smoke," Daphne added with an exaggerated sigh. "I think she's afraid it'll have a detrimental effect on my sex drive."

Neil and Shane laughed, delighted that some of the zest was beginning to return to Daphne's eyes.

"I hope you two dears are going to invite me to your wedding," he continued, pointing at the two visitors. "After all, I did do a little spadework on your behalf."

"You're going to be our best man," Shane said.

"Can I wear a dress?" Daphne asked with a mock sigh.

"You needn't wear anything if you don't want to," Shane told him.

"Oh now, I don't want to shock Neil's parents," Daphne said, winking at Neil. Neil was grinning away. He knew that Daphne was trying to drag him into the conversation, that he sensed the pity in Neil's eyes. And Neil wanted to say something to Daphne, something meaningful, but there was a look in Daphne's tired eyes that warned him that he wasn't going to entertain any attempts at pity.

"Speaking of dresses, I had Gladys and Penelope in to see me last week," Daphne said, rolling his eyes upward. "What a pair of pansies!"

Neil snorted.

"Of course, Mother only encouraged them, telling them that they looked wonderful."

Neil tried to imagine the reaction of the kids on the road when Gladys and Penelope stepped out of their taxi.

"I feel like Pinocchio," Daphne sighed, rubbing his nose.

"Lots of guys go for big hooters," Shane told him.

"Stop that now. We'll have none of your toilet talk in here," Daphne said, wagging his finger.

Neil's concentration drifted in and out of the conversation. He laughed loudly every time Daphne wanted a laugh, but his thoughts were about death. *He's going to die, isn't he, Jesus? He's going to just slip away unnoticed. And that cruel graffiti outside will remain to serve as a constant reminder to his family. A reminder of how much everyone loved him.*

His daydream was interrupted by Daphne's coughing fit. His fragile body went into uncontrollable convulsions. The poor fellow looked terrified. The rosary beads came free from his grasp and fell onto the floor. Neil picked them up and placed them on the bedside table. Both he and Shane were standing by helplessly when Daphne's mother came quickly into the room. She motioned them out into the hallway. Before he left the room, Neil turned to see her sitting by the bed, holding her son the way a mother would hold a newborn infant.

Neil and Shane went into the kitchen where the girl with the coloring book and a younger boy were sitting at the table. The effect of the coughing in the other room was written all over their worried faces. Shane and Neil struggled to engage them in small talk. The girl was Daphne's sister, and the boy, who had the most adorable brown eyes, was his nephew. *Got your Uncle Daphne's dark eyes*, Neil felt like saying to the kid. While Shane persisted with the small talk, Neil's attention drifted to the portable TV that was on in the corner of the room with the volume turned down. An enlarged image of an embryo in a womb came up on the screen. The tiny, wriggling, red-veined, saucer-eyed fetus fascinated him. It was hard to imagine that he was once like that, curled up helplessly inside his mum's womb. Going everywhere with her: down to the shops in Blackrock, into the church every morning, sunbathing in the back garden, driving in the car, and then snuggling up inside her in bed every night, with Dad snoring away beside them. The shy little girl tapped Neil's sleeve, and he had to turn away from the haunting TV image and admire her drawing.

The awkward interchanges ended with the return of Daphne's mother to the kitchen. "He's asleep now, God love him," she sighed, taking her apron off. "Move over there, Darren, love, and let the two boys sit down."

"Ah, it's all right, Mrs. O'Reilly," Neil said. "We better head off now anyway."

"Sit down there, I've made a little grub for ya," Daphne's mother insisted, taking a full plate of ham and cheese sandwiches out of the fridge. Neil smiled and shrugged his shoulders.

"Sure, look at ya," she said, prodding Neil's ribs, "you'd get more meat in a vegetable stew."

The two children made room for Neil and Shane at the table.

"Sit down there now and get them into ya," she added, rubbing her hands together heartily.

"Ya forgot the soup, Granny," Darren chipped in.

"Oh Janey, I don't know what I'm doing," the woman exclaimed, turning to get the soup. As he ate, Neil was conscious of the little boy's stare. But every time he turned to smile at him, the boy looked away bashfully.

"Ya know that he has it, don't ya?" Daphne's mother whispered out of the blue.

"Sorry?" Shane was puzzled.

"The virus…He's goin' to die, like."

"I'm sorry," Shane replied awkwardly.

"Please God, it won't drag on too long," she added, blinking back her tears.

An uncomfortable pause followed. The two children were sent outside to play in the back garden. All the jolliness returned to the woman's face when she started to talk about Daphne's younger days.

"When he was fourteen, he told me that he was gay," she said, chuckling to herself. "The poor fella, he thought he was tellin' me somethin' I didn't know already…Me, his mother!" Her eyes bulged for effect, exactly the way Daphne's did.

Neil and Shane smiled.

"Sure, he had pictures of George Michael plastered all over his bedroom wall!"

The two lads laughed out loud.

"And then it was Tom Cruise and Mel Gibson and, oh God, I lost track after that. But d'you know, lads, sometimes I think maybe I'm to blame for the way he is now."

"Don't be silly," Shane said firmly.

"Maybe I should've discouraged him," she sighed.

"I wish my mother was like you," Shane added.

Neil grimaced as he imagined what his own mum's reaction would have been if he had dropped such a bombshell at fourteen.

"You wouldn't think it now, but he was such a sweet, gentle little fella then," she continued lovingly, "sure if I didn't stick by him, God knows what would've happened to him." The tears had begun to well up in her eyes again.

Shane touched her hand gently. "He's lucky to have you."

"You boys are very good for visiting him," she said. "He doesn't have many friends."

Neil wanted to hug the poor woman. He wanted to tell her that he often spoke to Jesus, and that he was certain that a better place awaited her son.

"He gets very depressed…Especially at night, when the pain comes, and he can't sleep."

Neil swallowed hard.

"I love my boy—but I hope Jesus takes him home soon," she said, brushing the tears from her cheeks.

Neil noticed the huge bolt lock nailed to the foot of the front door. He was standing at the bottom of the narrow stairway, waiting for the taxi company to answer the phone. The door to Daphne's makeshift bedroom was slightly ajar. Neil was tempted to sneak upstairs and check how many people were actually crammed under the one roof. Judging by the photos on the mantelpiece, he guessed that it resembled a refugee camp. Then, a bedroom door upstairs opened, and four girls in their mid-teens appeared at the top of the stairs. Their giggly chatter halted abruptly the moment they spotted him. Each of them smiled shyly as they passed him. The last one down was a double for Daphne. The same dark eyes, thin features, and mousy brown hair.

"Hiya," she said, obviously feeling it her duty as the one who lived in the house to speak to the stranger.

"Hiya." Neil blushed, conscious that his accent didn't go unnoticed by the girls. No doubt they'd have fun imitating him once they got outside. Daphne's sister went into the kitchen and her three friends stood in the hallway, doing their utmost to pretend that they weren't listening to Neil.

"I'd like to book a taxi please…"

Daphne's sister had rejoined her friends by the time Neil had finished his phone call.

"You're Neil, aren't ya?" she smiled.

"Yeah." Neil was taken aback.

"Me bruds told me all 'bout ya."

"Did he?" Neil felt his face burning.

"Don't worry, we don't give a fuck if yer gay," she said. "Do we, girls?"

Her three friends shook their heads, and Neil could see that they meant it. Then Daphne's sister stretched up onto her tippy toes and kissed Neil's cheek.

"Thanks for visitin' him," she said.

Neil just grinned at her. He couldn't think what to say.

It wasn't every day that he met four young girls with such liberal views. Good old Daphne had obviously been influential in the formation of these views. Neil pictured the four girls, lounging on a bed upstairs, squealing with delight as Daphne painted the vivid kaleidoscope of his nocturnal adventures, some of which Neil had no doubt featured in.

"See ya, Eddie," each one of the girls whispered through the open door before squeezing past Neil and out the front door.

Neil and Shane barely spoke on the taxi journey back into town. The taxi driver soon realized that any attempts at making conversation were futile. They came upon a wedding in Fairview. The traffic had come to a virtual standstill. Car horns hooted, crowds of passersby stopped to look, everyone wanted to join in the special day. The pretty bride, dressed all in white, was smiling brightly and waving to the throng of confetti-throwing well-wishers while the groom struggled to lift her into the wedding car. Her happy, radiant smile seemed to transcend all the gloom of the day. Clinging on to each other, the lovers posed for endless photographs. "The happiest day of my life," his sister Kate had once said about her wedding day. Neil remembered the bitter, stinging pain he felt inside his thirteen-year-old heart when she uttered those words. And how he went to bed that night and prayed that Jesus would take him up to heaven, that it would be better than facing the years of always being the outsider that lay ahead of him. But those days all seemed so far away now.

Across the road, the white wedding car finally began to pull away slowly from the church. Smiling to himself, Neil wondered what Daphne would've said if he were there with them. "Sister! Sister! It should've been me!" he probably would've shrieked. But in the backseat of that taxi Neil made one of the biggest decisions of his life. Seeing Daphne the way he was had changed his life forever. He was going to tell his mum and dad.

––––––––––

Yo Jesus! What's happenin', dude? This is your old pal Neil. Remember me? Course you do. Listen, sorry for calling on you at such short notice, but we're talking something major here. I'm going through with it, so you better stick around. I'm standing in the hallway, trying to muster up the courage to go in. They're in the living room watching the television. What's new? says you. Anyway, you probably want to know why I'm doing it. Well, it's simple. I'm tired of telling lies. Maybe it's because of Daphne, I don't know, but I can't live with this pretense any longer. You see, I'm happier now. Well, sort of, anyway. I've been staying the night over at Shane's gaff quite a lot recently. I never really believed that anything like this was ever going to happen in my life. I thought beautiful moments were the preserve of the rhyming couplets. Like the first night Gary climbed in through Trish's bedroom window. God, I thought he'd never stop going on about it. Of course all my friends think I've gone weird. They never see me now. I told them I had a new girlfriend named—wait for it—Daphne. I couldn't resist it. Then, Gary kept asking when they were going to meet this mysterious Daphne, so I told him that it was a bit awkward, because she was married. You should've seen the face on him! I thought he was going to drop a litter of kittens on the spot. And my mum, well she's starting to ask questions. She's worried, she doesn't know what's happening. Or maybe she does. She must've noticed my beard rash. I don't know. But what I do know is that I'm in love. Well, I think I am, and I want to celebrate that love, not hide it. I know what you're thinking; it's wrong, it's against nature, it's whatever. But you see the thing is, J.C., you or your old fella made me this way, and I can't help it, the feelings are too strong…Maybe you don't think it's wrong. I doubt that you're the type that would want to see me miserable again. I don't know, but it doesn't really worry me whether you do or not. No point in lying to you, is there? Things are never going to be the same again after this. They're always going to look at me and wonder where I was the night before, who I was with, what I was doing. And, of course, they're always going to imagine the worst. Wouldn't surprise me if my mum becomes a twice-daily communicant, so that's good news for you. Anyway, I have my bag packed upstairs just in case. Something tells me that I might be leaving home tonight. Stick close, J.C., here I go.

His dad's face turned ashen and he stared down blankly at his shoes. His mum sank her face into her hands and started to whimper. The television had been switched off. Neil shifted uncomfortably; he had never seen his parents react like this to anything before. It was as though he had told them that he was going to die. Not even Paul's motorbike crash shook them as much as this. Then his mum hugged him. Tears were streaming down her cheeks. Even his speechless dad's eyes were glistening.

"It's okay, Mum, it's not the end of the world."

There was no reply. Neil swallowed the lump in his own throat. He wanted to tell them that worse things could happen. That a fire could burn the house down that night and frizzle them all to cinders. So what was the big fuss?

Then his dad spoke sensitively. "Look, Neil, a lot of young fellows your age are often uncertain about their, eh…their sexuality…But it's probably just a passing phase."

"It's not a passing phase, Dad, I've known for ages."

Neil felt sorry for his father. This was the first time he had ever seen him look so lost. His life's foundations had been rocked. But Neil braced himself. It was now time to tell them the truth about being beaten up, and more importantly it was time to tell them about Shane.

"Jesus Christ!" His dad slammed his fist down angrily on the small coffee table.

"Brendan." His mum tried to appease him.

"You mean to say that you've been going into those queer pubs!"

"You heard what I said, Dad," Neil said, averting his eyes from his father's furious glare.

"And that you and that…that Northern pervert have been—in this house! Jesus Christ!"

Where are you, Jesus? Feel like crying now. They really don't know me at all. They're just like everyone else. Feel lonelier than ever before. Even thinking of Shane doesn't cure it. Better I die now. Make it something quick and painless, a brain hemorrhage or whatever. It'd be a huge funeral. All of Blackrock would be there, and the blokes on the rugby team would form a guard of honor. No one need ever know the truth. Let them keep this secret, let them keep their sweet memories of me.

"Look, I don't mind you thinking that you're homosexual or whatever, but no son of mine is going to start getting involved in all this queer carry-on."

Neil looked at his mum with pleading eyes. But she just gazed at him pitifully and shook her head.

"You shouldn't have told us all those lies, Neil," she said.

"I don't like it anymore than you do," he stuttered. "But I'm the one who has to live with it. It's the way God has made me."

"This has nothing to do with God!" his dad roared.

"Brendan, stop," his mum pleaded weakly.

But Neil was undaunted. "You don't know how unhappy I've been."

"Unhappy?" his dad snarled. "What've you got to be unhappy about? You've got everything laid on a plate for you: Brains. Sports. College. Jesus!"

"But I've always been alone."

"Alone? For Christ's sake, the phone never stops ringing for you."

"You know what I mean."

His dad snorted derisively. "Do I?"

"Please don't be like that." Neil's voice started to waver. "I love both of you, and I hoped that you would stand by me. But if you want me out of your life, just say it, and I'll go, and you need never see me again."

His mum started to sob.

His dad got up and stood at the fireplace, turning his back on Neil. "I'm not an idiot, Neil, I know your brothers are living with their girlfriends, and I know that Jackie is probably tucked up in bed with that long-haired boyfriend of hers right now. I didn't come down in the last shower. I've always allowed you all a certain amount of freedom."

His dad turned around and pointed at Neil, his eyes blazing. "But one thing I'll never tolerate is that queer carry-on. Never! Ever!"

Neil started to cry. "I can't help the way I am," he shouted.

His mum reached out and patted his hand.

"I told you, I accept you as a homosexual, if that's what you think you are. But I don't accept any of your homosexual practices. It's flying in the face of God," his dad replied coldly.

Neil felt the rage inside him rising. It was like he was talking to a complete stranger. "What's wrong with you? Why can't you just see who I am?" he roared.

"I told you, no son of mine carries on that way." His father was unusually calm.

"Well, whose son am I, then?" Neil was bawling now, and his mum draped her arm around him, attempting to soothe him. "Because I am going to carry on that way. I'm not going to change. I can't!"

His dad swore before he stormed out of the room, slamming the door behind him. Neil stood up weakly.

"He's as big a bigot as those bastards who beat me up," he said, looking at his mum. But she just stared up at him sorrowfully. Now she understood. All those lonely bike rides, all those silences, the stranger in their midst.

"I suppose you're going to turn your back on me now?" he snapped, uneasy under her stare.

"I'll never turn my back on you, love," his mum said. "You know that."

Neil wanted to snuggle up to her and tell her about all the little inconsequential things he had done that day. He wanted her to wrap her arms around him and shelter him from the world. He wanted her to rub his hair and call him her little man. But he knew from her tone of voice that she hadn't finished speaking yet.

"But your father's right, Neil. It is flying in the face of God."

Neil's heart sank right to the bottom of his stomach. But his sadness was quickly replaced by anger.

"You're just as bad as him!" he shouted, wiping the tears from his face.

"Neil, listen to me."

"The two of you hate me now, don't you?"

"Neil," his mum pleaded.

"Well, it's your problem, not mine!" he yelled and stormed out of the room and upstairs to his bedroom. He tasted the salty tears trickling into his mouth. *Why don't* they ask me how I feel, instead of always telling me how I should feel? Hey Jesus, should I bring Ted with me? That's everything. All your belongings. Bye-bye, bed. Good-bye, room. Down the stairs slowly, give them their last chance. No sound. Delay in the hallway. Fumble with the latch. C'mon, Mum, at least say "God bless." Open the door slowly to get the loudest squeak. Still no sound. Screaming inside, but they don't hear me. Why don't they understand? Good-bye, house. Close the door gently.

There's Gary's wagon of a mother, pretending to water her flowers. Walk faster, she's standing up. Pretend you don't hear her. Got to get out of this place. Stop crying, will you? Go through the school grounds, won't be anyone there. Sundown spreading its last burning orange glow across the sky. Lights twinkling out on Howth Head. What're the words of Daphne's song? "Every time we say good-bye..." They're going to play it at his funeral. Redser told me. Stop thinking about it... Look, there's some kids playing soccer. Put down the bag. "Hey lads, give us a game. Okay, me and this little fellow against the rest of you. You go in goals, small fry. No, of course I wasn't crying, it's from the chlorine in the swimming pool." Trusting excited faces chasing around, trying to get the ball off you. "Didn't your mamas ever warn you against the likes of me? It's Ryan Giggs, he beats one, he beats two, he beats three, it's there. One nil. I played for Manchester United, you know. Janey!" A gasp of amazement. "You're going into First Year *next year? What's it like?" "Ah now, it's a while now since I was in First Year." Laugh then. "It's great fun being in First Year, best time of your life, but you won't know it at the time. Okay, your tip-off. Oh, what a tackle, and the break is on. The keeper comes out, but Giggs sells a dummy and slots the ball home. Two-nil. What about that, small fry? Who's calling you? Your mum? You better go in. Right, see you, lads." Off they run, home to their glass of milk, their mummies' good night kiss, their snug little beds…Pick up your cross. On your own again.*

"You're not leaving us, are you?"

Startled, Neil turned around to face Father Donnelly. "How're you, Father?" he said with a grin.

"What's this?" Father Donnelly was pointing at Neil's multicolored canvas bag. Neil felt his face flushing. *There's no point in trying to lie to Donno*, he realized. *He can read you like a book, and anyway he's going to know that you were crying.*

"Bit of a row at home, Father," he said, fixing his gaze on his sneakers.

"Oh?" Father Donnelly was rubbing his wizened chin, as he always did, patiently waiting for the troubled boy to open his heart.

"So I'm going to stay at a friend's place."

"A friend in need is a friend indeed," Donno said, absently pointing across the grounds. "You know, Neil, that tree there is over two hundred years old."

Neil glanced over at the huge oak tree dutifully, but his thoughts were elsewhere. He knew that Donno always used tricks like this to disarm you, and when your defenses were down, he struck with all the cunning of a python.

"Look at all the colorful flowers growing around the bark."

Neil nodded. Maybe he wanted the python to strike.

"They're like the First Years, bright and vivacious. But that disappears all too quickly. And the old oak is left standing there, waiting for the new crop to come along and add color to his life…"

Neil sneaked a look at the elderly priest and he knew that Donno was pretending not to notice his look. He was like an old fisherman, biding his time before he started to reel in.

"Sometimes, the old oak sees a lot more than his flowers think."

The fisherman had begun to reel in. But the sad fish didn't fight or struggle. The silent cry for help rang out in the twilight. He broke down and the kindly priest draped his arm around his shoulder. They went inside and all the years of pain and frustration were poured out upon the benign listener. Then the wise old listener stood up and looked out the window as he spoke.

"Neil, there are some things in this life that we'll never understand. And I'm not going to start telling you what's right and what's wrong. But one thing you should always remember. You're part of God's beauty, and you have to respect that beauty, both in yourself and in others."

Neil dried his eyes and drained his coffee. The elderly priest crossed the room and held Neil's shoulders gently.

"And promise me one other thing," he said. "Promise me that you'll phone your mother tomorrow."

Neil nodded, knowing that he wouldn't be phoning his house in the near future. But his heart felt lighter. The moon had begun to rise. And as he traipsed through the silvery school grounds, he wondered how Donno would have reacted if he had told him about Shane. He'd probably just say, "Well, Neil, I didn't think you were going to go off and varnish your nails."

Neil sat on the steps outside Shane's flat for over an hour. Crowds on their way into the basement nightclub gave him odd looks as they passed. He pulled the peak of his baseball cap down to conceal his face. One slightly drunk girl stopped and asked him if he was okay. Her boyfriend stood behind her, impatiently shuffling from foot to foot. Neil assured her that he had just forgotten his key and that his brother would be home soon. He liked that, referring to Shane as his brother. But he couldn't help smiling when the concerned girl warned him to be careful, that a number of people had been beaten up in the area recently.

Around midnight, he saw Shane stumbling toward him with his arm draped drunkenly around another guy's shoulder. As soon as he spotted Neil, he unwrapped his arm.

"Neil!" He looked surprised, but Neil noticed his smile dim slightly when he spotted the canvas carrier bag sitting on the steps.

"Hi." Neil was subdued.

"Sorry, Neil," Shane swirled around drunkenly. "This is Rory, a pal of mine from Belfast."

"Hiya, Neil," Rory said.

"Hi," Neil muttered, barely glancing at Rory.

"We went to school together," Shane added quickly, sensing Neil's displeasure.

"A good Catholic school," Rory said in a funny voice, and Shane laughed at what was obviously a private joke between them.

Inside the flat, Neil felt worse. Shane and Rory talked about their school days, and Shane kept turning his shoulder on Neil, purposely excluding him. Nothing was even said about the heavy canvas bag that he had lugged up the stairs and that was now sitting in the middle of the room, visible to all. And it wasn't that Shane was hiding anything, because it was obvious that his pal Rory knew everything about him. Neil wanted to leave. But where to? *Go back home and tell them that he was only joking. Too late for that. Sugar's apartment? Bit more comfortable than this kip, and it'd give that fucker Shane something to think about.* If only Becky were still around. It would've been no problem staying in her place. At least he wouldn't have had to put up with this sort of grief. But there was no doubting it, he wanted to pick up the bread knife and stab Rory. He was a potential murderer as well as everything else.

Forget about yourself for once, he said to himself. *Join in the conversation. They don't want me to. Well, just sit there and look pretty then. They don't know that I'm admiring myself in the mirror. Admiring what? That sulky face? I can watch their faces in the mirror as well. Shane's face, you mean. Animated in a way that it's never animated when he's talking to you. Stop it, that's not true.*

Eventually Rory fell asleep on the sofa and this signaled a change in Shane's behavior toward him. Suddenly, he was all ears as he listened with concern to Neil's account of his parents' reaction. He laughed when Neil revealed that he suspected that maybe there was something going on between him and Rory.

"Even if he was the last bloke left on earth, I still wouldn't be interested." It was the old Shane again, and Neil quickly forgot about all his worries.

It took Neil ages to fall asleep that night. His mind was

a jumble of confused thoughts. What were his mum and dad doing now? Were they asleep?

Beside him, Shane slept soundly. Neil propped himself up on his elbow and watched his chest rising and falling softly and his face that looked so peaceful now, lost in a dream world. A stranger in the bed with him. Maybe he should go into the kitchen, pick up the bread knife, drive it through that smooth skin, and save himself so much pain.

He began to argue silently with himself. *Becky's right,* he thought. *It's only a matter of time before it ends. No, what does she know, she doesn't see the little magical moments that pass between us. Like in the song, magic moments, magic moments. What magic moments? Well, like the way he smiled at me outside the pub in Donnybrook last Saturday night. Yeah, when he was drunk. But what about those long silences between you while he was still sober? And when you did start to babble on, he wasn't even listening to you. Stop fooling yourself, Neil, he doesn't want you here. Did you see the face on him when he saw your bag? Stop, I don't want to know about these things, I have enough problems as it is. Everything will be all right in the morning, that's what mum always used to say. And everything always was all right in the morning. Go to sleep now, curl up like you did when you were a little boy, wait for Dad's stubbly kiss… Oh Jesus, what've I done? My life's in a bigger mess than ever before. Why is this happening to me? I can't take it any longer. What did I have to fucking well tell them for?*

chapter ten

Neil spotted his mum's blue hat instantly. She was sitting at the rear of the restaurant. Sipping her mug of coffee apprehensively with her handbag jammed between herself and the wall, she looked like a total stranger. All the confidence he normally associated with her was absent. She looked ill at ease, vulnerable even. Gone was the poise and control, the wagging finger, the look that had to be obeyed. Then he decided to do something he hadn't done in years: he leaned down and kissed her cheek lightly before he sat down opposite her. All traces of anxiety vanished from her face the moment she spotted him. They were in Bewley's on Grafton Street. It was three o'clock and the lunchtime rush had cleared. Two arty types, reeking with pretension, and wearing quasi-hippie-style clothing, sat at the next table. The guy was reading a book, and the girl, who was sporting a purple beret with a flower in it, was sketching with charcoal. A baby sat gurgling in a buggy alongside them.

"What did you do to your hair?" his mum asked.

"D'you like it?"

On Shane's suggestion, Neil had begun to gel his hair back off his forehead, so that their age gap wouldn't be so apparent. And he had also colored it with a pinch of henna.

"Oh yes, it looks fine."

Neil could tell that his mum was trying hard not to let her bewilderment show. He had let a week go by before he had phoned her. And when he did phone her that morning, her voice was fraught with worry and emotion.

Their initial exchanges were awkward, as his mum performed verbal gymnastics to avoid mentioning Neil's revelations. But Neil was also engaging in a degree of role-playing, doing his Mister Happy act, as though meeting his mum for coffee in town was a normal, everyday occurrence.

"D'you remember you and Dad brought me in here the day I had my confirmation?"

His mum smiled. "And you ate six sticky buns and nearly got sick afterward."

Neil was amazed at the accuracy of his mum's memory.

"And then we went to the spring show," he added, smiling at the memory of himself in his neat blazer, with the big red confirmation badge pinned proudly onto it, the brand-new pressed trousers, and the squeaky clean new shoes. They were on their second mug of coffee when his mum dipped her hand into her handbag and produced three crisp twenty-pound notes.

"Here, love, you'll need this." She was embarrassed as she slid the money across the table to him.

Neil felt his veneer of pretense wilting. "Thanks, Mum."

"I hope you're eating proper food now," she said quickly in an obvious attempt to divert attention away from the money.

Neil nodded, smiling to himself.

"I should've asked you to bring in your dirty clothes with you," his mum continued in her fussing voice.

Neil laughed. "There are laundromats in the city, Mum."

But the ice was broken. The unmentionable had been mentioned, indirectly at least. Neil realized that it was up to him to broach the subject more directly.

"Has Dad said anything else about last week?" he asked.

His mum shook her head, but he knew that she was lying to him. They had probably sat up every night since, discussing the moment that had ripped their hearts apart. It was funny though, he thought, he could never lie convincingly to his mum, and neither could she lie to him.

"We just want you to be happy, Neil," she whispered, reaching across the table to hold his hand.

"I know that," he muttered, keeping his head bowed to conceal his reddening face. He was conscious that the two art groupies at the next table were glancing over.

"He did make one suggestion, Neil. Your father."

"What?" Neil was wary.

His mum leaned forward and whispered, "He thinks that maybe you should go and see a psychiatrist."

Neil looked twice at his mum to check that she wasn't joking. Then he leaned back in his chair, shook his head, and expelled a quick rush of air through his nostrils. "You are being serious, aren't you?" he said incredulously.

His mum shifted uncomfortably. "Well, you never know, it might help, they're very good at—"

"Mum," Neil interjected, taking hold of his mum's hand. He saw that she was blushing when she lifted her head to look at him. "After I told you I was gay," he said quietly, "I swore to myself that I'd never lie to you again. No more pretense. I've done enough of that to last a lifetime."

His mum lifted her eyebrows in surprise.

"So believe me when I tell you, being gay is not a mental illness. It's the way I am, Mum, the way I've always been, and the way I always will be."

"Ah, you don't know that," she said, hitting his hand gently.

He spoke deliberately. "Mum, I do know that."

His mum managed a smile. "He was only trying to help, Neil."

"Sure," Neil sighed, and he turned to glare at the two art groupies who were listening intently. His mum looked sheepish now, so Neil changed the subject and started to ask about his nephew and niece. She told him that they both missed their Uncle Neil, and that they charged upstairs to check his bedroom every time they visited.

"Tell them that I'll take them in to see my new house one of these days," he said. The thought of their amazed little faces looking out onto Leeson Street from his bedroom window amused him. But this mention of his flat only prompted another inquisitive search for details of his new life.

"Tell me," his mum said in her soft whisper. "Do you and your friend…" She paused, holding her hand to her head.

"Shane?" he said, jogging her memory.

"Yes, of course, Shane."

Neil smiled to himself. His mum's feigned forgetfulness

often amused him. But years of experience told him that it usually meant that she was carefully maneuvering her way toward an awkward subject.

"Tell me, do you and Shane share a bed?"

Neil very nearly slipped off his chair. He wanted to laugh out loud, but he didn't. Suddenly, he felt so sorry for his mum. Why should he hurt her anymore? Surely the woman who had devoted so many years to him deserved a break. The woman who had carried him around as a tiny, wriggling, red-veined, saucer-eyed fetus.

"God no," he said and watched the warm glow of relief spread across his mum's face. *I'm doing the right thing, Jesus, aren't I? Why not let her believe what she wants to believe? After just telling her that I'd never lie to her again,* he said to himself. *Scribble it in my ledger as a very, very, small, barely noticeable, white untruth.*

"So, you're really just good friends then?"

"Yeah, just good friends," Neil nodded, still grinning.

"Ah, that's nice."

God, look at her, J.C., her world is worth living in again. But d'you think she believes a word of it? Aw, what the hell. You'd do the same for your mum, wouldn't you? Course you would. I'm not suggesting that you're gay or anything, now, don't get me wrong. But just imagine if you were. Imagine if you came back to earth in a blaze of glory. Most amazing light show ever seen in Dublin. It'd have to be the Phoenix Park, to cater for the

261

crowds. So anyway, there you'd be, with the whole country on its knees before you, and up you'd go to the mike, pause for effect, tap the mike a couple of times. Testing, one, two, three. Bit of hush now, the Main Man's going to speak. And then you go and tell them all that you're gay. Oh, I'm telling you, that'd put some spanner in the works…Hope you're not disgusted now. Are you? Well, I mean, let's face it, thirty-three and not married. If you lived on my road, the tongues would've drawn their own conclusions. You would've featured in a lot of their conversations. I mean, they wonder about me and I'm only eighteen. Imagine if I stuck around till I was thirty-three! Spare me.

"Neil?" His mum was waving her hand in front of his eyes.

"Sorry, I was miles away," Neil answered.

"What were you thinking of?" she asked.

"Ah, nothing really," he said.

His mum smiled. "You know, you look just the way you used to look as a little boy, when you go off on those daydreams of yours…"

But the moment between them was dashed when the arty woman at the next table spoke loud enough for the entire restaurant to hear her.

"Dermot, the child's name is Iseult, not Izzy! Speak to her properly, don't ever underestimate her intelligence!" The embarrassed man immediately stopped playing with the baby and returned to his book in a huff.

Neil and his mum exchanged looks, and Neil wanted to comment on how little the arty couple had to worry about. He wanted to ask them how they'd speak to their little girl if she turned out to be a diesel dyke.

Outside, the sun had emerged from behind the clouds. Grafton Street was in full flow. A guy in shorts strolled past them and Neil had to struggle not to turn his head. A passing girl smiled at Neil, and he felt his mum nudging his ribs playfully. Then she insisted on going into a newsstand and buying him a bag of apples and bananas.

"I don't want you getting scurvy," she said loudly, and Neil noticed a number of passing heads turn to look at them. Farther up Grafton Street, the friendly lesbian couple who had given Jackie the creeps waved across the street to him.

"Who're they?" his mum asked after he had waved back.

"Friends."

His mum looked at him, lifting her eyebrows in amusement. For some strange reason, he felt as though he was protecting her by not telling her who they were. He didn't want her thinking that the whole of Dublin had suddenly turned gay. Her world was in enough turmoil as it was. He walked up to St. Stephen's Green with her, up to where her car was parked. She sat into the car and rolled down her window. He rested his elbow on the car roof.

"Will you be out for Sunday lunch?" she had to shout to be heard over the din of the traffic.

Neil shrugged his shoulders. "I don't know, Mum. I'll phone you."

"Well, if you do come, make sure you bring out your washing with you. I don't want you wandering around looking like a tramp."

"Okay," he grinned.

"Oh, and have you got enough bedclothes?"

"Yeah," he said, trying his utmost not to blush.

"There's a bit of a nip in the air these nights."

"Will you stop worrying about me? I'm not a baby."

"You'll always be my baby," she smiled, punching his stomach lightly. He watched as she put her sunglasses on, turned the key in the ignition, and revved the engine up. Then she did something she hadn't done in years. She pointed at her cheek, her signal for him to kiss her. Neil leaned through the open window and duly obliged.

"Mind yourself, love," she whispered, ruffling his hair.

"Oh, now she tosses my hair," he said, feigning annoyance.

"Neiley Nook," she teased.

"I'll call you," Neil said, waving to her.

"God bless."

Once the traffic cleared, his mum reversed her car back out onto the road and drove off. Neil felt as if his nerve ends were scraping off the ground as he crossed the road.

He squatted down on his haunches and watched the ducks frolicking around the pond in St. Stephen's Green. He put on his tacky mirrored sunglasses so that the afternoon throng of sun worshippers wouldn't see his moist eyes.

Well, what d'you make of that, J.C.? Mother and child reunion. That's the sort of stuff you're into, isn't it? Madonna and child and all that. Here I am, making a public spectacle of myself again. But she's great, isn't she? I felt like telling her that I loved her. The moment was right. But I couldn't. Anyway, it wasn't necessary—she knows I do. The old fella will be a different matter. Shane says my dad probably sees it as some sort of reflection on his manhood. Pity about him, I hear you say. He's probably sitting at home, thinking of all the times he changed my diaper and wiped my bum, wondering where he went wrong. Crazy, isn't it?

"Hey, Neil!"

He turned around and saw Tom and Andrea strolling over to him. He blinked a number of times to clear his eyes.

"Long time, no see," he said.

"Love the sunglasses," Andrea laughed.

"What the fuck did you do to your hair?" Tom exclaimed.

"Looks great," Andrea said, kissing Neil's cheek.

"Don't ever wash your hair when you're locked," Neil said, pushing Tom's teasing hand away from his hair.

"What?" Tom was puzzled.

"I thought it was shampoo I was using."

Andrea laughed. "And it was henna?"

Neil nodded. They're happy now. Sighs of relief all around. Their friend isn't that weird. *Wonder what they've been saying about me. Let's go for lunch.*

"Anyone fancy an apple or a banana?"

"Where're you living?"

"Leeson Street."

"Why didn't you tell us? Are you really shacked up with a married woman?"

"Quiet now, the pair of you, I've got something to tell you about myself."

The story gets easier every time you tell it. Look at the faces on them, they can't believe it. Another kiss from Andrea. And then, couldn't believe it, Tom leaned over and hugged me.

"We're glad you told us, Neil, after all, we are your friends." He grinned, as always, but surely Neil didn't have to tell them that friends weren't enough.

chapter eleven

Sunday. Guess who's coming to lunch with his new earring? Wait till they see it. "It's a present from my boyfriend," you'll tell them, doing your best Daphne imitation.

Get lost, I'm taking it out before I enter the lion's den.

A young guy gets on the bus in Ballsbridge and he and Neil exchange just the slightest of looks. The sunshine brings it all out.

The moment Neil saw the expression on Gary's face, he knew that Tom and Andrea had spilled the beans. All his usual liveliness was absent, and he kept the garden gate between them as they spoke.

"How's your boyfriend?" he said, curling his lip into a sneer.

"Fine," Neil replied matter-of-factly.

"Jesus, you're not really queer, are you?" Gary blurted out, and Neil just looked down at his runners and smiled ruefully. Now, his lifelong pal seemed like a complete stranger.

"Tell me, what do the two of you do in bed?"

"Why? What d'you do in bed?"

Gary uttered a tense, jumpy laugh. He had both of his hands dug deep into the pockets of his jeans and he shifted nervously from foot to foot. Even though he was obviously repulsed, Neil could also detect a certain fascination deep below the surface. *Maybe you should just kiss him on the cheek and tell him that it's not really that important. Tell him that you're all going to be dead soon enough, that there's no point in fighting over things like this. Better still, kiss him on the mouth. Relax there, Gary duckie. Yuck, spare me. But could you imagine his reaction? He'd probably love it.*

"But why didn't you tell us about this before now?"

"You never asked." Neil couldn't resist the smart-aleck reply.

"I mean, you've been my closest friend growing up."

"I'm still your friend if you want me to be."

Gary purposely avoided Neil's gaze as he spoke. "I don't know. Listen, I've got to go, I was supposed to be over to Trish's half an hour ago." Gary kept five yards between them as he passed. Gone was his normal parting gesture of draping his arm around Neil's shoulder. Gone was the friendly grin and the playful punch. Gone was all the warmth.

"See you, then," Neil said weakly.

"Yeah, maybe." Gary flapped his arm nonchalantly before he headed off down the road. Neil wanted to shout after him, plead with him. *Please don't be like this, Gary, you don't realize how much you're hurting me. I'd never do anything to hurt you, you know that. I love you, Gary, and I know you love me too. As friends, I mean. I'm still the same Neil. We've gone through too much together to leave it like this. I could've mentioned the incident in the bed in Donegal, but I didn't, did I? I knew you'd be too embarrassed. You'd have probably denied it, but there's no point in fooling yourself, it did happen.*

Gary turned the corner without looking back. Then Neil noticed the shadows lurking behind the net curtains. Mr. and Mrs. Kelly gawking out at the freak show. The queer is home. Neil faced the window and, grinning, gave the lurking shadows a big friendly wave. The shadows evaporated instantly. *You should've given them a limp-wristed wave,* he thought. *That would've really given those tongues something to talk about.*

Neil's dad didn't speak to him during lunch. Neil and his mum exchanged smiles while the silent man pretended to be engrossed in his collection of Sunday newspapers.

"Oh, a girl called Mairead rang for you during the week," his mum said at one stage, bringing a snort of derision from his dad, who kept his eyes glued to his newspaper. Neil glared at his dad. Manners of a pig.

"She was the nurse from the hospital, wasn't she?"

Neil grinned at his mum and nodded.

"Put those papers away, will you, Brendan?" his mum said, but Mister Pig just snorted and continued reading.

"It's the height of bad manners," his mum added. "You should talk to your dinner guests."

"I've said all I have to say," Mister Pig replied pointedly before replacing his snout into his newspapers.

"Eat up some more potatoes there, love," his mum said, pushing the dish of roast potatoes toward Neil.

"I'm stuffed."

A loud snort of derision from Mister Pig, the liberal. *Wrong choice of words, Neiley Nook.*

"I'll get the dessert," his mum said, putting her napkin on the table and leaving the room.

Oh God, Mum, don't go, Neil groaned to himself. He's looking over at me. I know he is. I can sense it. Can't stop blushing. Why does he despise me? Can I rub my face against your stubble, Dad? Would you dive off a pier and save me now? Doubt it…The all-clear siren sounds. He's leaving the room. Had enough of you.

"Where's your father gone?" his mum asked, putting

her Neiley Nook's favorite dessert, baked Alaska, down on the table.

"Off to clean his snout," Neil said, and his mum grimaced.

"Don't mind him, love," she said, spooning him out an extra large helping.

"I wonder, does my liberal-minded dad still talk to his gay friend in the office?" Neil said.

His mum sighed wearily. "Give him time, Neil, he'll come around."

"Might be too late," Neil muttered, and his mum looked at him anxiously. Neil tried to smile to ease her tension.

"He loves you, Neil," she whispered, touching Neil's bare arm lightly.

"Could've fooled me," he murmured, lowering his eyes to avoid his mum's stare. The huge mound of baked Alaska now looked very unappetizing.

"Would you try and talk to him?" There was a hint of desperation in his mum's voice.

But Danny and Annie's squeals of delight prevented Neil from answering. They were playing with their grandfather in the hallway. The moment Neil set eyes on Kate and Dan, he knew that they had been told. He felt like an animal in the zoo. Kate went to extraordinary lengths to avoid looking at him. Dan kept sneaking so many furtive glances in his direction, that at one stage, Neil glanced at his reflection in the china cabinet to check that there weren't horns growing out of his head. They were having engine problems with their new car. Their world was in chaos. Neil wished that Jackie was there to knock the pair of them off their cruel pedestals with a blast of her rhetoric.

Then the two gleeful children raced into the room. They made a beeline for their Uncle Neil, but Dan stopped them in their tracks. Neil saw the flash of blind panic in his brother-in-law's eyes as he held the two protesting children firmly in his grasp.

"Stop that screaming!" Kate snapped, slapping Danny on the bottom.

Unclean, unclean, ring my leper's bell. Ding-a-ling-a-ling. Out of my way. Unclean, unclean. Mum is looking over. She's noticed. Kate's afraid to look at you. Old Mister Pig tries to talk about the new car, but the kids are shouting him down. They want their Uncle Neil.

"Good-bye, everyone, have to go now."

Thought they might relent, but they don't. Casual mutters of good-bye.

"Are you going already?" *The fake look of surprise on Kate's face. But still she can't look you in the eye. She knows you see right through her. Have a nice life.*

Mum comes to the door with you. "I'm sorry, Neil," she

says, hugging you. Hold her tightly. Salty tears flowing, nose sniffling. "I love you, Neil," she whispers softly. Can't answer. "God bless," she murmurs. Kiss her and walk away. Past your brother-in-law's gleaming new car in the driveway. Past the flowers in the garden. Past the lamppost you crashed your bike into once. Past the next-door net curtain shadows. Put on the tacky mirrored sunglasses. Don't look back. Don't let them see you this way.

———————

When Neil got back to the flat that afternoon, Shane was there. He could hear the loud classical music wafting through the building as he climbed the old, creaky stairs. A broad grin creased his face when he traipsed into the living room, but he couldn't bring himself to tell his lover how glad he was to see him.

"What's that?" He had to shout to be heard.

"Baïlèro," Shane replied absently without lifting his head from his book.

"What time d'you get back at?" he asked, flopping into an armchair.

"From *Songs of the Auvergne*."

"What?" Neil was puzzled.

Shane closed his book and looked at Neil. "You asked what the music was," he spoke slowly and deliberately.

Neil winced. He hated when Shane treated him like a kid, telling him to stop talking so fast and to stop asking so many questions at once. But try as he might, he couldn't stop himself when he was excited; everything just seemed to tumble out. He decided to try and say something meaningful.

"That's the type of music you'd like played at your funeral, isn't it?"

Shane barely nodded, leaving Neil feeling crushed. They sat in silence until the final note played. Then Shane rewound the tape and played the same piece again, at a lower volume. Now the sad haunting voice really sounded like funeral music to Neil.

"I'm going back to Belfast next week."

The words seemed to echo and reverberate around the room a million times before Neil actually heard them.

"I've got a job there."

Hey Jesus, do something, my world is falling apart. Stay calm, Neil, best to stay calm.

"Have you? That's great." Neil heard his own voice waver like a thirteen-year-old's as he spoke.

"There's nothing down here for me—workwise, I mean. And I'm sick of pissing around this stinking town on a bicycle."

What should I do? I have to ask him, but you'd think he'd have asked me already. No, I won't ask, I'll just assume.

"I wouldn't mind living in Belfast for a while. You know, the danger and all that could be exciting…" Neil heard his voice tail off weakly. The expression on Shane's face told him everything.

"You're eighteen, Neil, only just eighteen, and I'm twenty-three, almost twenty-four. We're at different stages of our lives."

I can't speak. I'm trying to, but no words come out.

"I'm sorry, Neil, I really like you—but it's just not working out, you're crowding me too much."

I won't do it anymore, I promise. Please don't look that way. Please listen to me. You don't know what you're doing to me. Please touch me, can't you see my eyes begging you. Why can't he hear me screaming?

"You'll find someone new, so you will."

Feel numb now. Can't think straight. All the world is spinning in a spiraling descent. Got to get out of here.

"Neil, come back."

He's still talking, but I can't hear him now. Throw everything in. Even you, Ted. What d'you think of that for a quick packing job? Shit, can't close the zip. Take out the new shoes Mum bought. A souvenir for him.

"Neil."

Let me out of here. Hide the tears.

"Neil, wait."

Bawling now. Don't look back.

Sunday. The seagulls rise majestically from the rugby fields as you approach. Up into the air like a billowing white carpet. Over to the building. Ring the bell. The old housekeeper with thin white hairs sprouting from her chin answers the door. Remember in school, all the lads used to say that she was having an affair with Donno.

"Yes?"

Speak to her. Ask her about her lover.

"Could I speak to Father Donnelly, please?"

Your voice sounds distant. She's looking at you oddly.

"Father Donnelly is away on a retreat for the weekend. He'll be back tomorrow morning."

Scratch your head. Tell her how sad you feel. Why not? Her face is kind. Who else do you have to turn to?

"Will I leave a message for him?"

Stare at your feet as you speak.

"Tell him that the flowers around the oak tree are withering."

Now she really thinks you're nuts.

"Are you one of the gardeners?"

Shake your head. Turn and walk away. She's watching you leave. Past the giant oak tree. Up through the grounds. There's the young lads playing soccer again. They're shouting over to you. Eager voices. They want you to play. Can't be bothered.

"Sorry, lads, in a hurry."

"Hey, mister, did you really play for Manchester United?"

How can you resist those innocent eyes. Long time ago. The others snigger. Can you blame them.

"What's your name?"

"Ryan Giggs."

"It is not!" *they roar in unison, except for Innocent Ryes, he believes you. There's always one. Take him with you and protect him from the world. How can his mother even let him step outside the door?*

"Bad day, lads, sorry, have to go."

"Ah, c'mon, mister."

"Maybe some other time." *They've forgotten you already. On you plod, there're places to visit. You're not going to? Are you? What does it matter now? The trees are bare now, the cherry blossom petals are all gone. Smell of freshly cut grass fills your nostrils. Naughty, naughty, cutting your grass on a Sunday. Press the doorbell. Ding-dong. Sounds the same as yours. We have something in common after all, me and Ian.*

"Yes?" his mother says from behind the half-open door. *Don't just stand there, say it. I can't. You have to.*

"Could I speak to Ian, please?"

The hardness drains from her face. Her face is pleasant now. She has his eyes and mouth, and even his cute little nose. Go on, tell her. "Hey, Missus, now I know where your son got *his heavenly looks from.*" Or, "*You don't know how lucky you are, sharing a house with that boy of yours.*"

"I don't know if he's in," *she says.*

Of course he's not. What did you expect, today of all days?

"Ian!" *she calls up the stairs.*

No reply.

"Ian!" *she calls again.*

Still no reply. She shrugs her slender shoulders and smiles.

"Oh . . . well, sorry for disturbing you."

She knots her brow and wonders if she's seen you before. "Who shall I say called?"

Decision time. Go on, go for it. Too late to turn back now. What does it matter? Take them out of your pocket and give them to her. You should've put them in an envelope.

"I just wanted to give him these."

"Oh wait, here he is now."

Everything goes cloudy as Ian drifts down the stairs, like an angel coming down from heaven. The frown leaves his brow when he sees you. A grin to brighten up the darkest day. Hand him the crumpled pages. That's it, ever so polite. Blackrock taught you something after all. Questioning look as he opens out the pages. It's the only way to lose these feelings. Watch it, Ian, your mum is looking over your shoulder.

"What are they?" *she asks, frowning as she takes your scribbled poems from her boy. What now? Why doesn't she understand? Please don't read them. That's my heart you're* holding in your hands. *She can't believe what she's reading. Look at her face. Now she thinks you're really weird. Tell her that you saved her little boy in Hollies the night of the fight. That'll win her over; he's bound to have told her.*

"Did you write these?" *she snaps, closing the door over slightly, pushing Ian back into the hallway. Would you blame her? She's glaring at you; you better say something. There's nothing to say, it's all in the poems.*

"Well, thanks very much anyway."

Oh my God, is that all you could think of? She's just staring at you. She loves her boy, can you blame her? His dreamy eyes are trying to tell me something, I know it. Turn and walk away. You don't belong here. The door closes behind you. Dejected, turn and see her standing behind the frosted window panes, reading your poems. She'll probably burn them and save her little boy. Oh Jesus, please let him see them. Just so he'll know.

The late afternoon strollers leave the pier when the rain begins to fall. Stand and watch the DART train emerge from the dark tunnel. Dial the number slowly. Please let Mum answer. It's ringing. Please let it be Mum. Please, please, please. "Mum, your little boy's heart is broken," *that's what I'll say, she'll understand.* "Mum, your little boy has never felt so alone."

Dad answers.

"Hello?" *A pause.*

279

"Hello, who's speaking please?" *Dad's voice sounds different.*

"Hello, who is this?"

Lips move, but no words come out.

Hang up. Another twenty pence, and dial the last resort. No surprise when Uncle Sugar's answering machine comes on. "Sorry, I'm out at the moment, please wait for the tone if you want to leave a message." *Sugar's businessman voice. Conscious of the lady waiting outside the phone booth. Want to say so much, but don't. Just hang up instead. Wish I had Becky's or Jackie's number with me. Pick up your bag and over to the ticket office.*

"Sorry, son, the next boat's not till tomorrow morning," *the man behind the glass window says. Bag hoisted up onto your shoulders, you begin your long trek.*

The hotel bar on the seafront is half full with Sunday afternoon drinkers. Children chase one another around the tacky bar. Sit over in the corner, away from everyone. Stick your bag under the table. The barmaid looks in surprise at the speed with which you knock the first pint back. "Got to feel something, babe," *you want to say in your American accent. Before the second pint arrives, the barman asks to see your ID. Everything's above board, pal. Order a double whiskey for good measure. Knock it back fast so you don't taste it. Yuck! Out with the pen and paper. Got a poem to write. A poem that will say it all. Another whiskey and a cigarette first. Jesus? Are you there? I* need some inspiration. *No reply. The sea is barely visible outside and it's supposed to be summer. Must look like some poseur scribbling away like this. Oh, turn up the radio, Sinead is singing my song. Painful to listen to now. Why are you doing this to me, Jesus? Down another quick whiskey. Throat burning. Head's going to explode. Imagine it. Bits of brains and flesh splattered all over the tacky bar.* "Don't worry, folks," *the barman would say,* "he was only a queer. Sit down there and enjoy your drinks, we'll have this mess cleared up in a minute. A bucket of water and a scrubbing brush will do the job."

I'm pissed out of my brains, got to get out of this kip. Out onto the wet street. Hoist the bag up on your shoulder and plod along the deserted seafront. There's a phone box. Call Uncle Sugar again. Last twenty pence. "Sorry, I'm out at the moment, please wait for the tone if you want to leave a message." *Where are you, Sugar? Hang up. Can't be bothered saying anything. Too fucking drunk. Up onto the main road. Windshield wipers going swish-swish, swish-swish. Car tires making a squelching sound. Mist rolling in from the sea. Can't even see Howth. Oh shit, there's Mal and Tony on the other side of the road. They've seen you, no escape now.*

"Hi, Neilly," *Mal says in an effeminate voice.*

"Hiya, darling." *Tony makes a limp-wristed gesture and blows a kiss across the busy road. People are looking.*

"Backs to the wall, boys!" *Their cruel roar drifts across the street. Pretend you can't hear them.*

"Faggot!"

They're laughing at you. Hands are shaking with fury. Feel like picking up that rock there and smashing it into their faces. Blood must spill. They're whistling after you now. Feel like crying. Why are you letting them do this to me, Jesus? Can't take it anymore. Just ignore them and walk on.

Darkness has fallen. Gloomy clouds almost touching the rooftops of the empty road. Misty drizzle drifts past the street lamps. Haven't eaten for ages but don't feel hungry. Nearly home now. There's Mr. Kelly, Gary, and Trish sitting like zombies in front of their blue flickering television light. God, look at them. And here's good old Mrs. Kelly now with the supper tray. Would anyone like a slice of the fresh fruitcake I baked? Look at Trish, pouring the tea, trying to impress. That fucker Gary says something and they all laugh. Bet it was about me. Something like, "Would anyone like a slice of Neil-fruit-Byrne-cake?" "Gary, stop, you're making me spill my tea." "He's a gas man, isn't he?" Trish would say. Ah no, Trish is okay. Look at the state of them, sipping from their dainty little cups. Put a brick through the window and shatter their smug lives. Lights are off in our front room. Leave your bag on the porch. Take Ted out and leave him sitting on top of the bag. There you are now, Ted, you sit there and keep an eye on my stuff. You tell my mum that I left this poem for her. Tell her I'm sorry it's a bit smudged, but it couldn't be helped. It's private now, so don't you go reading it, Ted. Not even as much as a peek. Sneak in by the side entrance. Lights on in the kitchen. Look in, no one there. Move on to the TV room. Oops, stood on one of Mister Pig's flowers. Calamity. There they are, staring at the screen. And they're sipping their tea as well. But look at their faces, they're not watching it at all really. Mum's chin is sagging, and her eyes are red. Dad looks different now. Jesus, what should I do? No answer. You're probably sipping your tea like everyone else. Only the lost souls are out on a night like tonight.

Climb up into the tree house. Safe from the world here. The tree house that Dad built. Cozy here, isn't it, Jesus? Still not speaking to me? Join the club. Hey, Jesus, d'you remember the first time I came up here with Paul and Joe? It was fine getting up, but climbing down again was the problem. D'you remember them all saying, "It's okay, Neil, just lower your foot down, the ladder's there." But I couldn't, I was sure I was going to fall. I was crying then. And d'you remember, I sat up there for hours, I wouldn't let anyone else lift me down, it had to be my dad. And then he came home from work, and he was laughing and calling me Mister Not-So-Happy as he carried me down on his shoulders…Only two smokes left, better smoke them, don't want Mum to know about my naughty habits. Know what, Jesus? I feel like I'm drunk. Well, I am drunk. But no, I feel like I did in hospital that time. Sort of floating. Free and floating, in a happy place, where I don't feel lonely. Where I don't feel anything.

A silent scream would ring out in the night air. The old tree branch would groan and creak as the noose tightened around the boy's neck. He'd fight to breathe, his feet dangling in midair. He'd try to reach his arms upward. His love bangle would hang limply on his wrist, covering his watch. The dizzy world goes around in circles, swirling and twirling like a merry-go-round. The happy children on the merry-go-round wave to their mums and dads. Round and round the little bobbing horses go. The happy mums and dads wave back to their passing children. The music of the fairground plays. The boy's life flashes before him. All the faces are smiling and waving to him as he passes, and he's crying out for help but none of them hear him. Round and round he goes, flashing pain from his eyes, but everyone keeps on smiling. Then the music fades. The boy would gasp his last breath. All the happy faces would disappear. The struggle would end.

Time would pass. The misty rain would keep on drifting down. The people in the house would switch off the television, lock the doors, and go upstairs. Out of habit, the woman would take a look into her boy's empty bedroom. The man would mutter a comment about where the boy is sleeping. Then the curtains would be drawn and the lights switched off. They'd tuck up warm in their cozy bed. The gloomy clouds creep down lower in the sky. The teddy bear gets wet and soggy on the porch. It's quiet now. Only the animals in the under-growth stir. The people in the house would be immersed in their peaceful dreams.

Night would pass and the darkness would lift. Birdsong would greet the arrival of dawn. The foghorn would sound far out at sea. A dog would bark. The gloomy clouds would be gone, and the glorious crimson sun would rise majestically up over the bay, spreading its pinky glow across the sky. Alarm clocks would chime. The rumble of early traffic could be heard in the distance. The man in the house would sit on the edge of the bed rubbing his sleepy eyes. He would stand up and stretch himself wearily. Then he'd walk over to the window. The woman would stir in her sleep. Feeling a cold shiver curdling her blood, she'd awaken with a start. The man would open the bedroom curtains and blink as his eyes adjust to the brightness. The woman would sit bolt upright in the bed. The man's pained cry would resound around the peaceful neighborhood. The woman would rush to his side. The man would clasp his arms around her. Her desolate scream would ring out. Their boy would really be talking to Jesus then and that would teach them all a lesson they wouldn't forget in a hurry... *Oh Jesus, what am I doing?*

"Neil."

A voice from down below.

"Neil, are you all right?"

Neil starts to cry. Uncontrollable salty tears stream down his cheeks, mingling with the rain. His whole body shudders as the rope is lifted from around his neck. He feels his dad's arm around his shoulder. He feels the bristle warm against his face. He sees the wetness in his dad's eyes as he helps him down from the tree house. His mum is standing in the light of the kitchen door, waiting for them.

"I'm sorry, Neil," his dad whispers, and Neil clasps his arms around him, burying his face into that safe shoulder.

His canvas bag is on the table, with Ted sitting proudly on top of it, like a king upon his throne, watching the happy family reunion.

"Someone named Ian called three times for you," his mum says. Neil's heart stops beating, his world stops revolving.

Say that again, Mum.

"He wants you to phone him immediately."

Jesus, you are cool, you know that.

His mum and dad wait in the kitchen while their boy makes the phone call that changes his life.

"Kate's bringing the two children over to see you in the morning," his dad tells him, but Neil is in another world now. He hugs his mum and dad again, and his tears are tears of joy this time. *Dreamboat Ian has been mad about me for years, he wants to tell them, we're meeting tomorrow.*

Never know, we might even ask Mal and Tony out on a double-date. You really do excel yourself sometimes, Jesus, you know that? You should've heard us on the phone, Ian and myself, stammering like two little kids. Well, one thing's certain, neither of us is going to get a wink of sleep tonight.

"Who's Ian?" his mum asks, her anxious voice charged with polite uncertainty.

Neil hesitates. The question hangs in the air like a grenade without a pin. Both his mum and his dad are staring at him.

"A friend from school," Neil says, placing the pin safely back in the grenade. This is the answer they want to hear. It brings the smiles back to the happy family faces. His dad turns to face him. "Your mother tells me that you and…eh, your Northern friend…"

"Shane," his mum prompts.

His dad nods. "Yes, Shane. She tells me that you weren't actually, you know …"

Neil watches his dad contort his face in embarrassment, unable to bring himself to say those words. But now Neil understands the conditions. We'll love you, providing you hide your love away. We know you've been through hell, but please don't bring us down into that hell. Just pretend. And Neil's grin of compliance brings a warm glow of relief to their faces. He realizes that they'll never understand him, that they don't want to. But only one image really matters to him now. That boyish grin, the red baseball cap, and the faded jeans. And now he was going to be a part of those dreams. Maybe they realized this, maybe they didn't, but their boy didn't really care anymore. They always told him to tell the truth, but now it was clear to him that they didn't want to hear the truth.

Irish slang and other terms

bender	derogatory term for a gay man. Similarly, bent: to be gay
bruds	brothers
chancer	person who is sneaky, mildly unscrupulous and opportunistic
cogging	to cheat on schoolwork or an exam by copying
Cooperation North	charity and exchange program dedicated to promoting peace between the Republic of Ireland and Northern Ireland. Secondary schools in both regions participate in class trips and activities similar to community service trips in many US high schools
cuppa	cup of tea or coffee
DART	Dublin Area Rapid Transit, the public transportation railway in Dublin
debs	formal dance for graduating students in Ireland, similar to prom
First Year	the equivalent to seventh grade in the US. Secondary education in Ireland lasts up to six years
fiver	currency note for five Irish pounds. Similarly, tenner: a ten pound note. The Republic of Ireland had its own currency until 2002
gaff	house or apartment
gobshites	despicable people, jerks
hard-chaws	tough people, thugs
Hot Press	a biweekly music and events magazine published in Dublin. Like many publications of its kind, it runs personal ads
IRA	Irish Republican Army, an often violent organization opposed to British rule in Northern Ireland

Jacks	men's bathroom
kip	a run-down place, a dump
knackers	originally a derogatory term for Irish Travelers (nomadic people similar to gypsies), also denotes lower-class people with rough attitudes
knickers	underwear
locked	drunk or wasted
nappy	diaper
Northern	person from Northern Ireland
pint	pint of beer. The drinking age in Ireland is eighteen, but the law conditionally permits sixteen-year-olds to enter pubs
pissed	drunk or wasted
po-faced	overly serious, humorless, disapprovingly pious
row	argument or quarrel, often domestic in nature
runners	athletic shoes
scats	derogatory term for gay men
semi-D	semi-detached house, similar to a duplex. A common type of home in the suburbs of Ireland and the UK
snogging	kissing, making out
snug	a booth or private nook in a pub
spoofed	joked or kidded
tearaway	delinquent or hooligan
wagon	derogatory term for an unpleasant woman

Ireland in the 1990s

When Love Comes to Town takes place in Dublin, the capital of the Republic of Ireland. Belfast, where Shane is from, is the capital of Northern Ireland, a politically separate region that is part of the United Kingdom. Since 1920, Ireland has been divided as a result of conflict between Catholic nationalists and Protestant unionists regarding Ireland's relationship with Great Britain. After the violence of the Troubles, which began in the 1960s and took place mainly in Northern Ireland, the 1990s were a time of negotiations and cease-fires, though tensions continued. Dublin enjoyed relative peace throughout this period.

SUPERSTAR LINEUP

ARNOLD SCHWARZENEGGER
HERCULES IN AMERICA

ROBERT LIPSYTE

HarperCollins*Publishers*

Acknowledgments

Every effort has been made to locate the copyright holders of all copyrighted materials and secure the necessary permission to reproduce them. In the event of any questions arising as to their use, the publisher will be glad to make changes in future printings and editions.

In addition, the publisher acknowledges the following institutions for the illustrations provided:
Page vii: The Bettmann Archive. • Pages 15 and 16: The Strong Museum, Rochester, New York, © 1992. • Pages 18 and 19: UPI/Bettmann. • Page 30: AP/World Wide Photos. • Page 39: Reuters/Bettmann. • Pages 40 and 46: UPI/Bettmann. • Page 65: AP/World Wide Photos. • Page 70: UPI/Bettmann. • Page 73: Springer/Bettmann Film Archive. • Page 74: Reuters/Bettmann. • Page 76: UPI/Bettmann. • Page 81: Washington Post Writers Group, © 1992. Reprinted with permission. • Page 83: UPI/Bettmann.

Arnold Schwarzenegger
Hercules in America
Copyright © 1993 by Robert M. Lipsyte

Library of Congress Cataloging-in-Publication Data
Lipsyte, Robert.
    Arnold Schwarzenegger, Hercules in America / Robert Lipsyte.
        p.   cm. — (Superstar lineup)
    Summary: A biography of the Austrian-born world champion bodybuilder who went on to become a Hollywood star and active in the politics of his adopted home.
    ISBN 0-06-023002-9. — ISBN 0-06-023003-7 (lib. bdg.)
    1. Schwarzenegger, Arnold—Juvenile literature.   2. Bodybuilders—United States—Biography—Juvenile literature.   3. Motion picture actors and actresses—United States—Biography—Ju[venile literature. [1. Schwarzenegger, Arnold.
2. Bodybuilders.   3. Actors and actresses.]   I. Title.   II. Series.
GV545.52.S38L57   1993   92-46901
646.75'092—dc20   CIP
[B]   AC

Typography by Tom Starace
1   2   3   4   5   6   7   8   9   10

First Edition

★

This page is for my team.

Robert Warren, my editor, and Theron Raines, my agent, were smart and steady coaches.

Kathy Sulkes, my wife, was the photo researcher who never quit.

Professor Peter Levine of Michigan State University checked the manuscript with his Captain History eye.

Benjamin Kabak, a student at the Horace Mann–Barnard School in New York, was a very helpful reader.

And without the editing, writing and research of Sam Lipsyte, there would be no pages after this one.

★

The greatest hero of Germanic mythology was Siegfried, who slew the dragon Fafnir and was immortalized in Wagner's opera cycle The Ring of the Nibelungs. Can you imagine how this handsome, muscular hero could fire the mind of a young Austrian?

Prologue

The myth of the strong man, the larger-than-life hero who can protect us from our enemies and teach us to be better than we are, was told at campfires in prehistoric caves. It lives today in our craving for real and imagined role models, from heavyweight boxing champions to generals to presidents to movie stars.

We remember the names of the ancient strongmen.

There was Atlas, leader of the giant gods called Titans, who fought the Olympians for control of the universe in the first great battle in Greek mythology. When the Titans lost, Atlas was condemned to spend eternity holding up the sky on his shoulders.

There was Hercules, most popular of the Greek heroes, who, as a baby, strangled two huge serpents in his crib. He went on to perform the mighty twelve labors, which included slaying many monsters. He wore a lion skin and carried a huge club.

There was Samson of the Israelites, who slew

the Philistines with the jawbone of an ass. Because he believed his strength came from his long hair, which symbolized his godliness, Samson became feeble when Delilah cut it off. Blinded and chained, he regained enough strength to pull down a temple, killing himself and his enemies.

There was Milo of Croton, who, as a young boy, gained his strength by lifting a calf every day. Eventually the calf was a full-grown bull and Milo was the strongest man in the world. He struck such terror that all he had to do was don a lion skin and carry a club, like Hercules, to rout an enemy army.

There was Siegfried, the mighty folk hero of Germanic sagas, who slew the dragon Fafnir, and the gigantic lumberjack Paul Bunyan, the legendary American strongman who created rivers and canyons with Babe the Blue Ox.

Some of the strongmen were gods and some were human, but all were idealized versions of the authority figure, the king, the dad. There were female heroes, too—Diana the Huntress and Atalanta and Brunhilde, among others—but they did not come equipped with cannonball shoulders and stomachs that looked like rows of bricks.

In modern times, the word "strongman" is more often used to describe dictators such as Stalin and Franco and Hitler, who are often small and not muscular, but who rule with power.

We tend to admire brains more than brawn these days, particularly if our hero becomes rich and famous by inventing something new or solving a problem.

For most Americans in the twentieth century, being physically powerful is not as important as it was when people depended on the strength of their bodies, as hunters or farmers or warriors.

Of course, for some Americans, especially those in prisons or in dangerous communities, big muscles can still be important; no wonder there are so many weight lifters in jail yards.

But few of us are not impressed by, or at least interested in, the potential of the human body to become bigger and stronger. We are enthralled by mammoth weight lifters like Paul Anderson and enormous football players like William ("Refrigerator") Perry, by Hulk Hogan or the American Gladiators, men who could crush most of us with their bare hands, who can pick up cars. (These days, there are such women, too.)

Of all the musclemen, perhaps the most fascinating are the bodybuilders. They look as though they could tear down stone walls with their fingers, but they are not as powerful or as healthy as they look. They pump themselves up for show rather than for strength.

Yet with their sculpted muscles and the symmetry of their bodies, they come closest to resembling the mythic strongmen. Nevertheless, for most of this century, there seemed to be something phony about bodybuilding contests, something cheap. These were men in oiled skins flexing to music; it was more of a beauty pageant than an athletic event.

And then a strongman appeared whose fierce desire to win every contest turned pose-downs into cockfights, and whose commanding presence evoked Milo and Hercules. Arnold Schwarzenegger brought bodybuilding to the general public, and he helped change the way people thought about their bodies.

Arnold Schwarzenegger has become the most famous real strong man in history. How he shaped his body and his destiny—and created his own myths along the way—is a story of our times.

1

> Ever since I was a child,
> I would say to myself,
> "There must be more to
> life than this."
> —ARNOLD SCHWARZENEGGER

The boy was thirteen years old, large for his age and known in his little Austrian mountain town of Thal as a bully. The people who were afraid of him would never know how small and fearful the boy really felt. He was afraid of not measuring up to the harsh standards of his police-chief father. He was afraid of disappearing in the shadow of his handsome, athletic older brother. He was afraid of being marked a loser.

Whenever he could, the boy ran down the mountain to the nearby city of Graz to escape into a Technicolor dreamworld. He imagined himself as confident and powerful as the figures on the movie screen. He loved the Hercules adventure movies, especially when a champion bodybuilder named Reg Park played the ancient Greek hero.

Thirteen-year-old Arnold Schwarzenegger squirmed with pleasure as Hercules/Park flexed his enormous, oiled muscles in the sun, broke men in half with his bare hands and tossed boulders as if they were basketballs. This was power. There was no way Reg Park wet *his* pants when his father roared his name. With those rippling arms and that granite chest, not even a father could ever scare him. Who could stop Hercules from doing anything he wanted? Who would ever dare call him a loser?

In 1960, thirteen-year-old Arnold was living in a land of losers struggling with guilt and shame. It had been only fifteen years since an Austrian, Adolf Hitler, had been defeated in World War II, a war he had started to make Germany the dominant world power.

Millions of men, women and children died because of Hitler's war. Many Austrians had joined Hitler's gang, the Nazis, either because they believed in its evil racism or they wanted to be on what they thought would be the winning team. Gustav was a young police officer with musical talent when war broke out. Although it has been reported that he served in the losing army, to this day his wife, Aurelia, and his son Arnold deny they know what he did during the war.

After the war, Gustav became police chief of Thal and leader of the local police marching band, an honor in that rural region called Styria, where the old songs and colorful native costumes set people dreaming of bygone national glory.

Gustav and Aurelia's first child, Meinhard, was born in 1946. Arnold was born a year later, on July 30, 1947. The brothers grew close, but everyone remarked on how different they were: Meinhard was blond and charming, the object of instant affection, while Arnold was darker and less outgoing. Gustav made his preference clear.

"Arnold is a bastard child!" Gustav would bluster, so terrifying Arnold that sometimes he wet his pants.

On weekends, Gustav pitted Meinhard and Arnold against each other in running races, boxing matches, ski races. Umpired by Gustav, these events were not mere fun or exercise; they were lessons in domination.

"Let's see who's the best!" Gustav would shout, and the games would begin. Meinhard, older and stronger, usually was better, and Arnold learned to dread the final ritual. Bowing in defeat, the loser was forced to admit his own inferiority to the victor, while Gustav would try to weave some lesson around the humiliation, some moral about discipline and dedication. On the rare occasions Arnold won, Gustav might go so far as to start the contest all over again. Arnold did not need a footrace or a boxing match to know who was the best in his father's eyes.

More than anything, it seemed, Arnold wanted to shine for Gustav, to win some of his father's love. Arnold threw himself desperately into those little games. He knew he had to play twice as hard to be "the best." A tie always went to Meinhard.

Even worse than the contests were the judgments after the Sunday outings. Every week after church the whole family would visit a local the frozen lake; in spring, they hiked in the hills.

The brothers outgrew their bully phase, but while Meinhard discovered a talent for art, Arnold found nothing to absorb his energy. It would be later that he committed himself to honing his mind. Now he was frustrated in school. It is not hard to imagine him sitting dreamily at his desk, fantasizing about being someone else, a strong, beloved someone else without a father who picked on him or a brother he envied: He dreamed of being someone whom other people admired, respected, were afraid of, like the mythic German hero Siegfried, or the mythic Greek hero Hercules.

"Ever since I was a child, I would say to myself, 'There must be more to life than this,'" Arnold later told interviewers. "I wanted to be different. I wanted to be part of the small percentage of people who were leaders, not the large mass of followers. . . . I was always fascinated by people in control of other people."

2

A real-life Hercules named Kurt Marnul oper-
ated a bodybuilding gym near the movie theater
in Graz where Arnold dreamed of happiness
through power. Marnul was a former Mr. Austria on the lookout for young talent. Impressed
by Meinhard's looks and Arnold's enthusiasm,
Marnul invited the boys to train under him.

At first, Marnul was more interested in
Meinhard, whose easygoing personality, slender
hips and broad shoulders made him seem like a
natural bodybuilding star. But it was Arnold
who showed an almost fanatic dedication to the
often painful routines of the gym. Early on,
Arnold was willing to make promises he forced
his body to keep. Marnul encouraged Arnold to

push himself even further. Meinhard began to lose interest.

Maybe because everything had always come easily to Meinhard—friends, school, girls, sports, his father's affection—he didn't have Arnold's need to become SOMEONE. Maybe those years of being held up as the favored son were more damaging to him than to Cinderella. Soon, Meinhard drifted back to loafing and drawing while Arnold focused on weights, lifting to exhaustion, then lifting some more. He watched the boy in the mirror begin to swell. He couldn't stop now. He had to get bigger. Bigger. BIGGER.

Bodybuilding, the art of exercising not so much for strength or health as to create large sculpted muscles, dates back to ancient Greek and Roman ideals of "perfect" human physiques. At different times in history and in different parts of the world, the "perfect" male body was huge and hairy or sleek and smooth or bulging with muscles or as lean and wiry as a marathon runner's. Throughout history, most people didn't have any free time to spend on their bodies—they were too busy just trying to

Just-add-milk breakfast cereals for busy, health-conscious families revolutionized eating habits in the early twentieth century, during the first great fitness movement. Note the female basketball player; the game was young but already catching on.

Lifting weights as a hobby was a joke to most everyday folks in the days when they did manual labor from sunup to sundown to survive. But as the twentieth century offered more and more tedious jobs that did not fully exercise the body, dumbbells became the new symbol for health and strength.

survive by hunting or farming or working at hard jobs.

But in Europe and the United States by the late nineteenth century, more and more people were becoming "brain workers" in offices and shops. They needed to get fit, get thin or gain weight, relieve nervous tension; and they had the money and leisure time to "work out." They were encouraged by religious organizations (such as the YMCA, where basketball was invented), anti-alcohol groups and businesses that wanted healthier workers.

Immigrants brought the fitness techniques of their old lands—yoga, t'ai chi, karate. German immigrants brought their *Turnvereine*, or gym societies, to the Midwest. Their focus on increasing strength and sculpting the physique with dumbbells and heavy clubs coincided with a growing American passion for power, or at least the appearance of power. The country was flexing its muscles in the world arena. During the fifty years between the Civil War and World War I, the United States swelled into a military and economic force. People believed then, and still do now, in the slogan on the wall of an American gym where Arnold once trained: "Bodybuilding is important for Nationbuilding."

The American physical-culture movement had undertones of racism and nationalism— white people had to develop their strength and

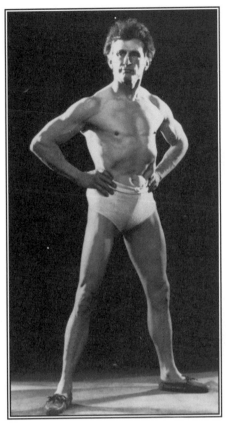

Bernarr Macfadden (1868–1955), the so-called father of physical culture, was a weak and sickly boy who grew healthy and strong through regular exercise, natural foods, pure water and abstention from alcohol, smoking and drugs. He grew rich and famous selling his ideas. When this picture was taken, he was fifty-five years old.

stamina so that "lesser races" would not threaten their dominance. The Muscular Christian, a mythical white superman popular in serial books and cartoons, was symbolic of the goal of preserving white power.

The fitness wave that swept the United

A self-described "97-pound weakling" from Italy, Angelo Siciliano read Macfadden's magazine, Physical Culture, and used "dynamic tension," in which one's own muscles were pitted against each other, to win Macfadden's "America's Most Perfectly Developed Man" contest. Siciliano changed his name to Charles Atlas and made a fortune with a mail-order bodybuilding plan that promised other "97-pound weaklings" that bullies at the beach would never again dare to kick sand in their faces and embarrass them in front of girls.

States a hundred years ago was very much like the fitness wave that has swept it in recent times. Gyms were built. New magazines advertised special foods and exercise equipment, including the spring-and-pulley grandparents of modern Nautilus machines. Serious teachers of strength and health competed with crackpots and crooks for consumer dollars. Just like today, it wasn't easy to separate what looked good from what was good.

There were gurus like Sylvester Graham (the cracker was named for him), whose almost religious regimen of calisthenics and vegetarianism was too strict for most. There were showman strongboys like Bernarr Macfadden, who used lights and makeup and hype to reinvent the art of bodybuilding and posing. Macfadden's life was as flamboyant as Arnold's would be. He came from the hardscrabble poverty of the Ozark Mountains of Missouri to become a celebrity millionaire.

"Weakness is a crime," Macfadden always said, and if Arnold ever heard that motto, he surely would agree.

3

You must go on the salt diet.
—ARNOLD SCHWARZENEGGER

Aurelia worried about her son Arnold. He didn't go to church with her anymore. He seemed to have found a new religion. Sometimes at night, after finishing his homework, Arnold would wait until Gustav was asleep, then hitchhike down the mountain to Graz for another workout.

He grew distant from Meinhard. He resented his parents' disapproval of his new passion. He found a new family at the gym.

A local Jewish businessman and bodybuilding promoter, Alfred Gerstl, invited Arnold to his house for good advice and more red meat than Aurelia and Gustav could afford to feed him. Arnold knew he had to eat as vigorously as he trained.

Meanwhile, Marnul and his friends at the gym made Arnold feel like he could be SOME-BODY someday, perhaps even a champion. They also encouraged his personality to develop. Once Meinhard had been the leader of pranks and tricks, with Arnold tagging along. But now, as Arnold's muscles began to emerge, so did his charm and humor. But inside the new joker of the gym still lurked something of the old bully, the boy who helped beat up the milkman.

A famous story that Arnold often told was about his notorious salt joke. A young man from a rich family had come to train at the gym and developed an athlete's crush on the older, bigger Arnold. He annoyed Arnold by constantly following him, studying his lifting, badgering him with questions. Arnold and the older men mocked the kid, but he would not quit pestering his hero. Finally, Arnold motioned him over.

"You must go on the salt diet," Arnold whispered.

"What's that?" the kid asked breathlessly.

The gym fell silent and everyone perked up.

You see, Arnold explained, you crush up

some nutshells and eat them with one table-spoon of salt the first day, two the second, three tablespoons the third day, and so on. Do it for thirty days.

When the kid thanked Arnold and burst out of the gym to start his new diet, the other lifters exploded with laughter. Everyone else knew that salt, besides being poisonous for anyone who takes too much, makes you retain water, the last thing a bodybuilder wants drowning those rip-pling muscles. The cruelty of the trick made Arnold an instant hero in the macho atmos-phere of the gym. Later in his career, he would repeat the cruel prank with the "ice cream diet" and the "sugar diet."

According to Wendy Leigh, who relates the salt story in her unauthorized biography *Arnold*, the kid realized he'd been tricked after a few weeks, but not before he was nearly hospital-ized.

If the salt victim learned a lesson about blind hero worship, Arnold also learned that he could be mean and funny when he wanted, and that this gave him power over other people. He must have noticed the relief in the eyes of fellow bodybuilders when they found themselves on Arnold's side of a joke.

Those he spared became his circle, his friends and protectors, the court where he was both jester and king. All his life he would keep a circle around himself by playing with people—you were either his friend or a target.

It was the art of the psych out. Bodybuilders are always psyching themselves up for more lifts, heavier weights, the confidence to pose half naked before a crowd. So they learn to psych out their competition, deflate their egos, make them weaker, less confident, ready to lose.

Arnold stayed in Graz for a few years, often living in the gym. He laid bricks for a while, and borrowed money from friends to support himself as he learned the techniques of bodybuilding and its tricks. Bodybuilding contests, like beauty contests, are subjective, the outcome decided by the opinion of a few judges. While there are standards for muscle tone and definition and symmetry that every bodybuilder must meet, there are also intangible qualities—presence, musical choice and stage power—that make the difference between winning and losing.

Already Arnold was making his talent known. The judges at his very first regional contest named him runner-up.

After he turned eighteen, Arnold began his compulsory service in the Austrian army. Gustav got him stationed near Graz in a tank division. Arnold had always dreamed of driving tanks, but he continued to train as well, packing away lots of free army food to grow on.

Meanwhile, a buzz about Arnold started in the bodybuilding world. Some German muscle magazines decided to sponsor Arnold if he would go to the city of Stuttgart to compete in the Junior Mr. Europe contest, a major event for young bodybuilders.

Arnold knew he'd never get permission to leave the army base. But he knew this contest was a crucial step toward becoming somebody. It was a big, risky decision. When he left the base for Stuttgart, he was AWOL, absent without leave.

Arnold returned with the Junior Mr. Europe championship. His officers were angry enough to lock him up in a stockade cell for a week. But he was a hero to the other soldiers, for challenging the system and for being a winner.

Winning at Stuttgart not only made him a rising star but introduced him to some people who would play important roles in his life. One was Franco Columbu, a short former boxing champion from Sardinia who was also on his way to stardom. They would become best friends. Another was Rolf Putziger, a magazine publisher who invited him to train at his gym in Munich, a much bigger city than Graz or Stuttgart.

In the spring of 1966, when Arnold finished his year in the army, Gustav and Aurelia confronted him. They were proud of his trophies and muscles, but now it was time to settle down, to make a plan. Bodybuilding was a fine hobby, but Arnold needed a real job. He was nineteen years old. Maybe he could reenlist in the army or work with some of his old friends at the pencil factory in Thal.

Arnold held back a nervous laugh. He had a plan, all right; but if it involved pencils, they would be the ones reporters used to write about his ascent to stardom. But first he would have to leave little Thal.

The time had come to go down the mountain for good.

4

It's like someone putting air in my muscles. It blows up. It feels fantastic.
—ARNOLD SCHWARZENEGGER

Arnold worked hard in Munich, lifting for six or seven hours a day with Franco, one day for chest and back, the next for biceps and triceps, paying particular attention to the calves and thighs, traditionally weak areas for European bodybuilders. Arnold and Franco pointed out each other's flaws, the "cut" of a muscle here, a gesture or movement during a pose. There could be no weaknesses, no soft spots. The goal was perfection. Arnold was methodical and precise in his work habits. If Gustav had approved of bodybuilding, he would have been proud of how well Arnold remembered the lessons he had learned in Thal.

And Arnold was not afraid of pain, which, he said, "divides a champion from someone who is not a champion. That's what most people lack, having the guts to go on and just say they'll go through the pain no matter what happens."

For Arnold, pain was not a signal to stop. It was a flag waving him on to more repetitions, heavier weights. Pain meant he was getting bigger.

"I have no fear of fainting," he has said. "I do squats until I fall over and pass out. So what? It's not going to kill me. I wake up five minutes later and I'm okay. A lot of other athletes are afraid of this. So they don't pass out. They don't go on."

Arnold was determined to go on. After lifting all day, he swept and mopped Putziger's gym to pay his training fees. Other lifters were in awe of his energy, passion and drive. Had his need to succeed come out of his childhood? And had those years of dreaming produced the Master Plan?

"I will come to America. . . . become the greatest bodybuilder in the world . . . learn perfect English and educate myself," went the Master Plan, according to his friend the photographer George Butler, who directed the movie *Pumping Iron*.

As the Master Plan continued, Arnold would invest in real estate, go into the movies as an actor, producer and director, and be a millionaire by thirty.

These predictions appeared in Butler's 1990 book *Arnold Schwarzenegger, A Portrait,* but it is not hard to believe that Arnold was already saying, or at least thinking, such words in 1966, at nineteen.

He was not only psyching himself up for the hard, painful climb to the top; he was practicing psyching out his competitors, making them nervous, leading them to quit in fear, or overtrain, or lose their concentration as they stood on the stage and posed for the crowd and the judges.

After all, who wants to compete against a madman who is willing to collapse after every workout? Arnold was casting himself as the superhero of the movies in his mind. How much of what he says should we take seriously?

Young lifters certainly should stop at pain and never allow themselves to pass out.

Believing Arnold's stories about himself may be harmless fun, but believing everything he says about his training could be as dangerous as following his "salt diet."

But it wasn't all psych and pain. Arnold was feeling the joy of "the pump," that moment in the lift when the muscles "become really tight with blood. Like the skin is going to explode any minute. It's like someone putting air in my muscles. It blows up. It feels fantastic."

To feed those muscles, Arnold and Franco ate vast amounts of food. To earn money for

In 1975, Arnold and one of his oldest and best friends, Franco Columbu, combined two of their favorite activities, showing off muscles and meeting women.

those monster meals, most bodybuilders of their time posed for photographs. There were many older men, bodybuilding fans, who paid to observe and shoot posing routines. Dinner and drinks were often included.

The way Arnold and his friends figured it, all their hard work was directed at posing in competition anyway, so why not practice for the camera and some easy cash?

Once in a while, Arnold would return to Thal, only to realize how different his life had become.

He had lost touch with Meinhard. Even when he went home, Arnold did not see much of his older brother, who seemed to be drifting through life, borrowing money he could never repay. Gustav kept a disappointed watch on his favorite, bailing him out of trouble more and more often. Meinhard hardly ever mentioned Arnold, and people assumed he resented his younger brother's escape from Thal. It may have been true, but there was still a bond between them.

Once, while Meinhard was strolling with a new girlfriend, according to Wendy Leigh's book, a member of a group of boisterous body-builders gave him a long, silent stare. Mein-hard's girlfriend snickered at how silly the bodybuilder looked with his grotesque propor-tions.

"Don't say that," snapped Meinhard. "That was my brother."

His girlfriend had thought Meinhard was an only child.

Bodybuilding was not taken seriously by the general public in the sixties. Sportswriters con-sidered bodybuilding in the same class as such "exhibitions" as roller derbies and professional wrestling, and much closer to a beauty contest than to Olympic weightlifting. There was no governing body, such as the Olympic Commit-tee or the National Football League, to make rules and award championships. While there was a National Amateur Bodybuilding Associa-tion (NABBA) in the United States, it seemed as though promotors and dumbbell manufacturers and power-pill salespeople had the real control.

But within the sport, the Mr. Universe con-test was as important as any Super Bowl.

Arnold went to the 1966 Mr. Universe contest in London hoping to meet people who could help him, and to learn some new techniques. Barely out of his teens, up against veteran body-builders, he did not expect to do well. He had conquered the junior circuit but this was the big league.

But as Arnold swelled into his final poses, his body pumped and glistening with oil, huge muscles straining to explode through his skin, as he smiled and turned and flexed with just the right attitude of cocky good nature, the crowd went wild.

He felt their screams, their applause, their awe wash over him like a wave of heat.

He loved it.

From now on this would be his fuel, and more than anything else, this would make him grow. The noisy, frenzied adoration of a crowd was the most powerful thing he could imagine.

All but one of the judges voted him runner-up. Did they think he was too young, were they frightened by this unknown newcomer's ability to move the audience?

The crowd booed the decision, and Arnold, who had not expected to win even second place, now felt cheated.

Afterward, the one judge who had voted for him, the British gym owner Wag Bennett, told Arnold that he had deserved to win. He took Arnold to his home for a visit. Wag and his wife, Dianne, a promoter in the growing women's bodybuilding movement, became surrogate parents for a while. They both believed in Arnold, especially after he revealed the Master Plan. After all, here was a potentially great young bodybuilder who was already thinking beyond bodybuilding. In his mind, Arnold had already won every title and was now getting bigger in movies, real estate, maybe even politics.

Arnold was impressed with Wag Bennett. Though older, Wag prided himself on being able to outlift his younger friends, including Arnold. Then Wag *really* impressed Arnold. He introduced Arnold to his boyhood hero, the Hercules of those movies in Graz, the retired bodybuilder Reg Park.

When they met, Reg Park gave his biggest fan the once-over and predicted a great future.

He invited Arnold to visit his palatial estate in South Africa—but only if Arnold won the 1967 Mr. Universe title.

Reg Park is supposed to have said, "Win it and I'll bring you out."

And Arnold is supposed to have replied, as he dashed off to Munich and more training, "See you there!"

5

I was a nut, a psycho constantly out of control—and then, thank God, the contest came, and I won it and got off the juice, and suddenly became human again.
— STEVE MICHALIK

Arnold at twenty was young for an international contender, but he was already very big—6 feet 2 inches tall, 235 pounds. His biceps were 22 inches around, his thighs 28 ½ inches. He had a 34-inch waist and a chest that expanded to 57 inches. Every inch of Arnold seemed molded from oak, his nickname.

Once, a fellow bodybuilder, confused by the scientific formulas for computing body fat and muscle mass, asked Arnold for the best way to make the calculations.

"Jump up and down," said Arnold. "If it jiggles, it's fat."

Nothing jiggled on Arnold. There was no fat. And no wasted motion in his training, just pure effort until he puked and fainted and woke up and started again. No one was surprised that he had gotten so big or "ripped," his muscles so defined or "chiseled," so fast.

He was determined, dedicated, talented; and like almost everyone else, he had gotten help from steroids.

From ancient Greek Olympians through nineteenth-century French bike racers to modern American baseball players, athletes have used various chemicals to enhance their performances, but nothing has worked so well as steroids for performers who need strength and sudden bursts of power.

Steroids are laboratory-manufactured derivatives of the male hormone testosterone. They have a psychological effect—an increase in aggressiveness—and a physical effect—they speed up and enhance the capabilities of human muscle.

During World War II, the Nazis injected steroids into their storm troopers to pump them up for battle. In the fifties and sixties, East German Olympians became notorious for using steroids to help them win so many gold medals. By the seventies, even though medical experts declared that steroids didn't work, elite athletes knew better. World records fell as juiced jocks proved that the line between winning and losing could be measured on the gauge of a syringe. Athletes stopped listening to doctors.

In the 1988 Seoul Olympics, when Ben Johnson tested positive for steroids and lost his gold medal for the 100-meter dash, the general public learned how effective the drugs were. In just a few years, Johnson's muscles had enlarged as dramatically as his times had shrunk.

Steroids have never been a substitute for training; in fact, users tend to train harder because they tire less easily and their muscles repair more quickly after injury.

Steroids rev up a natural function. The synthetic testosterone flows through the bloodstream and clings to muscles along the way, creating a chemical effect that increases their size and stamina. When you look at photographs of nineteenth-century strong men, notice how much smaller and less defined their muscles are compared to those of some modern athletes and movie stars, often thanks to steroids.

The Canadian sprinter Ben Johnson became the world's best adver-
tisement for steroids when he won the 100-meter sprint at the
1988 Seoul Olympics with this pumped-up body. But victory was
brief. Suspended after a postrace urine test, Johnson made a clean
comeback, but was caught again and banned for life.

The death of former professional football star Lyle Alzado in 1992 was a wakeup call to thousands of youngsters using steroids. Before he died, Lyle attributed his brain cancer to the drugs he took to bulk up for the game.

Arnold has admitted to steroid use, although he says he stopped many years ago and even then used far lower dosages than people use now. He warns against steroids, pointing out how they can cause impotence and sterility, destroy vital organs and perhaps cause cancer. The football star Lyle Alzado thought so too, before he died of a brain tumor in 1992.

Because steroids are a male hormone, the effect on a woman is even more dramatic than on a man; her muscles grow bigger faster, but menstruation can be disrupted, her voice may deepen and she can sprout hair on her face.

Psychological effects can also be devastating. Steve Michalik, an ex-Mr. Universe who was expected to replace Arnold as the reigning champion during the late seventies, almost died from steroids on several occasions, yet went back to the drug after recovering, despite his doctor's warnings. In a *Village Voice* article by Paul Solotaroff, Michalik remembered the "'roid rages" of destructiveness and invincibility.

"Here I was, a churchgoing, gentle Catholic, and suddenly I was pulling people out of restaurant booths and threatening to kill them just because there weren't any tables open. . . . I was a nut, a psycho constantly out of control—and then, thank God, the contest came, and I won it and got off the juice, and suddenly became human again."

During one period of rage, Michalik cut off a truck on the highway, ripped off its door, and smashed the driver's face with one punch. Michalik and the truck driver were luckier than the 'roid-crazed lifter who tried to stop a speeding Buick head-on with his bare hands.

Even in Munich in the 1960s there were rumors of violent incidents involving bodybuilders. Arnold admits to scrapes with the police, but he was able to bail himself out.

Arnold did not become a champion because he injected more steroids than other bodybuilders; he won because he worked harder, lifted more weight, spent more time studying his poses in the mirror, and dedicated his life to his goal.

It paid off in 1967, when he became the youngest man in history to become Mr. Universe. Arnold was twenty and his career was made. He would never again have to mop the gym floor.

He accepted Reg Park's offer and visited South Africa. He was impressed by his old hero's luxurious life-style and numerous servants and was probably inspired to work even harder toward his own fortune. He offered no public indication that he was disturbed by a society in which the majority of people, blacks, were oppressed by a white minority. Although Arnold's political views would not be well known for some years, this was a man who could say: "People need somebody to watch over them and tell them what to do. Ninety-five percent of the people in the world need to be told what to do and how to behave."

Arnold returned to Europe the hottest property in bodybuilding. Because he could sell out an arena, contests were created around his schedule. Muscle magazines put him on their covers. He was begged to endorse exercise equipment, clothing and nutritional supplements. He was en route to his first million.

He was happy but he wasn't satisfied. It was just the beginning.

6 I was just off the boat, you see, and someone asked me if I wanted to be in a movie. It seemed like a dream.

—ARNOLD SCHWARZENEGGER

By 1968, the Master Plan was clearly working. After winning his second straight Mr. Universe title, Arnold was the top bodybuilder in the world. And he was living in the United States.

He arrived in a turbulent time, the so-called "hard year," during which the Reverend Martin Luther King, Jr., winner of the 1964 Nobel Peace Prize, was shot dead in Memphis, and Senator Robert F. Kennedy, campaigning for the presidential nomination, was shot dead in Los Angeles, and during the Democratic Convention, the streets of Chicago ran with the blood of young demonstrators protesting against racial injustice and the war in Vietnam.

Not that life was calmer in Europe, where Arnold had just come from. The so-called "troubles" between Catholics and Protestants in Northern Ireland had resurfaced, Czechoslovakia was rising up against Soviet domination, and French students were rioting in Paris.

The sports world was no sanctuary. Before the Mexico City Olympics, police had machine-gunned student protesters; the Games themselves are best remembered by some for two African-American runners, Tommie Smith and John Carlos, raising black-gloved fists on the victory stand in solidarity with civil rights goals. Meanwhile, the single richest prize in sports, the heavyweight boxing crown, was up for grabs because the rightful champ, Muhammad Ali, had been illegally stripped of the title when he refused to be inducted into the U.S. Army.

It's not hard to imagine how Arnold felt about all these rebellious acts of conscience against authority. He supported U.S. policy in Vietnam, he was a veteran of his own country's army, and as the son of a police chief he would not be sympathetic to college students who called cops "pigs."

Not that anyone was interviewing him on politics in those days. In fact, few people outside

Raising the Black Power salute on the victory stand at the 1968 Mexico City Olympics was how American gold medal winner Tommie Smith and bronze medalist John Carlos showed the world that some athletes stood for more than just winning—in this case for civil rights.

bodybuilding paid much attention to this bulky twenty-one-year-old with his heavily accented English.

But those in the know paid attention. Arnold had the body and the mind to capture the emotions of the audience and the judging panel, to seem relaxed and intense at the same time, to exude victory before achieving it. As the defending Mr. Universe, he brought some new muscles and some fresh psychout strategies.

"Boy, what happened to *you*?" Arnold asked one bodybuilder as he was about to take the stage. "I've never seen you look so bad!"

Then Arnold waved over a familiar official.

"Come and meet my skinny friends," he said, laughing and pointing to his competition.

Who could pose with confidence after that? Of course, he won again!

Arnold understood that even an experienced eye had trouble determining whose muscles really were the biggest, the best toned, the most perfectly proportioned. So much depended on the attitude and stance of the bodybuilder, how his poses meshed with his music, how his routine compared to others. Even when he wasn't in top shape, Arnold knew exactly how to manipulate the other elements of his performance.

Among those paying careful attention to Arnold was Joe Weider, head of a new group, the International Federation of Bodybuilding (IFBB), a rival to the NABBA. Weider understood Arnold's dreams; Weider had been raised poor and scrawny in New York, and he grew strong lifting discarded machinery parts in an empty lot. Weider started the first magazine specifically for bodybuilders. He was a prime mover in the sport's attempt to get beyond its old image of a freak show.

Weider sensed that Arnold had the looks and personality to make the sport respectable to the general public. And Arnold was ready, after all those years of building an imaginary vision of the United States as an immigrant's El Dorado, to leap the ocean. After all, the music Arnold posed to was from the movie *Exodus*.

Arnold arrived with just a gym bag and his homegrown arrogance, convinced he had timed everything perfectly. His last words to Weider's European representative are said to have been,

"I'll eat them up in America. I'll eat them up, baby."

But the day after he arrived in Miami for the IFBB version of the Mr. Universe contest, they ate him.

Pasty and a little soft, Arnold lost to an American, Frank Zane. Humiliated and far from home, Arnold slunk back to his hotel room and cried himself to sleep.

Arnold's defeat humbled him. Briefly. Then he set out, as usual, to become even bigger and better. He signed a contract with Weider that paid him a good salary plus training expenses. In return, he promoted Weider's magazines, events, and products. Arnold's name appeared on a monthly column of training techniques written by someone else.

It seemed a typical promoter-athlete relationship, with Weider's mentor status giving him the upper hand. But Arnold would never be under anyone's thumb for long. Unlike most athletes, he asked questions, studied and learned until he could make his own deals. He took college courses to improve his English and his grasp of business and finance. He took control of his career as precisely and methodically as he had taken control of his body.

Arnold lived in Santa Monica and trained every day at the now-famous Gold's Gym. He was twenty-two, in the middle of America's bodybuilding capital. He convinced Joe Weider to send for Franco Columbu and give him a contract, too. Soon the two old friends were carousing again.

California was a perfect place for Arnold in the sixties and seventies: brimming with beautiful bodies and sexual openness, but still gripped by reactionary U.S. politics. The popular Californian Ronald Reagan was governor. The soon-to-be unpopular Californian Richard Nixon was president. Arnold supported them both, as he would later support President George Bush.

Arnold has never been shy about expressing his opinions. "Black people are inferior," Arnold is reported to have told black bodybuilder Dave DuPre. It was not clear whether he really believed this or was saying it to psych out DuPre.

In either case, Arnold's alleged racism could

not hide the fact that the only man he truly feared, the only man who knew how to beat him, was black.

Originally from Cuba, Sergio Oliva was a respected champion who possessed not only a magnificently sculpted physique but the rare power to mess up Arnold's mind. Arnold later admitted that at the IFBB Mr. Olympia contest, when he saw Oliva take off his trademark overalls and subtly flex in his direction, Arnold felt his own pump sag. Even the butterflies in his stomach collapsed. It is impossible to maintain a winning flex without total confidence. Afterward, Arnold vowed he would never again let Sergio intimidate him.

But first, time out to star in a movie.

It was originally titled *Hercules Goes Bananas*, but it was released as *Hercules Goes to New York*. By either title it was a silly, boring, poorly made, unfunny comedy. A muscleman-god listed in the acting credits as Arnold Strong comes down from Mount Olympus to cavort around Manhattan. Arnold's English was so bad that his voice had to be dubbed. It's hard to tell if he had any acting ability at the time, because he had little to do besides look confused, flex and beat up bad guys.

But he had starred in a movie. Another check off on the Master Plan.

More than twenty years later (by this time his real name was on the videocassette), a very different-sounding Arnold discussed his first film on David Letterman's show.

"I was just off the boat, you see," he said, "and someone asked me if I wanted to be in a movie. It seemed like a dream."

When he made *Hercules*, in fact, Arnold had been in the country some time and, of course, had arrived by plane. It's a good example of Arnold at work, shaping his myth the way he shaped his body.

7

An ego that was slightly bigger than the Austrian Alps.
—GEORGE BUTLER

Call it "Hercules Meets Hercules."

Only ten years after he sat in that theater in Graz wishing he looked like Reg Park, only three years after he visited South Africa and wished he was as rich as Reg Park, Arnold Schwarzenegger met his childhood hero in competition.

Reg Park picked the wrong year, 1970, to try a comeback. He entered a Mr. Universe contest after seeing pictures of a soft, pale Arnold, a pasty ghost of himself. Reg thought they were up-to-date pictures, but they were several months old. Arnold arrived in the best shape of his career, and Reg could barely finish his poses.

One can imagine Arnold's mixed feelings

after beating Reg Park—the joy of surpassing a former champion and the sadness of humiliating an old hero. As it turned out, they remained friends.

Arnold had no mixed feelings at his showdown with Sergio Oliva. Both men had peaked for the 1970 Mr. Olympia contest. Everyone, even Arnold's screaming fans, wanted to know once and for all who was best.

Backstage, Arnold unleashed his psych-out skills, spreading the story that while Oliva was desperately pumping up before the final posedown, Arnold and Franco had coolly strolled out for french fries. Oliva was shaken but he held his poise. Finally it was just the two of them left, flexing for an audience that responded as wildly as any rock fans at a concert. The two men fired their muscles at the crowd, twisting into poses that sent volcanic ripples across their backs and out along their arms.

After a while, Arnold leaned toward Sergio and whispered, "I'm tired—let's stop now."

"Okay," said Sergio.

"You lead off," said Arnold.

Oliva turned and left the stage and Arnold

began to follow. The crowd screamed for more poses. When Oliva reached the wings, Arnold turned back and walked to the lip of the stage. He started posing again, alone, to ecstatic applause. Was it just a spontaneous gesture for his fans or a planned dirty trick? In any case, the judges named Arnold Mr. Olympia. There would be only victories from now on.

Arnold returned to California a rare triple crown champion—Mr. World, Mr. Universe and Mr. Olympia—but he continued to train as if he were just a kid on the way up. Other lifters might have thought he was lucky or a natural until they saw his iron discipline, his "torture routine." He worked harder than anyone else.

Bad news came from Austria in the spring of 1971. His brother Meinhard had been killed in a car wreck. Cables from his family pleaded with Arnold to return for the funeral, but he refused. Some people were angry. Arnold was cold, they said, selfish. Others explained that he had spent so many years constructing a suit of armor for himself, a suit built of muscle and discipline and pride, that he was now unable to let his emotions emerge.

More news. Meinhard had left behind a little boy named Patrick. Arnold offered to support his nephew.

When George Butler, a free-lance photographer, met Arnold in the fall of 1972 at a Mr. America contest in New York, he knew he was onto something special. He was working on a book about bodybuilding with the writer Charles Gaines. They had finished most of their research on the inner world of international competition. It would document a sport and a way of life just edging its way into mainstream American culture. But the book needed a strong central character, a hero.

Then Butler and Gaines met Arnold. He had humor, charm and, according to Butler, "an ego that was slightly bigger than the Austrian Alps."

They shaped the story of bodybuilding around Arnold. The book would become popular, but the movie *Pumping Iron* would be a sensation, helping millions understand the sport, and transforming Arnold into a star.

Arnold went into hard training for the next Mr. Olympia contest, to be held in Essen, Germany, where he would meet Oliva once again.

Oliva wanted this one badly; he was angry that Arnold was getting all the prizes, the endorsements, the glory, and he had even hinted that Arnold's white skin had given him an edge in their rivalry. The judges, he intimated, preferred to have white champions.

Whether or not that was true, Arnold himself was not above exploiting the difference in skin color.

Before the competition began, Arnold used his clout with the officials to have the color of the stage backdrop changed from white to dark blue. As he had planned, Arnold's tanned white body was vividly contrasted against the dark blue, while Oliva's dark skin blended into the background. The magnificent size and definition of Oliva's muscles were simply harder to see against blue. Once more, Arnold was champion.

Arnold barely had time to enjoy his new victory before more bad news came from Austria. Just before Christmas 1972, his father, Gustav, died of a stroke at sixty-five. Despite his attachment to his mother, Arnold did not go to the funeral.

In the movie *Pumping Iron*, he explained that

he couldn't break training. Even his closest friends were shocked. They didn't believe that was the whole story.

Whatever the truth, there was one certainty: The discipline, the win-at-all-costs philosophy, the dedication to power that enabled him to brush aside everything but the commitment to victory, was Gustav's legacy. Arnold had learned it all in Thal.

I wanted every single person who touched a weight to equate the feeling of the barbell with my name.
—ARNOLD SCHWARZENEGGER

By the time Arnold Schwarzenegger captured the public imagination as the most famous bodybuilder of all time, his own imagination was moving him beyond the sport. On January 18, 1977, when the movie *Pumping Iron* was released, Arnold was taking acting lessons and studying the lives of Elvis Presley and Muhammad Ali as avidly as the thirteen-year-old boy had once studied Hercules.

At the time, only Arnold and those who knew how determined he was to be a megastar would have even dreamed of comparing a bodybuilder with two of the most famous celebrities on the planet.

But there were important similarities among

the singer, the boxer and Schwarzenegger. All three had been raised without money or connections, yet they had maintained absolute faith in the power of hard work, single-minded dedication and self-confidence to bring their talents to public attention. Also, each was lucky enough to be the right man at the right time.

Elvis's time was the fifties and sixties when rock 'n' roll music provided the anthems for a generation rebelling against postwar American values. People found new ways to express themselves, to live, to dress, to sing.

Ali's time was the sixties and seventies, when the boldest of the rebels stood up for their beliefs. It was a time to fight for equal human and civil rights for racial, ethnic, and religious minorities, for women, for the handicapped, for the poor. There was a sense of hope that problems could be solved.

After the Watergate scandal in which President Nixon and his closest advisors were disgraced and thrown out of office, people who were easily discouraged discarded their high hopes of quick-fixing the world and went about fixing themselves in many different ways, from making money to experimenting with drugs to improving their bodies.

Everyone seemed to be jogging. Natural-food stores and health clubs sprang up, and as they had a hundred years before, dozens of spiritual and physical-culture movements competed for attention and money. The bodybuilding world wanted a piece of this new action, and it counted on Arnold to lead it out of the dank gyms into the shining lights of TV.

Just as Elvis was bigger than rock 'n' roll and Ali was bigger than boxing, so Arnold was bigger than bodybuilding. He was a symbol for those who wanted authority and control over their bodies and their politics. In a time when the United States and individual Americans seemed to be losing their way, Arnold was a man with a plan.

Early in 1974, Arnold beat Lou Ferrigno, a rising young contender, in the Mr. Olympia contest at New York's Madison Square Garden. Ferrigno later became champion and played The Incredible Hulk on television. But this show was Arnold's. When he ripped off his final poses, fans went bananas. It was as if his exploding muscles touched them.

In 1976, Arnold got a real movie role, as a bodybuilder in *Stay Hungry*, and his first good reviews. The Hercules disaster was forgotten. But he still hadn't convinced Hollywood that he was a box-office attraction. Agents, producers and directors thought his body was too big for the screen, his accent too thick, his name too clunky. Couldn't he be "Arnold Strong" again?

And then *Pumping Iron* opened.

It was called a documentary, but it was carefully constructed to show bodybuilding as an intensely competitive sport whose star was Arnold Schwarzenegger.

Some of it takes place at an actual contest, the 1975 Mr. Olympia in Pretoria, South Africa, and there was controversy over this venue. Many black and white bodybuilders could not compete in good conscience while a majority of South Africans suffered under apartheid. For this reason, there had been many boycotts of South Africa in other sports, and the country had been barred from the Olympic Games.

But none of this seemed to bother Arnold as he posed and preened and joked and flexed his way to another championship. And then announced his retirement.

It was shocking, but it made sense. In his book *The Education of a Bodybuilder*, Arnold wrote: "I wanted every single person who touched a weight to equate the feeling of the barbell with my name." The film *Pumping Iron* made that wish come true. There was nothing more for bodybuilding to give him.

The film opened to rave reviews and was a hit. Arnold and bodybuilding became synonymous, and both boiled with new popularity. As Americans became fascinated by Arnold's body, they began to imagine the possibilities of their own. It was not likely you could make your body look like Arnold's, but you could certainly take charge of it, make it better, bigger, more muscular.

Arnold's popularity was based on more than just his body; his humor, charm and seeming honesty complemented his image of brute force.

When Barbara Walters, in a *Today* show interview, asked if he used steroids, he admitted that he had. But he said it without apologies or shame, with such an affable, invincible air, that Walters and the audience were charmed.

He had critics. Some thought his success would lead youngsters to steroid use. Others thought his physical proportions were ridiculous, grotesque. He was described as resembling an ape, as looking like a rubber bag stuffed with nuts and bolts. Some argued that his size was unhealthy. Was he really fit? Or did he just look fit?

Why dedicate your life to developing enormous muscles that could even hinder your movements when there were so many other interesting and important things to do in the world? Bodybuilders are generally not as strong as power weight lifters, and few of them have the agility to play other sports. Critics went on to claim that the "pose" in bodybuilding is just that, a pose, a sham of strength, not the real thing.

But even after the hoopla over *Pumping Iron* died down, Arnold remained a superstar. More

When Pumping Iron *was shown at the 1977 Cannes Film Festival in the south of France, the star of the film was the hit of the beach.*

and more people followed him into the gym. Bodybuilding was no longer a seedy shadow sport for muscle-bound oddballs. It was a respectable pastime for the rich and trendy. More and more women began to flex.

Over the next few years, Arnold traveled to promote events and products, and to bask in his rising fame and fortune. He continued to train, although not so passionately, and he kept taking acting classes and auditioning for movie roles. He was a celebrity now, invited to parties and openings. He was someone whose presence could "dress up" an occasion.

At one such celebrity event, a charity tennis tournament honoring the late Senator Robert F. Kennedy, Arnold met the woman who would change his life, and the public's image of him, two things forever intertwined in a celebrity. Her name was Maria Shriver.

> That which does not kill us
> makes us stronger.
> —FRIEDRICH NIETZSCHE

Maria Shriver is beautiful, intelligent and strong, an independent person, yet also part of the old Master Plan, the perfect mate for an Arnold determined to become even bigger— richer, more famous, more in control of his fate.

Maria was the niece of President John F. Kennedy, assassinated in 1963, and Senator Robert F. Kennedy, assassinated in 1968, two of the most mythologized U.S. politicians of the century. She is the daughter of their sister, Eunice, and of Sargent Shriver, who was the Democratic nominee for vice-president in 1972 running with George McGovern. (Arnold, the Republican who backed Nixon, would not have voted for his future father-in-law.)

Maria is a member of the Kennedy clan, which over three generations has used the kind of determination, intimidation and cunning Arnold knew so much about to become the first family of the United States, a royal family in a land that was supposed to have no kings.

Maria's maternal grandfather, Joseph P. Kennedy, made his fortune smuggling rum into the United States through the 1920s and early 1930s during Prohibition, when alcohol was illegal. In less than fifty years, the Kennedys had achieved an enduring fame and respect in politics and public works.

It has been said that Arnold and Maria felt an instant current between them. Maria saw a powerful man who seemed to possess the shrewdness, the charm and the toughness that personified the Kennedy masculine ideal. Arnold saw a smart, glamorous, tough-minded woman determined to pursue a career in television journalism rather than rely on her family's wealth and power for an easier life.

The very fact that Arnold's reactionary politics often clashed with the liberal Kennedy tradition made him more attractive. Even in the company of such powerful people, it was said, the Austrian Oak could not be bent from his own ideas.

Arnold worked with longtime Kennedy projects such as the Special Olympics, and he gave clinics on fitness and weight training in prisons. He took Maria to visit the tiny house in Thal. He was moving forward but was holding on to his roots.

And as far away as the world of pumping iron now seemed, his pride would demand one more night on the posing stand.

During the fall of 1979, Arnold was doing color commentary for the CBS coverage of the Mr. Olympia contest. Arnold was delighted to see an old rival and friend, Frank Zane, win the title, and he shouldered his way down to the front of the crowd to get an interview.

Arnold asked Zane a routine sportscasting question, one he had heard himself a thousand times. "How does it feel to win, Frank?"

Maybe Frank Zane felt incredible relief at this moment, not only from winning the title but at seeing Arnold here beside him, in a suit and tie, holding a microphone, a legend, sure, but

Arnold became involved in one of the Kennedy family's favorite causes, the Special Olympics. At the United Nations in New York in 1986, he supervises a weight-training demonstration.

no longer an invincible monster.

"It feels great," said Zane. "Better than the last time I beat you, Arnold!"

Did Arnold reel back, flabbergasted? Did his eyes turn tiny and red?

Zane probably meant it as a friendly, light-hearted jab, but it struck a painful memory of

1968 in Miami, when Arnold had cried himself to sleep. Arnold left the auditorium vowing to show them all once again why he was Arnold and they were not.

But the world of competitive bodybuilding had changed. New drugs and training techniques had produced a new breed of massive musclemen. Champions who had taken up the sport because of Arnold heard the rumors of his comeback with a mixture of pity and resentment. Why couldn't he just be happy with everything he already had? They didn't know how fiercely his competitive flame burned.

The competition was held in Sydney, Australia, in 1980. Arnold brought Maria along. He nearly came to blows with a young favorite during a debate over a rule change, and though many contestants were bigger than Arnold, he managed once more to psych everyone out before the competition began.

Last but not least was Frank Zane, the defending champion. Noting that Zane was extremely tense, Arnold told him a joke in the middle of a posing routine. Zane burst out laughing and lost points.

Still, Arnold had trained for only eight weeks, and many said he didn't look good enough to win. They treated him like a great old fighter whose reflexes were shot, who everyone was afraid would get hurt in the ring. But it was Arnold who did the hurting. Fans might think he was washed up and opponents might think he was beatable, but after Arnold turned on his triumphant smile and popped his muscles, the judges named him Mr. Olympia.

The crowd booed. They threw chairs, chanted curses, and screamed that the contest was fixed. Arnold stormed out of the Sydney Opera House, arias of rage in his wake. He was finished with competitive bodybuilding.

Now he totally committed himself to becoming as big a movie star as he had been a bodybuilder. *Conan the Barbarian*, released in 1982, established his credentials as an action-film star. The film grossed more than $100 million. Not all the reviews were good; some critics thought he acted like an oak. But there was no doubt he had the physical presence of an ancient warrior. And the opening line of the film, a quote from the German philosopher Friedrich Nietzsche,

Arnold didn't have much to say in Conan the Barbarian, *but he looked powerful and he moved well. The movie was a hit and Arnold had star quality. Later, moviegoers would learn he also had humor and could deliver a line.*

Arnold and his future wife, Maria Shriver, the television journalist, on the day he became a U.S. citizen.

including such old pals as Wag Bennett and Franco Columbu. It was a grand occasion, marred by only one incident.

Arnold and Maria received a gift from Kurt Waldheim, the former secretary-general of the United Nations and soon-to-be president of Austria. Waldheim had just been accused of concealing his past as a Nazi during World War II.

Arnold not only acknowledged the gift at the wedding but made a little speech reiterating his friendship for the absent Waldheim.

Most people just let the controversy pass. Arnold was royalty now, a member of the Kennedy family, a star heading up into the sky with Ali and Elvis.

10

You have to look at your-
self in the mirror and then
visualize what you can be.
—ARNOLD SCHWARZENEGGER

When President George Bush appointed him
chairman of the President's Council on Physical
Fitness and Sports in 1990, Arnold seemed to
take the unpaid job seriously. He traveled the
country preaching the importance of good
health and mental attitude through exercise.

He told kids that "it's just as important to
grow up fit as it is to grow up smart." He
warned against drugs, including steroids, and
urged them not to become couch potatoes ad-
dicted to TV, starting the heart problems that
could kill them in middle age.

He also made the critical distinction between
a good sports program for elite competitors and
a good physical education program to get every-

one else in shape. In the United States there are thousands of talented young athletes who are supported by state-of-the-art equipment, dedicated coaches and rabid fans.

But there are also millions of kids who don't get the gym time necessary to learn the games and exercises that can help them be happy and healthy their whole lives.

What Arnold said was important but not new. The President's Council had been created in 1956 because U.S. political and business leaders felt threatened by the Soviet Union; they thought American youth wasn't fit enough to battle Soviet youth, in war or Olympic Games.

But by the time the Berlin Wall came down and the Soviet Union fell apart, American youth was in no better shape, despite the jogging, stretching and pumping boom of the seventies and eighties.

Consider this: In 1970, only 126 runners, all men, ran in the first New York Marathon. Richard Nixon was president then and Arnold was winning the triple crown of bodybuilding; in 1992, when President Bush lost to Bill Clinton and Arnold was the world's biggest movie star,

25,000 men and women ran in the New York Marathon.

Yet young people of the nineties seemed less fit than ever. According to an article Arnold wrote for *The New York Times*, U.S. children are fatter than they were in the 1960s, and most teenage girls can't do even one pull-up.

He thought there were lessons to be learned from *Kindergarten Cop*.

In that 1991 movie, Arnold played an undercover detective who becomes a kindergarten teacher to track down a murderous drug dealer. He was funny and likable in the role; his charm and humor came through. That movie proved he could go beyond the action film and, once again, shape himself into something new—a romantic comedy star.

But some of his critics wondered if there wasn't a secret message in that movie. They wondered if "Conan the Republican"—who has called Democratic politicians "girly-men"— might be using this action comedy to sell his own notions of iron discipline. As the teacher, he uses his authority and a metal whistle to intimidate a class of rambunctious five-year-olds into running, doing calisthenics, getting into shape.

Is this really the way to get children interested in healthful play and exercise? Is the man who lived by the "torture routine" the right leader to follow? Should entertainment movies be used in such a way?

Other critics pointed out the hypocrisy of

Some political commentators wondered how Vice President Dan Quayle could attack the TV character Murphy Brown in 1992 for having a child without getting married but not criticize Arnold for making all those violent movies.

performing in gory, violent movies such as *Conan the Barbarian* and *Commando* and *Predator*, yet still offering himself as a role model. By playing take-charge heroes, was he setting himself up as an authoritarian leader? After all, hadn't he said that most people want to be told what to do?

Arnold separates these aspects of his life as if they have no relation to each other, as if Arnold the Movie Star and Arnold the Health Guru and Arnold the Politician are different characters. In fact, when reporters try to probe this area, another character, Arnold the Bully, reappears. He can be as nasty as Conan to someone who asks a question he doesn't want to answer, especially if the reporter questions whether he joined the President's Council to promote the nation's health or to promote his movies or himself as a future politician. Interestingly, Arnold, a staunch Republican, resigned from the position of Chairman of the President's Council on Physical Fitness and Sports four months into the new Democratic administration of President Clinton.

Arnold Schwarzenegger came to the United States from a struggling nation, a refugee from

Arnold on the White House lawn. After he campaigned for George Bush's election in 1988, he was appointed chairman of the President's Council on Physical Fitness and Sports in 1990. People started calling him "Conan the Republican" and wondering if he had his own political ambitions.

an unhappy childhood, a relative unknown in a low-rent "sport," and became the greatest body-builder in history, an icon of the New Age body culture, a Hollywood superstar, a presidential appointee, and one of the most recognized faces on the planet. How many other people are known only by their first names?

His timing was perfect. Not since Jim Thorpe's turn-of-the-century United States has there been such an explosion of sports opportunity, at every level of skill, and such an infusion of new energy from other countries.

In New York, Dominican-American youngsters are surging onto baseball sandlots. In California, Vietnamese-American youngsters are scrambling over tennis courts. A Korean American is playing on a National Football League team, and Africans and Eastern Europeans are playing on National Basketball Association teams.

Arnold Schwarzenegger has showed them all the way. He has learned from every failure and every success, and there is no reason why he cannot reshape himself again and again, like the quicksilver morph he battled in *Terminator 2*.

And we can learn from Arnold. As long as we remember that he is a master psych-out artist, that he is in the business of creating his own myths for his own reasons, what he says and what he does is worth our attention. He had a plan, he worked hard, he had faith in himself, he wouldn't change his name or his friends, he held on to his roots even as he moved forward.

He had a dream, and it began with taking control of his own body.

His best advice may be this: "You have to look at yourself in the mirror and then visualize what you can be."

For Further Reading

Butler, George. *Arnold Schwarzenegger, A Portrait.* New York: Simon and Schuster, 1990.

Gaines, Charles, and Charles Butler. *Pumping Iron.* New York: Simon and Schuster, 1981.

Ernst, Robert. *Weakness Is a Crime.* Syracuse University Press, 1991.

Green, Harvey. *Fit for America: Health, Fitness, Sport and American Society.* Baltimore: Johns Hopkins University Press, 1988.

Leigh, Wendy. *Arnold, An Unauthorized Biography.* Chicago: Congdon & Weed, Inc., 1990.

Levine, Peter. *American Sport: A Documentary History.* New Jersey: Prentice-Hall, Inc., 1989.

Schwarzenegger, Arnold and Douglas Kent Hall. *Arnold: The Education of a Bodybuilder.* New York: Pocket Books, 1977.

INDEX

Page numbers in *italics* refer to illustrations.